D0071596

HELL
OF A
Lady

Hell of a Lady
Annabelle Anders

Print Edition

Dedication

I dedicate this book to none others, than my readers. Without your encouragement and support I'm not sure I would have persisted so diligently. Ever so humbly, I thank you for reading.

HELL OF A LADY

By Annabelle Anders

A Most Outrageous Wager

1824, April 7th

Betts placed below naming whom Miss R.M. will next bestow S. favors upon.

Minimum. Bett £1000

*Proof must be provided. Wager remains open until winner is confirmed.

£1000 on FN (Ld. K)

-April 7th Ld. Mimms

-April 8th £2000 Ld. FN (Ld. K)

-April 8th RS (Ld. Q)

£1000 on DB (Ld. W)

-April 8th Ld. Bn.

£1000 on … RY Ld T

£1000 on FN (Ld. K)

-April 7th Ld. Mimms

-April 8th £2000 Ld. FN (Ld. Ps)

-April 8th RS (Ld. Q)

£1000 on DB (Ld. Wh)

-April 8th Ld. Bn.

And so forth… And so on…

CHAPTER ONE

Crabtree Ball

"I DON'T UNDERSTAND it, Emily! It's not as though I'm any different this year. I'm the same person I've always been. Heaven knows my dowry's as small as it ever was." Normally, Rhoda wasn't one to question good fortune, but the past year had turned her into something of a skeptic.

For upon her wrist, attached to the string her mother had tied earlier, Miss Rhododendron Mossant possessed a full dance card for the first time in all of her ten and nine years. Not once since coming out two years ago had she ever had more than a third accounted for.

Tonight, a masculine name was scribbled onto every single line.

"Likely something to do with you garnering Lord St. John's notice last year. If a marquess finds you interesting..." Her friend and fellow wallflower, Emily, scrunched her nose and twisted her lips into a wry grimace.

The gentlemen of the *ton*, usually oblivious to her presence, had pounced upon Rhoda the moment she set foot in the ballroom, vying to place their names upon her card. Once they'd procured a set, a few even requested sets with Emily, although with less enthusiasm.

Rhoda had not gone out of her way to flirt or fawn. She hadn't been nearly as friendly as she'd been in the past. So, why now? The question niggled at her as she bent down to adjust her slipper.

The supper dance was next to commence, and her feet already ached. She hadn't prepared to partake in such vigorous exercise this evening. Nor had her life prepared her to be the belle of the ball.

"Miss Mossant."

Rhoda peeked up to identify the owner of the polished boots that appeared before her. The voice sounded familiar, but she didn't immediately recognize the rather fine-looking gentleman executing a stiff and formal bow.

As she sat upright again, a flush crept up her neck and into her cheeks. Rhoda usually didn't forget a handsome face. Blond hair, blue eyes, perhaps nearing the age of thirty. Ah, yes!

"Mr. White." Mr. Justin White, *the vicar*. She stopped herself from gasping. She'd not met with him since the day Lord Harold died last summer at Priory Point, easily one of the worst days of her life.

Second only to the day she'd been informed of St. John's tragic demise. She shivered as she pushed the thought aside.

"Please, sit down." She indicated the chair Emily had vacated. Rhoda glanced around the room. Where had she gone?

Not much time presented itself for conversation as the next set was soon to begin. She'd promised this one to Flavion Nottingham, the Earl of Kensington, of all people. She could endure the vicar's company until Kensington came to claim her. Mr. White was a *vicar*, after all. One could not simply *ignore* a vicar.

He smiled grimly and lowered himself to the seat. "I trust you are doing well." He cleared his throat. If he felt as uncomfortable as she, then why had he approached her?

Likely, he felt the need to inquire as to her spiritual

health. The collar he wore set him quite apart from the other more ornately dressed gentlemen.

And as for the condition of her spiritual health?

She would have laughed, but if she were to begin laughing, it might turn to hysteria. And quite possibly, she'd be unable to stop.

She wasn't sure her soul would ever be *well* again. Not since that weekend Harold had fallen off the cliff. And less than a fortnight later, when a river of mud and rain had swept the steep narrow road near Priory Point into the sea, along with the Prescotts' ducal carriage. St. John, his father, and uncle had all been riding inside.

"I am well. And you, Mr. White?" She studied him from beneath her lashes. He'd been witness to Harold's death that day, too. The men were all cousins, from what she remembered. Mr. White had nearly jumped into the sea to rescue poor Harold. He'd remained hopeful longer than anyone else. Even longer than Harold's own brother.

Mr. White's persistence might have had something to do with his faith.

"It has been a trying winter," the vicar answered. "But with springtime always comes hope." He spoke sincerely. No mockery in his words whatsoever.

Hope was something she'd given up on. The greater a person's hope, the more pain one experienced when disappointment set in. No springtime for her, just one long, endless winter.

"Is it presumptuous of me to hope I might claim a set with you?"

Her heart fluttered ever so weakly. This handsome, kind, wholesome man showing interest in her… Laughable, really. She smothered any pleasure she'd normally have enjoyed upon his request.

Likely whatever had come over the rest of them affected him as well.

"I'm afraid, sir, they have all been spoken for." When his eyebrows rose in surprise, she held out her wrist. She could hardly believe it herself. "I'm not fibbing, Mr. White! I wouldn't lie to a vicar!"

He shook his head, not bothering to examine the card. Instead, he stared down at his hands, clasped together at the space between his knees. His blond hair, longer than was fashionable, fell forward, hiding his profile from her gaze.

"I am to be disappointed, then." He spoke as though mocking himself but then sent her a sideways glance.

"Hope does that." She couldn't hold back her opinion. "Eventually."

He held her stare solemnly. "I would not have taken you for such a cynic, Miss Mossant."

She turned to watch a few ladies promenading around the room. "Disappointment does that, you know. Too many letdowns tend to stifle one's optimism."

He scratched his chin. Perhaps she confounded him. She certainly wasn't engaging in typical ballroom conversation. She ought to be flirting. Complimenting him, widening her eyes, and feigning enthusiastic agreement with all his opinions.

"I'll wager you're an optimist." She'd redirect the conversation back to him. "A man of God. Your prayers are likely given top priority." She stretched her lips into a smile.

He did not smile back. Again, that sideways glance. Her heart jumped at the startling blue of his eyes.

"I seriously doubt it works that way, Miss Mossant."

"It's not an insult." She'd be certain he hadn't taken her comment that way. "Rather the opposite, really." Those who were good deserved to have their prayers answered. He was obviously one of the good ones. At this thought, she remembered the desperation with which he'd climbed down the side of the cliff, hoping to save Harold.

Hope had driven him. Even then.

And he'd been disappointed. As they all had been.

He cleared his throat. "I'd like to think God does not favor any one of us over others. Are we not all undeserving? Are we not all sinners?"

"Some more than others." She could not be in complete agreement with him. People discriminated. They passed judgment upon one another, upon themselves. And they were made in God's image, were they not?

She met his gaze steadily and shook her head.

"You believe me naïve?" He raised his brows.

"I believe your faith gives you confidence. And your goodness." Neither of which she could lay claim to. "But I suppose that is why you wear the collar. A true calling."

Those blue eyes of his narrowed. "I hope someday you allow yourself to hope again. You are far too young to be so cynical." His gaze, after searching her face, dropped to her bodice. "And too beautiful."

She shivered. Her lack of hope had nothing to do with her age or her looks. Rather to the circumstances life had handed her. She would not thank him for the compliment. "And you a vicar," she scoffed, feeling defensive at his comment. She didn't like feeling vulnerable, and he'd somehow caused her to feel just that. Why had he chosen to sit *here*? What did he want?

He turned his gaze downward again, and, as though she'd voiced her thoughts, seemed to decide it was time he stated his purpose.

"I do not wish to bring to mind unhappy memories, Miss Mossant." He remained focused on the floor. "But I never had the chance to tell you how much I admired your composure and compassion on that dreadful day. I do not know that your friend could have endured it without your strength and comfort. I've often wanted to tell you this, and when I realized you were here tonight..." His throat worked as he swallowed what else he might say.

His words surprised her.

Again.

She barely remembered the accident itself, often dwelling instead upon everything that happened afterward.

Their assembled group had been sitting atop the cliff, drinking wine and sharing a lovely picnic. Rhoda had been upset with St. John's attention to another lady. Today, she could not even recall the woman's name. Her presence, however, had mattered greatly at the time.

Lord Harold had been in a good-humored mood as he joked about falling into the sea, and St. John had goaded him, it seemed.

And then it was not a joke anymore. "It was all so senseless," she said through lips that felt frozen.

Lord Harold had lost his balance and tumbled over the edge of the cliff. He'd been standing there, laughing one moment, and the next, he'd simply disappeared. He'd ceased to exist.

His wife of less than a fortnight, Sophia, had lurched forward, as though she would jump into the crashing waves below to save him.

Yes, Rhoda had caught her friend, held her back as Sophia sobbed and cried out her husband's name.

"She is my friend," Rhoda added into his silence. "I would do anything for her." And she had. *God save my soul.*

What else was there to say?

"Miss Mossant, my set, I believe." The words crashed into her thoughts almost violently.

Dressed in a cream-colored jacket and an embroidered turquoise waistcoat, the Earl of Kensington could not be more dissimilar to the vicar. His breeches were practically molded to his thighs, and she thought that perhaps he wore padding beneath his stockings. The heels on his buckled shoes would ensure that he stood taller than her, despite her own above-average height.

Rhoda had wanted to refuse him, but in doing so would have had to decline other offers as well. A lady could not deny such a request. Not if she wished to dance with any others that night.

Rhoda twisted her mouth into a welcoming smile.

Her friend Cecily wasn't here. Regardless, she'd understand.

The despicable earl had lied and tricked Cecily into marrying him, and then betrayed her in the worst possible manner. Rhoda knew he was not to be trusted. And yet, here he stood, all affability, affluence, and charm.

Although Kensington had paid for his misdeeds, Rhoda could never forgive what he'd done to one of her best friends. Even tonight, he'd put Rhoda in an uncomfortable position. He should not have claimed a dance with her. He ought to have remained in the country with his new wife and baby.

If she refused him, she'd be forced to sit all other dances out.

Might as well get this over with.

She turned to Mr. White and nodded. "If you'll excuse me, sir."

She rose hastily, uneasy with the emotions the vicar evoked.

He remained sitting, unwilling, it seemed, to remove himself from the memory they had been reliving together. Scrutinizing her, he nodded, almost imperceptibly.

Regret caught at her to leave their conversation unfinished. She brushed it away. The past must remain in the past. For all of their sakes.

She dipped her chin, signaling the end of their conversation.

Placing one hand on Lord Kensington's arm, she allowed herself to be whisked onto the dance floor for the lively set. Taking her position, she determined to forget the unnerving encounter with Mr. White. She ought to be having the time of her life!

"Your looks are even more dazzling tonight than ever." Lord Kensington stood across from her. His compliment only reminded her of what he'd done to Cecily.

"Thank you." She'd appear sullen and prideful if she failed to respond. And others were watching them. Both the ladies and the gentlemen.

The music commenced, and he reached across the gap to take her hand. Thank heavens they wore gloves. Her skin might have crawled if she'd had to endure the touch of his flesh.

She wished he'd not singled her out this evening.

Dancers all around her smiled and laughed as they executed the well-known steps. Several ladies' gazes followed her partner covetously. Despite his despicable past, no one could deny Lord Kensington was a most handsome and charismatic gentleman.

Initially, as they executed the steps of the dance, he kept his distance and did not attempt to hold her gaze for longer than was considered appropriate. The second time they came together, however, his hand lingered at her waist, and he brushed too close to her body for comfort.

"I cannot identify your scent, Miss Mossant." He leaned his face into her neck. "Roses? But there is a hint of something else? Your own particular magic? Are you casting spells?"

The words struck her as more of an accusation than anything else. She did her best to widen the gap between them. His flirtatiousness set her skin crawling. He persisted in closing the distance between them and leaving his hand on her longer than necessary.

She hoped no one else noticed.

A lady's reputation was all she had.

Except, he was an earl. Surely, he wouldn't do anything to dishonor her in public. He'd mended his ways. Or so everyone said—and by everyone she meant the *ton*.

A time or two, she spotted Mr. White watching them with a scowl. Obviously, he disapproved. Of her? Or of her dance partner?

The question needled.

She barely knew Mr. White. She hoped to never speak with him again, as a matter of fact. They had shared one afternoon, one tragic afternoon together, and each time she saw him, the terrible emotions of that day would resurface. Such a phenomenon did not lend itself to friendship.

Lord Kensington caught her gaze, and she stretched her lips into a smile. She'd always loved dancing, moving to the music, talking and flirting with those around her.

Tonight, she merely endured it. She wished for nothing more than to return home, change into her night rail, and climb under her counterpane.

The music slowed to a halt. One dance over, two left in the set.

Lord Kensington tucked her arm into his, his face flushed and eyes bright. "My dear Miss Mossant, it's ever so hot in here. Shall we forgo the remainder of the set and take some air?" Without allowing her to answer, his hold upon her elbow tightened, and he led her toward the terrace.

When he went to set his hand at her back, she arched forward. She did not welcome his overly familiar touch.

Lord Kensington's scent clawed at her. At one point, a lifetime ago, she'd considered him desirable, indeed. Now he stirred only disgust in her. She knew him for who he was.

But he was an earl, an influential one, and for that reason, he would never be turned away by society.

Despite the scandalous duel that had grievously injured his… male parts.

"How is Daphne, er, Lady Kensington?" She'd remind him of the lady he'd ended up married to.

No need to flutter her eyelashes at him or encourage his preening boastfulness. Even though that was what gentlemen wanted. They wanted to feel their superiority. It was at least half of what made a man feel worthy.

"My countess is well," he answered tersely.

"And your baby daughter?"

He grimaced but did not answer, unusually intent, it seemed, on steering her away from the ballroom guests.

She had no need to be wary of the earl. She reminded herself that she had nothing to fear. Flavion Nottingham was no longer, in truth, a man. So, why was she suddenly feeling so uncomfortable?

Her mother had attended the ball and would be seated with the other matrons. Would Rhoda be overreacting if she demanded that he take her back inside?

But, no, Kensington was harmless.

He guided them away from the terrace and down a dark path. In the distance, she caught sight of a tall fountain surrounded by lanterns. Was it an angel or a devil? An odd work of art for such a pretty setting. Water shot up from the wings, and mist hovered around the stone creature.

She shivered to think an angel could appear satanic, as well as the opposite.

People were like that, too.

With an invisible moon, stars twinkled dimly in a mostly black sky, making for a very dark night. Furthermore, the glow of the candles inside the ballroom failed to illuminate much through the windows. Rhoda shivered as the earl's arm slid around her waist.

His breath blew hot behind her ear. "Much better, don't you think?"

Much better for what? The air? Was that what he referred to, the fresh air?

She doubted it. His too-familiar touch sent a shiver of fear creeping along her spine. "I'm fine. Nonetheless, my lord, I wish to return inside now." She must return to her mother. She slowed her pace and resisted him at last. She ought not to have come outside alone like this.

He chuckled but held fast to her, his grip becoming almost painful. "Ah, so, you wish to pretend reluctance, Miss Mossant? Does that make you feel more like a lady?" His words confused her, but his tone set her heart racing in fear.

Without warning, he spun her in his arms and dragged them both off the path, behind one of the tall hedges.

And then hard, cold lips landed on hers.

Stunned, Rhoda pushed against his chest and twisted her head. The taste of whiskey and cigars evoked a wave of nausea.

"Don't play games with me." He was stronger than he looked. One arm held her in place, and the other hitched her skirt higher. "I have too much to gain."

How had this happened? In the matter of a few seconds, she'd gone from casually strolling through the Countess of Crabtree's garden to fighting off a vicious attack! She kicked out at him, but as her slippers encountered his boots, realized the futility of such a strategy.

"Stop it, my lord!" she tried imploring him. Perhaps she had been too passive, allowing him to touch her as he had throughout the dance. Had he thought she *wanted* him to do this? "My lord, stop! Please! I don't want—" His mouth smothered her pleas.

Real panic set in. The earl's hand was now clutching at her bare leg. "Ah, yes, you like a little fight, eh?" He ground their teeth together. Rhoda didn't know if the blood she tasted was his or her own.

Why would he do this? Surely, he couldn't expect any gratification? At that moment, it didn't matter that he lacked the necessary equipment. His hands roved over her arms, and he sought to touch her intimately. Rhoda squirmed and pushed at him, crying, angry and terrified at the same time.

JUSTIN HAD RESENTED Kensington for the set he'd reserved with Miss Mossant. He'd seen the look in Kensington's eyes even before the dance began—a lasciviousness that belied any good intentions.

Perhaps Justin identified it so easily because of his own improper inclinations toward her.

Watching the dancers turn and step to the cheerfully paced music, Justin admitted that he'd been attracted to her the first time they'd met but then been disappointed upon hearing St. John's boasts. He hadn't wanted to allow his cousin's words to dictate his opinion, but was human, after all.

His gaze searched the dancers making turns about the

parquet floor and inexorably settled on the chestnut-haired beauty again. Miss Mossant did not appear excessively flirtatious, but she didn't shun Kensington's advances either. After the first dance of the set ended, the bounder led her off the floor and toward the doors that opened to the terrace. As they disappeared, she put up no argument.

Justin gazed into his glass. He was not mistaken, she considered him naïve. He'd heard it in her voice.

But if she knew his thoughts, she would not think him so benevolent. Even now, his imagination ignored his conscience.

If she'd go walking alone in the dark with *him*... He shook his head, dismissing his untoward thoughts.

When the second dance of the set commenced, a few matrons were tittering and pointing at him with interest. God, he hoped news of his recent inheritance hadn't been made public yet. He'd prefer to bide a few more days in anonymity.

Damn. They looked to be heading his way... with purposeful intent.

Before he could be cornered, he placed his wine on a sideboard and then slipped through the French doors. The air outside the ballroom met him in a refreshing gust. Perhaps he could make his departure with the hostess being none the wiser.

The door closed behind him and he didn't look back to see if the matrons would be so bold as to follow.

His collar scratched uncomfortably. It hadn't done that before. He'd always felt more than comfortable wearing it. Guilt, likely.

Jamming his hands into his pockets, he turned onto a poorly lit pathway. What the devil? Rustling sounds stirred from behind a barrier of foliage. Likely, he had nearly stumbled upon a tryst.

"Does that make you feel more like a lady?" snarled a gruff-sounding voice from the dark area off the path.

Justin crept closer. If this wasn't a consensual encounter, he'd feel compelled to intervene. Not that he was a confrontational man. As a vicar, he'd learned to stifle violent impulses that came over him. He preferred using words to settle most disputes.

He'd also learned, however, that without a willingness to use his fists, talking could be futile.

In an ideal world, neither would be necessary. Hopefully, his suspicions would be proven wrong and he could return inside to finish his wine.

More rustling, and then all of his senses came alert. "Stop it, my lord! My lord, stop! Please! I don't want—"

Miss Mossant's voice. Apparently, she'd issued an invitation she wasn't willing to entertain in full. But she sounded distraught, frantic. Justin lengthened his stride until he came even with the couple. He could barely make out two shadowy figures.

Dash it all, she appeared to be resisting the earl. Yes, the situation had turned ugly indeed.

Although he'd heard rumors of the earl's infamous history, he'd never been introduced. According to most of the *ton*, Kensington had been something of a rake before his emasculating injury. Obviously, the extent of it had been exaggerated. Otherwise, the man would lack the motivation that seemed to have overcome him with Miss Mossant.

What would members of the *ton* think if they knew the extent of debauchery practiced by some of their beloved so-called gentlemen?

The scene before him did not appear consensual.

Justin tensed. "The lady has asked you to stop, Kensington. I suggest you honor her request."

Kensington stilled for a moment upon hearing Justin's words. "Walk away, Vicar. You know nothing of these matters."

Hell and damnation. Justin took one step forward, but before he could grab hold of the bounder's collar, Miss Mossant lifted her knee and landed it with surprising accuracy. The earl stumbled back and then bent over forward, gasping.

Although Kensington deserved it and would receive no pity nor assistance from Justin, his own dangling parts retreated considerably at the thought of experiencing a similar blow.

It seemed he'd not have to bruise his knuckles after all.

Miss Mossant met his gaze, a combination of fear and anger burning in eyes that looked almost black. Her lower lip trembled, and she hugged her arms in front of herself protectively.

With a moan, Kensington dropped to the ground and curled himself into a ball.

What this situation required, Justin assessed, was finesse.

To prevent Miss Mossant from becoming the subject of yet more gossip, he needed to lead her away from watchful eyes, to someplace where she might repair herself. An alluring array of chestnut curls had escaped her coiffure, tumbling down her back. More troublesome, her dress appeared disheveled and had torn in one place. A trickle of blood dripped from her swollen lips.

His gut clenched at the sight.

Justin stepped around Kensington to where Miss Mossant stood frozen. She nearly collapsed before he took hold of her arm. As unobtrusively as possible, he tugged her bodice back into place and then dabbed his handkerchief at her lips. Although his hands were steady, his heart raced.

"Remind me never to anger you, Miss Mossant."

She didn't laugh, blink, or respond in any way to his attempt to break through her lifeless trance.

Others strolled nearby, at a distance of fewer than twenty yards.

Maneuvering her so that she would be indistinguishable in his shadow, he tucked her hand through his arm and led them along the veranda away from the ballroom entrance. They had no choice but to pass a few other guests.

"Is everything all right there?" a tall, elderly gentleman turned away from his companion to inquire.

"Positively delightful evening for a stroll." Justin nodded toward the couple standing near one of the large potted plants. He blocked them from getting a good look at Miss Mossant. "My Lady, My Lord,"

Tall glass-paned doors beckoned at the far end of the terrace, and from what Justin could remember, they led into one of the Crabtrees' drawing rooms. With any luck, the doors would be unlocked and the room empty.

He steered the passive young lady in that direction and released the breath he was holding when the door swung open. Miss Mossant stepped inside but then stood unmoving while Justin lit a few of the candles.

"An unusually dark night." Best to burn only a few. He didn't plan on remaining here long. Just enough time for Miss Mossant to gather her calm so that he could escort her to a ladies' retiring room.

Her stillness gave him pause. Caramel eyes stared straight ahead, unblinking. She wasn't trembling or shaking, but she seemed frozen from the inside.

Justin could have gazed upon her silhouette all night long. If he were that sort of fellow, that was. He turned away from her and examined a painting placed at eye level. She needed a moment. He'd give her a level of privacy to compose herself.

The urge to comfort her, to hold her tightly against him, was strong. But with a woman such as she, his initial desire would hastily be replaced by another, less platonic one.

He was a man of the church, but a man, nonetheless.

But that would make him no better than Kensington.

Finally, the rustling of her skirts signaled that she'd cast off whatever spell she'd been under and had crossed farther into the room. Perhaps she was ready to face him now.

When he turned and caught sight of her expression, he tried to interpret her thoughts. Finely arched brows lowered in concentration, and she seemed baffled. Confused. "I–I thank you for your most timely arrival, Mr. White. I cannot imagine... If you hadn't come along..." Her hands fluttered.

A shiver ran through her, and he glanced around for a quilt. "Are you cold?"

She shook her head.

And then her soulful eyes widened to stare at him. "I must find my mother! She'll be worried if she doesn't see me at supper." The mysterious beauty went to take a step but caught herself on the back of a chair when her knees nearly buckled. "I..."

When he moved to assist her again, she stayed him with one hand, grimaced, and then seemed to shake off her confusion. Moving slower this time, she lifted her skirt as though she'd carefully pick her way to the exit.

Justin seized her by the arm. "First, the retiring room, I think." If she were to reenter the ballroom in her present condition, her ruination would be complete. He held her gaze steadily, making certain she understood his meaning.

Comprehension dawned, and she nodded slowly. "Yes. Yes, of course." At least the corridor wasn't well lit.

"Thank you, Mr. White." Shaking him off, she turned again to leave.

"Miss Mossant?" He stopped her with his voice this time. "You would do well to avoid such circumstances in the future. Not all men are so easily thwarted." She really was too beautiful, too *sensual,* for her own good.

Her jaw tightened but she did not meet his gaze again. She nodded. "I am ever so grateful for your kind advice."

And then she was gone.

CHAPTER TWO

A New Lord

RHODA FUMED AS she strode toward the retiring room. The vicar's condescending advice had shaken her out of the dazed shock left over from Kensington's appalling behavior.

Mr. White ought not to deserve any of her wrath, really, as his arrival had given her the opportunity to escape. And then he'd led her to safety. But she rebelled inside that he'd taken it upon himself to imply that she had somehow been at fault.

Why was it always the woman's fault when a man ran afoul? When Kensington had lied to, married, and then cheated on her dearest friend Cecily, Cecily had been the one shunned. She'd been shamed and blamed by the *ton* not only for her low birth, but because she'd failed to hold her husband's attention.

And when poor Sophia had been harassed by her stepbrother, no one had protected her either. It had been *her* responsibility to keep him at bay. *Her* responsibility to make certain her bedchamber door remained locked at all times.

Rhoda huffed out an irritated breath. Kensington's impertinent attentions had not been welcomed by her, had they? But of course not! Still, a niggling of doubt plagued her.

Had she done anything that might have given Lord

Kensington reason to believe she'd be receptive to such advances? Had she, by not chastising his touch during the dance, inadvertently given him reason to suggest…?

But, no! That was ridiculous! She understood the difference between mutual attraction and unbridled lust. Kensington had acted solely upon his own impulses.

Apparently, he'd recovered from last year's injury.

Rhoda's hand shook as she repinned an errant curl. He'd suggested that her protests were some sort of playacting. His assumption had been wicked, vicious… perverted!

Her dress was wrinkled where he'd gathered it into his fist. She moistened her hands and tried smoothing the creases away. She wished she could wash away the remembrance of his touch. Her stomach lurched sickeningly at the thought of his hand on her leg, reaching under her gown…

She'd been so stupid! She should know by now that men were not to be trusted!

She ought to have learned from St. John!

She stifled a groan. Surely, he'd loved her, hadn't he? Surely, he'd had every intention of meeting with her father?

But he had not. He'd recklessly delayed. And then died—leaving her alone to deal with what she'd done—what *they'd* done.

She could never forget what had transpired between them, how it had felt to be with him, skin to skin; how it had felt to give herself to him. At least no one had known. She'd told no one that she had given in to him. Not Sophia, not Cecily, not even Emily, who'd known something was off.

She'd been incredibly lucky he'd not left her with child. She dared not contemplate the condition of her circumstances if a pregnancy had resulted. And even so, she'd cried the morning her menses arrived.

Women were fools.

Satisfied with her reflection in the looking glass, if not the reflection of her soul, Rhoda deemed herself presentable enough to return to the ballroom.

She needed to locate her mother and then make up an excuse for having lost Lord Kensington's escort. The expectation would be that she'd sit with him. He'd reserved the supper dance with her, after all.

But Rhoda would not dine with him now if he were the last man alive. She never should have agreed to the dance.

Maybe she could plead a megrim. She felt even less like dancing now than she had earlier in the evening. But she'd promised all those sets.

To all those gentlemen.

"I wondered where you'd gone off to." Emily appeared at her side. Practical, outspoken Emily. "Are you trying to ruin your reputation intentionally? I was looking for you, but Lord Kensington told your mother you'd abandoned him after the dance. Said he thought you'd gone off with some other man." Emily frowned and adjusted her spectacles. "Horrid of him to request a dance with you!"

Admittedly, Rhoda had always been something of a flirt, but in the past, it had always been harmless. Fun.

She was not having fun tonight.

"I needed to go to the retiring room. I am not feeling quite the thing this evening. Too much dancing perhaps?"

In the past, she might have told Emily everything. She might have told her about St. John.

And Dudley Scofield.

With a shiver, Rhoda pushed the memory of Sophia's stepbrother to the darkest crevice of her mind.

She, Emily, Sophia, and Cecily had shared everything. They'd been bosom friends and dedicated confidantes.

Before the horrific events that occurred at Priory Point last year, Rhoda likely would have told Emily right off what Kensington had attempted in the garden tonight.

But too much had transpired since then. All of these incidents had changed Rhoda into a stranger, someone she, herself, didn't recognize. That flirtatious, carefree girl she'd once been had disappeared.

Emily examined her closely. "You do appear somewhat green."

"I'm not!" Rhoda wasn't *really* ill and so, of course, her complexion would not be green. "Really, Emily, sometimes you know exactly the wrong thing to say to a person!"

"I'm only trying to help. If I tell your mother you look green, then perhaps she'll believe this cock and bull tale you're spouting about being ill." Emily could be far too astute for Rhoda's comfort.

But not astute enough.

Rhoda sighed. "I wish Sophia were here. And Cecily." Rhoda dropped onto one of the plush sofas that lined the presently empty ballroom. The guests wouldn't return from supper for a while. "It isn't the same without them."

Emily joined her, striking a similarly dejected pose. "Mother says this is to be my last Season. If I don't land a husband, she'll send me back to Aunt Gertrude in Wales. I can't do it, Rho. She's a horror!" Both girls sat silently mulling over their less than optimistic situations.

For the past two years, landing a husband had been the four girls' main concern. With two of them married off, Emily and Rhoda ought to have felt somewhat hopeful.

"What has gotten into all of them tonight, anyhow?" Rhoda asked the question that had plagued her as soon as the gents began lining up to partner them. "I don't think all four of us put together have *ever* received so many offers."

Emily shook her head. "I've been wondering the same all evening. You don't suppose it's some sort of joke, do you?" Rhoda had to ponder this, for it very well could be! "Perhaps it has something to do with St. John setting his sights upon you last year, before, you know, the accident. Perhaps they believe that if a duke's heir saw something fetching about you, there might be something about you that they've been missing."

"Perhaps," Rhoda agreed softly. As always, the mention of St. John twisted her emotions.

Perhaps Emily had the right of it.

Her dear friend clasped her hand. "The reason doesn't matter. The night is just beginning, and you have throngs of gentlemen vying to dance with you. I even have a few names upon my own dance card. It is up to us to make the most of it."

Rhoda couldn't disappoint Emily. Dear Emily, whose worst fault was her honesty.

Surely, Rhoda could find it within herself to put on a good show for the rest of the evening. She'd better prepare herself. The entirety of the Season awaited them.

"Very well." She followed Emily toward the large dining hall.

"Did Flavion say anything about Cecily when you danced with him? I wondered if he might be remorseful after all he put her through."

Rhoda choked on a disbelieving laugh. Lord Kensington likely never felt an iota of remorse his entire life. He'd been a liar and a cheat when he'd married Cecily. Had he since become something even worse? "He didn't say anything I found interesting."

JUSTIN RUBBED HIS chin in an abstract manner as he watched the so-called gentlemen boasting and drinking heartily across the room. They clustered around the betting book, notes exchanging hands, jovially slapping one another's backs.

"It is bewildering to me that White's, England's most exclusive gentlemen's club, has renewed Kensington's membership." His cousin, Devlin, now the Duke of Prescott, dropped into the empty seat beside him. Leaning forward, Devlin poured them each a splash of scotch. "If my duchess hears of his return to Town, she'll go into conniptions."

"It isn't an exaggeration, then?"

Dev shook his head, requiring no clarification as to what Justin asked. Any time a man took such a gruesome injury on the field of honor, his story would become legendary for certain.

Justin had heard the rumors. He doubted many members of the *ton* had not. Flavion Nottingham, the Earl of Kensington, it was said, had been rendered a eunuch in a duel last year.

With the image of the man groping Miss Mossant the night before, Justin could not help questioning the validity of the story. Kensington's intentions with the young woman had not been consistent with that of a gentleman lacking sexual urges.

Disgust unfurled in his gut. The earl had been a scoundrel before and now, having returned to Town, seemed even more so.

And yet, society persisted in embracing him.

Rather unfair that Miss Mossant couldn't be given a second chance as well. His cousin, St. John, had done her no favors before dying. Even less so by boasting of his conquests before doing so.

"Good God, not one man present that day will ever forget it," Dev commented. And then, catching sight of someone behind Justin, he gestured with his drink. "Blakely, here, was present as well. Good to see you, old man. Join us if you've nowhere else to be."

Justin had known Lord Blakely since Eton. Considerable time had passed since he'd last seen him and they'd gone their separate ways; Blakely into industry and Justin, the church.

"Prescott, White." Marcus Roberts, the Earl of Blakely, claimed the seat on the other side of Justin. "The duel? I presume that is to what you are referring? Oh, yes. I was present that day. What in the hell is he doing in Town again?"

"Stirring up trouble, from the sounds of it. And now this disgusting wager."

Justin had wondered what all the activity at the betting book was about. "A gentleman's favorite entertainment," he commented non-committally. Justin had done some gambling before entering the church but seen enough damage since to keep his distance.

Families ruined. Estates fallen into disrepair. Ladies left to live in squalor.

In general, he didn't approve.

Dev swirled the amber liquid in his glass. "The damned thing puts me in something of a quandary." Justin waited for Dev to continue speaking. A duke now, his cousin must feel greater responsibility than ever before. Devlin's title was new to him. He'd been fourth in line to inherit and nobody, least of all the man himself, had ever considered inheriting a likely possibility.

"What sort of quandary, Prescott?" Blakely leaned forward.

Dev set his jaw. "Before his untimely death last year,

our cousin did irreparable damage to an innocent young woman's reputation. St. John couldn't keep his mouth closed regarding his conquests and has besmirched this particular young lady's, ah, virtue. And now," Dev lifted his glass to indicate the activity around the betting book, "Kensington and other so-called gentlemen have initiated a wager on who might next impose upon her favors."

Justin did not need to inquire as to the identity of the young lady.

No wonder Kensington had been so confident, so bold last night with Miss Mossant. Dash it all, once these louts got a hold of such information, whether there was any truth to it or not, they weren't likely to leave it be.

And once everyone else got a hold of it... Miss Mossant's entire family could be ruined.

Blakely broke the silence that had ensued upon Dev's statement. "But why is this your problem?"

But Justin understood.

Sophia was Dev's wife, his duchess, and she was one of Miss Mossant's closest friends.

"The young woman is very dear to my duchess. Her friends are everything to her. If she learns of this, she'll be deeply distressed, and anything that distresses my wife, distresses me." And then he added, "Deeply."

"Ah." Blakely raised his brows but nodded. "Is she in Town with you, then?"

"At Prescott House." The ducal townhouse was one of the grandest estates in all of Mayfair. "Along with our one-month-old daughter and a few other relatives. What with the speed this sort of nonsense travels, it's only a matter of time before she gets wind of it." Prescott gestured with his drink toward the betting book.

The duke and duchess were a thought-provoking couple. Devlin, former military, had always been considered something of a rogue. He was tall, with black hair and eyes—brawny enough to make most think twice before giving him cause for displeasure. The duchess, petite and blonde, was quite the opposite—in nature as well as looks. Justin remembered hearing something about difficulties throughout her confinement.

"What can we do to assist you?" Justin asked. The lady in question was obviously Miss Rhododendron Mossant. The thought of her disquieted him. She appealed to him much the same as she did most other men, he supposed, but mystery lurked in the depths of her dark gaze. Was that mystery nothing more than sorrow over St. John's death?

Justin chastised himself for feeling jealous of a dead man. And him a vicar.

Such a shame, really. She'd deserved better. She still did.

From his own discussions with St. John, shortly before the man's death, he'd understood his cousin had had no intention of offering for the girl. In fact, he'd told Justin he had no imminent plans to marry. He'd enjoyed sowing his oats.

"Anything to stifle the gossip," Devlin suggested, but they all knew just as well how futile that would be.

"Get the chit out of Town," Justin offered. "Perhaps your wife could plan a house party down at Priory Point."

"Not Priory Point," Dev said. But he seemed inclined to like the idea. "At Eden's Court, perhaps."

Last night's ball at the Crabtrees' had been the first of the Season. "Will the ladies be amenable to leaving so soon? The festivities here in Town have just begun."

Examining the contents of his glass in the light, Devlin contemplated Justin's question. "I will speak with Sophia. She will want whatever is best for her friend, and her friends will wish to accommodate Sophia as a new mother."

Recalling the voracity with which Kensington had pursued Miss Mossant, Justin could not help but believe it would be best for her to get out of Town. There might yet be hope for her reputation as long as the wager never played out.

And if she ceased inviting trouble for herself.

If the more genteel members of society got wind of the story, her situation would be beyond repair. The elderly biddies were worst of all.

"Congratulations are in order, as I'm to understand." Dev turned to Justin, changing the topic of conversation. "Or condolences… I'm never sure which is most appropriate."

He'd rather not be reminded.

"I'll accept the latter, for now anyhow." Three days earlier, he had discovered he'd inherited a distant uncle's title and estate. Dev, as the Duke of Prescott, would, of course, be privy to such information. Upon reading the official documents delivered to the vicarage, Justin had made arrangements with his curate and left immediately for London. He hoped the reports hadn't caught up with him already. He was in no hurry to make any announcements.

As it was, the task of meeting with his uncle's grieving sisters and examining the estate books loomed akin to contracting the plague. It would change everything. He'd be expected to resign from his current position.

The reading of the will had occurred without him, but as the new Earl of Carlisle, the family would expect him soon. He'd thought to consult with Prescott before opening that Pandora's Box. In due time, he'd arrive at his new estate, Carlisle House.

"Ah, so you had hoped to remain a member of the clergy indefinitely then?"

Justin dispensed the contents of his own drink in one swallow. Dev leaned forward and refilled the glass. Not until Justin downed the second pour did he answer, "I had."

Justin initially had wanted to join the effort against Old Boney. He'd been barely seventeen at the time, however, and his mother had persuaded him to go into service for the church instead. Justin was all that she had, and her wishes had weighed heavily on him.

Since then, he had become content at the vicarage while his mother traveled extensively. Presently, she had set up residence in Paris.

He enjoyed writing sermons, visiting parishioners, and assisting those in need.

But all that was to change, it seemed. No public announcements had been made yet, but it was just a matter of time. He preferred his altered status go unnoticed. Perhaps a sojourn to the country would benefit him as well.

"Percival Howard," he said into his glass. "He wasn't much older than me. Never married."

"What's the title?" Blakely asked. Justin had no concerns that Marcus would spread his news. He'd always been something of a tightlipped chap.

"Carlisle. The deceased was my father's cousin. I only met him once, and I've never visited the estate. Apparently, Percy had an abundance of unmarried sisters but no brothers, and no sons... obviously."

"Have you been in contact with the sisters yet?" Dev crossed one leg over the other.

"I sent a letter with my condolences this morning. I cannot imagine them anxious for my arrival." He'd always heard Percival was something of a spendthrift. And a gambler. From what his mother had told him, the lust for gambling had run in the family.

Justin was none too eager to dig into the details of his new financial circumstances.

Dev watched him with narrowed eyes. He, of all people, would understand the extent such an event might turn a man's life upside down. "The announcement will likely appear in the *Gazette* tomorrow, if it isn't there today."

This was not what Justin wanted to hear.

But Blakely apparently found humor in Justin's plight. "The ladies will be after you soon enough, White. Doesn't matter if the estate is broke. You're a titled gentleman now. And to a chit and her mother looking to rise in society, you might as well be fresh meat."

"Still on the run yourself?" Justin deflected. Marcus Roberts, the heir to a dukedom, was as confirmed a bachelor as could be. It was common knowledge that his father had drawn up a betrothal for him years ago, but it was equally well known that Marcus would never honor it.

"Ah, but I am well practiced in this area. You, my dear Mr. White, despite your good looks and noble blood, haven't learned the tricks required to keep yourself free of the parson's noose. Beware of the traps, my friend. Beware of the traps."

Dash it all. Marriage was the last thing on Justin's mind. "Let me know if your duchess is amenable to the country, Dev. I'll happily join you." He'd delay the inevitable for a few more weeks by such an opportunity and assuage some of his guilt over doing so at the same time.

"Ahem." None other than the esteemed manager of the exclusive club had approached quietly. "My dear Lord Blakely? Might I have a word?"

Justin chuckled as Marcus rose from his seat. "Forget to pay your dues, old man?" Neither the manager nor Marcus laughed. Justin met Dev's eyes and both men raised their brows.

"Might have something to do with his father. They're still on the outs with one another," Dev suggested. "Dicey situation for the clubs... what with father and son both members."

"Perhaps not much longer," Justin observed. Marcus looked none too happy as the manager escorted him toward the front entrance. "Perhaps Lord Blakely will be interested in the duchess' house party as well."

And then a cheer arose from the collection of men at the betting book and some sympathy stirred in him for the mysterious beauty. Perhaps her friends would be of assistance in guiding her to change her wayward behavior. He imagined remaining chaste might be more difficult for a girl with her sort of looks.

Hell and damnation, God knew he lusted after her for himself.

CHAPTER THREE

A Country House Party

RHODA LEFT HER maid on the park bench with the two other lady companions who'd followed Sophia and Emily to the park. As usual. Sophia, Emily, and Rhoda met weekly at the shores of the Serpentine to feed the ducks whenever they were in Town. Every Wednesday, in fact. Today was to be the first time Sophia had joined them in several months, having given birth to a beautiful daughter recently. Lady Harriette Brookes was barely one month old. Tiny and fair skinned, the infant surprised everyone when she peered out from her blankets with eyes as black as the night.

"You didn't bring the baby?" Rhoda greeted with a grin. Sophia had brought her little dog, Peaches, however, and so Rhoda bent down to pet the squat-but-long, red-haired pup she'd not seen all winter.

Sophia grinned. "Dev insisted I spend too much time indoors. He's so good with her. When I left, she was sleeping peacefully upon his chest." Love shined from her friend's eyes.

Rhoda was terribly happy for Sophia, and yet a part of her wished things could have stayed the same, wished all four of them were still wallflowers, making jokes about the absurdities of the *ton*.

Foolishness!

With a sigh, she rose and hugged Sophia tightly. "I've

missed you so." An overwhelming urge to cry struck her. Stepping back, she realized Emily was watching her curiously from behind her spectacles.

"Such an interesting evening, last night, wasn't it?" Rhoda lifted the corners of her mouth. "Did you tell Sophia that you danced all of four sets?"

Emily's gaze widened and then she laughed half-heartedly. "What of you, Rhoda? Dancing with nearly every bachelor in attendance?"

Astonishment persisted at the notion that her dance card had filled so quickly. That it had filled at all! She was doing her best to squash the memory of the unfortunate event in the garden. Shame swept through her at the mere thought of it. She shouldn't have gone outside with him. It had been unwise of her. She *knew* better.

But her dance card, ah, yes. Some gentleman or another had claimed every last dance. Should she tell them about the eight elaborate bouquets delivered this morning?

"So I heard," Sophia mumbled, somewhat surprisingly. "I've decided to host a house party," she declared, ever so casually as she handed Rhoda a slice of bread.

Rhoda took the bread but ignored the increasingly impatient ducks upon hearing Sophia's announcement. "Surely, not right away? The Season's just begun."

Her two dearest friends shared a conspiratorial glance before Emily asserted heartily, "I, for one, am happy to get away. I'm already bored with the usual inane conversation."

Rhoda glanced back and forth between her two friends. "I thought you said this was to be your final Season, Emily. Don't you want to make the most of it? You danced with *four* gentlemen last night!"

Emily met Sophia's eyes again and then bit her lip. "Ah, well, yes, yes, but I… um, I am so out of practice that I do believe I am in need of a refresher course. And Sophia has, er, said she could hire a dancing master for all of us to work on our dancing skills. Isn't that right, Sophia?"

Sophia tilted her head questioningly and then her brows rose. "Oh, Oh, yes. Indeed. A dancing master. Yes, of course. You know, Rhoda, those two years sitting with the wallflowers eroded our skills something fierce."

"But, Emily. You made a fine show of yourself last night. Aside from a few missteps with Lord Blakely, you were more graceful than ever!" Rhoda wondered what her two friends could possibly be thinking.

"Ah, well." Emily pushed her spectacles higher upon the bridge of her nose. "You did not see yourself. You seemed about a half step off from all the other dancers. I'm surprised nobody said anything."

"I was not! Was I? Surely, you cannot be right? I've always been comfortable dancing." Doubt crept in. Her friends wouldn't tell her this unless it were true, would they?

"Not to worry!" Sophia gave her a pinched smile. "As one of your dearest friends, I am more than happy to provide all of us with a dancing master at Eden's Court next week."

"Humph." Rhoda was still not entirely convinced.

"It will be marvelous. To get away from London." Emily tossed a few pieces of bread toward a cluster of curious brown ducks.

"Sophia." The ducks could wait. "What will the dowager say about you hosting a house party while the household remains in mourning?" Harold's demise had been in early August, and St. John, the duke, and the duke's brother had died a few weeks later.

As it was only April, a full year had not yet passed since Sophia's first husband's death.

"She is not the dowager, technically. Since Dev inherited, and not one of her sons, she is still the duchess. We are both referred to by the title. Confusing at times, I admit. I'm surprised you didn't know that, Rhoda," Sophia explained, a trifle condescendingly. "She keeps to herself, anyhow. I do my best to lure her away from the dowager house, but she prefers to be alone most of the time."

Rhoda nodded. The duchess had lost a great deal over the past year. Rhoda understood all too well.

"We'll refer to this not as a house party, rather as a 'quiet removal to the country.' This shall deem it entirely respectable." Sophia lifted Peaches off the ground so that the ducks would feel safer approaching them. After all this time, the pup still occasionally took it into her head that one of them would make for a delightful meal. "And the air is so much better there for your sister," she cooed while gazing into the dog's face. "Isn't it, Peaches?" Only Sophia would refer to the daughter of a duke as being the sister to a small dog.

Perhaps Sophia was concerned about the baby's health. The air in London could be unpleasant. "Fine then," Rhoda conceded. "But not until the end of the week. I've promised my mother I would attend the Snodgrass Garden Party tomorrow afternoon, and I'll need to convince her of this sudden dire need to head to the country. Emily, won't your mother object to you missing opportunities to land a husband?"

"That's the beauty of it." Emily's attitude turned quite cheerful. "Sophia was just saying, before you arrived, that His Grace had informed her of a few eligible bachelors she ought to invite as prospects for both of us. Isn't that right, Sophia?"

Peaches caught sight of one of the larger ducks and let out an outraged bark. Sophia scowled. Rhoda wondered at how very different Sophia's life had been just one year ago. As was the other former wallflower, Cecily's. "What about Cecily? Have you heard from her lately?" Cecily and her husband, Mr. Stephen Nottingham, the Earl of Kensington's cousin, had also recently increased the size of their little family by one. Cecily had given birth to a son a few months before little Harriette had come along.

"Of course, I'll invite Cecily and Mr. Nottingham." Sophia must be quite serious about this impromptu house party. Rhoda hadn't considered how frustrating it must be for her friend to be in London and yet unable to attend any of the *ton* events. And if she could host a 'quiet removal to the country' within the confines of her mourning, well, then, who was Rhoda to argue?

"And those eligible gentlemen that His Grace told you about," Emily reminded her.

"Oh, yes. Those." Sophia sent a chagrined expression Emily's way, but Emily simply smiled and tossed more bread toward the water.

"Yes. Those," Emily agreed with an impish smirk.

Peaches took that moment to leap out of Sophia's arms and before any of them could stop her, go chasing after one of the poor ducks who'd been so trusting.

"Peaches!" Sophia dropped the bread, sending the ducks into a frenzy.

A few of the ducks began flapping their wings in excitement. When Emily reached down in an attempt to save some of the loaf, her spectacles went flying.

"Don't move! They'll break if you step on them!" Emily's horrified exclamation froze Sophia in place.

"I'll get Peaches." Rhoda took off at a run after the surprisingly speedy short-legged rat. "Peaches! Come back here! Peaches! No! Leave Lady Milestone alone! Oh, dear." Rhoda navigated around bushes and trees and ladies with parasols as the little devil continued to elude her.

"Come back here!"

And just as Rhoda was closing in on the diminutive imp, masculine hands reached down and scooped Peaches off the ground.

Rhoda nearly skidded to a halt in order to keep from plowing the gentleman over.

"I'm so sorry. Thank you," she gushed and reached her hands around the tiny sausage-like body at the same time that she realized Peaches' savior was Mr. White.

"My pleasure."

Rhoda kept her gaze pinned firmly upon his cravat as she lifted Sophia's dog free of his grasp. She hadn't been prepared to see him again so soon. Heat rushed to her face at the remembrance of what he'd witnessed the night before. She couldn't meet his gaze. It was as though he could see into her thoughts.

"Um. Well. She got away…" Rhoda fumbled for polite conversation before she could return to Emily and Sophia.

"I've met Peaches before." He chuckled. "We're the best of friends, I assure you. And I do understand her desire to take flight on occasion."

Ah, those eyes of his. She'd not been able to help herself, hearing him laugh. Knowing he had befriended the little dog.

And Peaches did seem to like him. Even now, the pup strained to be back in his arms, tongue peeking out and tail wagging.

Not likely the only female to ever do so.

"She wants to eat the ducks." Rhoda shrugged, unable to keep herself from grinning up at him.

Mr. White gave in to the dog's wishes and took her back from Rhoda again. Peaches attacked him mercilessly with kisses, but he merely tilted his head back, exposing the sinewy muscles of his neck for the dog to lick.

With a firm pat, he tucked the dog into his arms and managed to somehow wing his other for Rhoda to take. "Might I escort you back to your chaperones?"

Was he implying she'd been acting inappropriately again? Some of her pleasure subsided at the thought, but she took his arm nonetheless.

"Her Grace and Miss Goodnight are near the flower beds," she ground out. "As is my maid."

Damn him. Why did he make her feel this way? Like she had to defend herself—her actions.

He shortened his stride and walked them at a leisurely pace. Rhoda wanted to drag him along more quickly, but some ridiculous part of her enjoyed having his strength beside her, his masculine scent.

"You seem to be in good health and spirits this afternoon. I ought to have ensured your safety back to your mother myself, last night after..." He cleared his throat. "Please accept my apologies. It was inexcusable of me."

Rhoda turned her head to study him in surprise. How could she be angry at the man with Peaches tucked beneath his chin?

"I was fine. I am fine." She wished she could forget the entire incident. It angered her that the fear she'd felt had entered her dreams the night before.

"Nonetheless, I am sorry." This time, when she glanced at him, he met her gaze earnestly. He swallowed hard, halting their steps. "Will you forgive me?"

She'd not been angry with him for failing to escort her to the retiring room. She'd been angry that he'd seemed to judge her. That he'd pointed out that which she'd already been chastising herself.

"I did not invite his advances, Mr. White." Rhoda stiffened beside him. "I'm not..." Only she had been. Once.

Last summer. And now she felt like a fraud to defend herself.

"I did not mean to imply..."

Rhoda stared at the ground now. "I'm not..."

She didn't know how to explain. She couldn't tell her closest friends, so why did she even begin to feel compelled to tell him?

"Then I am sorry for that as well. I am sorry if I made you feel in any way—"

"Of course," she cut him off. He was a vicar. "Of course, you have my forgiveness." But who would forgive her?

Sophia's arrival prevented them any further conversation. Which was a relief. Left alone with the vicar much longer and she'd likely regale him with her every sin.

"You bad girl, Peaches. Bad girl," Sophia reprimanded the dog, who merely looked at her lovingly. And then she turned to Mr. White. "Thank you Justin! She does that sometime. Runs off. I can't tell you how often I've had to go chasing after her."

"Miss Mossant may simply require a tighter leash." His joke caused Rhoda's eyes to widen in astonishment and Sophia to erupt into a fit of giggles.

"Not amusing, Mr. White." Rhoda narrowed her gaze at him. "Not amusing at all." But his eyes twinkled back at her in a way that made her heart skip a beat.

Sophia quieted enough to glance between the two of them meaningfully.

"I thank you again, Mr. White." Rhoda dropped her lashes to stare down at the ground. His presence disquieted her.

"I'm happy to be of assistance."

Rhoda stepped back from him so that Sophia could attach Peaches' leading string and set her on the lawn. "It is greatly appreciated." Sophia smiled up at him after securing Peaches.

He nodded solemnly and tipped his hat. "I'll bid you both good day, then."

"Good day." Rhoda bit her lip as he backed away and then turned to stride toward wherever he had been going in the first place.

When he finally disappeared, she turned to see Sophia watching her with a suspicious gleam in her eyes.

"Justin, My husband's cousin, recently inherited a title. He is Carlisle now. As in the Earl of."

"How very delightful for him," Rhoda responded. Such things didn't matter to her anymore.

As she strode back to where Emily was chatting with one of the maids, Sophia practically skipped alongside her. "Marriageable. That's what I'd call him."

Rhoda couldn't help but laugh at that. He was also a vicar, for heaven's sake. "You ought to introduce him to Emily, then."

RHODA WAITED FOR the perfect moment to inform her mother of Sophia's invitation. A house party so early in the Season, really, was quite extraordinary. She must present the excursion in such a way that her mother could not refuse.

Thus, two days passed before Rhoda broached the subject.

She and Coleus, the eldest of her two younger sisters, sat quietly crocheting while Hollyhock, just ten and five, practiced at the pianoforte. Although Coleus had wanted to have her come out this Season, their mother had refused.

She'd been emphatic that Rhoda must secure a husband first.

Rhoda's mother and both of her sisters, therefore, had experienced the disappointment of St. John's untimely demise along with Rhoda last summer. Unsurprisingly, her mother remained undaunted. With the knowledge that her eldest daughter had attracted a marquess, she now would set her sights on nothing lower than a viscount.

"Mama, Sophia is hosting a house party at Eden's Court," Rhoda mumbled vaguely, as though this was nothing unusual.

"I imagine Kent will be lovely during the summer months." Her mother remained focused on her knitting, keeping her dark head bowed and her efficient fingers moving. Of course, her mother would assume the event would be held at the end of the Season.

"The party commences in four days."

At this, her mother jerked her chin up and stared at her with disbelieving brown eyes, so similar to her own.

Rhoda plowed ahead, undeterred. "His Grace has invited some *very* eligible bachelors." Sophia had informed her the duke had invited Mr. White—Lord Carlisle, she'd do well to remember. The very day after Sophia had informed her of this piece of news, an announcement had appeared in the papers. And Lord Blakely would be in attendance, although she'd wager that particular bachelor would refuse to marry until he became an octogenarian.

"Hmph." Her mother did not seem entirely convinced. Well, of course not.

"Two unattached earls, Mother."

A gleam of excitement emerged behind her mother's eyes. This was not the first time Rhoda had witnessed this effect. If there was one thing that excited her mother these days, it was the prospect of Rhoda landing a title. "Who?"

"Um, Lord Blakely," she began.

"That rake!" Her mother wasn't all that impressed, apparently. But then she twisted her lips and scrunched up her nose. Lord Blakely was an *earl*, after all. "Well, I suppose he's going to have to marry eventually. And who is the other? Certainly not the new one?"

"Yes, Mother, the vicar, Mr. Justin White. He is now Lord Carlisle."

"Hmm..." Her mother set her knitting in the basket beside her. "Quite often a lady shows better away from the crowded balls. Gentlemen are less distracted and more able to notice those finer characteristics. And this will be hosted in Kent? By the Duchess of Prescott?"

"In four days. Coleus and Hollyhock are invited as well. Sophia says it will be mostly informal."

And when such news reached their ears, both of her sisters went to work on Rhoda's behalf. Rhoda grinned as she watched them swarm around their mother.

"Please, Mama!" Hollyhock clutched her hands to her chest, looking quite sorrowful really.

"There is nothing for us to do here! Until you allow me to come out, London offers me nothing but tediousness." Coleus dropped to her knees. "Please, Mother, please?"

"Don't be so melodramatic, Coleus." Her mother rolled her eyes heavenward.

Before two minutes passed, however, her mother was shaking her head. "Give me the dates, dear. I'll send notice to the hostesses I've already accepted. Excepting the garden party tomorrow, however. I do expect you to make the most of such a picturesque setting. Just in case."

"Of course, Mother."

It had been decided.

The Mossant ladies would be attending the Duchess of Prescott's midseason house party.

CHAPTER FOUR

A Good Dunking

WITHOUT EMILY—WHO'D CRIED off at the last moment—by her side, Rhoda had no choice but to attend the Snodgrass Garden party with her mother.

She wore one of her newer day dresses, a creation she'd collected the day before from Madam Chantal's shop. Not given to false modesty, Rhoda knew the bold jonquil yellow color set off her hair and skin perfectly. It even drew out the little golden flecks of light in her plain brown eyes.

Not many women could carry off such tones, Madam had effused, while draping the material down Rhoda's front. Rhoda would be envied.

Rhoda smoothed her skirts while an unusual collection of nerves attacked her as her mother alighted from their coach.

She'd received an inordinate amount of attention at the Crabtrees' ball. And then so many flowers arrived afterward.

She didn't trust any of it—not the dance offers, nor the bouquets. Despite the gorgeous weather and the prospect of a delightful party, Rhoda wished she were already in Kent.

"You will outshine all the other ladies here today." Rhoda's mother grasped her by the elbow and led them around the path other guests were already following. "I must admit, Madam Chantal has outdone herself with that one," she added with a sideways glance at the new dress.

"And yours." Rhoda reached out to touch the fine silk of her mother's understated day dress in deep Pomona green.

For a moment, Rhoda experienced a nostalgic comfort of going somewhere with her mother. Perhaps the familiar scent of her mama's perfume brought it on. Mrs. Mossant had worn the same scent as long as Rhoda could remember.

"Such a shame St. John didn't live to see you in it."

Whoosh.

The warmth and security disappeared in one fell swoop. Any mention of St. John, or the events of last summer, never failed to drop Rhoda's heart into the soles of her shoes. The edges of her vision clouded, and the world tilted awkwardly.

"I still cannot believe Miss Beauchamp landed the title. A duchess! You were so very close to having it yourself!" Rhoda wished her mother and sisters would forget about St. John. She wished even more that she could.

Nearing a cluster of guests, Mrs. Mossant patted Rhoda's gloved hand as though she were a child. "There are Mrs. Potter and Mavis Torrey. I simply must express my regrets to them. Both are hosting parties next week that we're going to miss. An apology is always best made in person." She then pressed Rhoda onto a nearby bench and took her leave.

Mrs. Mossant had never made for a very good chaperone. She was too much of a socialite herself. Rhoda sighed and gazed around at the lovely setting. Lady Snodgrass had obviously planned her soiree so that it coincided with the blossoming of the most colorful flowers in her garden. Pink, purple, deep blues, and golden yellows matched the colorful bows tied to the canopy that had been set up a ways from the manor.

Rhoda didn't know the actual names of the flowers. That was her mother's particular talent.

Despite the sun, the stone bench felt cold on her backside. She pressed her knees together and studied some of the other guests. With Cecily and Sophia married, Rhoda found herself regretting the fact that she hadn't attempted to make many other friends. Even the few ladies she'd conversed with on occasion didn't seem to recognize her.

Which was odd… because, whereas none of the women met her gaze, a considerable number of the gentlemen present seemed to be brazenly staring at her.

An ominous shiver ran down her spine, and she swallowed hard.

Suddenly, despite sitting in the sunshine, on the edge of Lady Snodgrass's exquisitely decorated courtyard, in the presence of over a hundred reputable members of the *ton*, Rhoda felt ill at ease. Frightened, somehow.

And Rhoda was never frightened.

Foolishness! Nonsense. Likely, she was imagining things.

"Miss Mossant."

Rhoda jerked her spine ramrod straight when she realized Lord Kensington had crept up behind her. "Fortune is shining upon me today! How is it that I am so lucky as to find you sitting here alone? And looking so fetching?"

Surely, he wouldn't! Not after his actions the other night. He moved around the bench to stand directly before her and presented a stockinged leg.

She'd not acknowledge him. Blond hair, perfect features, and sparkling blue eyes—such looks were wasted on the lout.

She'd give him the cut direct.

His arrogance, his *nerve*, knew no bounds.

"Come now, Miss Mossant. Surely, you don't fault me

for being overcome by your beauty." Lord Kensington turned and dropped onto the bench beside her. He then had the audacity to attempt to take her hand in his.

Rhoda was no weak-willed simpering young miss.

Not anymore.

She snatched it away before he could wrap his fingers around hers, but he persisted. "A diamond such as yourself mustn't ruin your countenance with such an ugly scowl."

She would not be pleasant to this… person. She couldn't even think of him as a gentleman. "If you do not enjoy seeing my scowl, I suggest you find another lady to harass." She spoke in polite tones, staring straight ahead.

And then his hand landed on her leg.

Enough!

Bolting off the bench as though burned, she'd like to have called him out for his audacity. Unfortunately, she knew these people. They'd look the other way. As an earl, Lord Kensington would escape censure. As always, the *ton* would take his side.

She'd been lucky to escape him before. She'd not make the mistake of being alone with him ever again. She covered her mouth briefly, stifling the gagging sensation the incident provoked.

She hated this. Why was everything so… off?

Fighting the inclination to run away, to have their carriage brought around, Rhoda lifted her chin and stifled her urge to sprint in the *opposite* direction. To sprint away from all these people who suddenly acted like strangers.

But she could do no such thing, so she strolled in a leisurely fashion through the small clusters of people. She simply needed to find her mother.

One by one, as she approached familiar faces, heads turned away.

Other ladies recognized her easy enough but refused to

acknowledge her. A cold vise began squeezing her lungs. What was going on? What had she done now?

What do these people know?

And where on earth was her mother when she needed her? Good heavens, if Rhoda experienced such treatment, it was more than likely her mother might be experiencing it as well, but for her few close friends.

But even then, scandal could end many a friendship.

If only she knew which scandal had come out.

"SUCH AN HONOR to meet you, my lord! This is my daughter, Miss Louella Rose. Louella, dear, make your curtsey to the earl." Justin cringed inside as the young woman dropped obsequiously before him, her smooth mahogany ringlets falling forward.

He'd been introduced to the mother, once, he believed, and she'd looked down her prominent nose at him. He believed the father to be a viscount. The girl really was beautiful. A perfect English Rose. Too perfect, in fact. As though she'd been groomed with the express purpose of attracting an acceptable title. He imagined he now fell into that criteria. God, he wished he could have kept the news under wraps a bit longer, or better yet, not inherited at all.

If not for Prescott's request, he would not have attended today. The duchess would have come herself if possible. She'd implored her husband to provide some sort of protection for Miss Mossant. It was the last event Miss Mossant would attend before being swept away to the country by her concerned friends.

"My pleasure, ladies." He bowed, all the while trying to catch sight of the tall chestnut-haired beauty who'd taken residence in his mind as of late. Although having witnessed the way she'd handled Kensington, he doubted she needed anyone.

He frowned, uncertain whether he admired her unconventionality or was repulsed by it.

Perhaps some of both.

"Such a beautiful day." Lady Redfield, a round and rather buxom woman, tilted her head back, indicating the clear blue sky. "Perfect day for a boat ride, don't you think, Luella, dear?"

Miss Luella Dear gazed toward the lake and then glanced down at her wrists. Oddly enough, she had silk ribbons tied around them. Odd fashion these debutantes sported these days. "Oh, yes, Mother. The conditions are divine."

Not at all what he wished to do. Except he could not in good conscience disappoint the girl—or her mother.

One more search for Miss Mossant and then he cleared his throat. He couldn't exactly explain that he had attended only to protect another lady from the very gentlemen who ought to be most trusted. "Miss Redfield." He bowed. "I'd be honored if you would allow me to row you around the pond."

A perfect smile, and then perfect blue eyes peered up from beneath long, dark lashes. Slim and just the perfect height, the younger woman took hold of the arm he'd extended and fell in beside him. "Have you just arrived in London, my lord?"

Justin took a breath and began to respond but was interrupted before he could get a word out.

"Papa brought us an entire week early so that I could shop. He insists I dress in the finest England has to offer. You wouldn't believe the dresses I've ordered. Do you like this one, my lord?" She released him and halted her steps in order to skim her hands over her skirt and twirl around. The dress looked the same as every other dress worn by the other debutantes that afternoon.

"It's lo—"

"Because Mother declared the pink perfect, but I'm not as certain."

Justin nodded and smiled. He could see he wasn't going to have to search for topics of conversation with this chit. As the thought struck, a flash of yellow caught his eye.

The color had somehow captured Miss Redfield's attention as well. She turned her head and then grimaced. "It's Miss Mossant! She has such lovely coloring. I don't believe I could ever wear such a color, but it doesn't look quite so horrible on her. Mother says I'm not to converse with her though. Mother didn't tell me why; she only mentioned that Miss Mossant had tainted herself forever. I'm surprised Lady Snodgrass received her today." And then she met his gaze conspiratorially. "Do *you* know what she's done to kick up so much scandal?"

Justin pursed his lips in disapproval. A convenient set down he'd learned from the vicar who'd retired before him. "I'm certain your mother is mistaken."

Miss Mossant did indeed have lovely coloring. And the dress perhaps would have made most other ladies appear sallow. But not her. It set off the golden highlights in her russet locks and made her coffee-colored eyes appear even darker. Mysterious.

He imagined it would bring out the golden lights hidden there and itched to take a closer look.

She held herself proudly even though no one approached her.

Justin winged his elbow to Miss Redfield and firmly changed their direction.

The determined debutante did her best to tug him, once

again, in the direction of the jetty where the boats had been left out, but Justin's mind was set.

Best for him not to appear to have singled one particular lady out today, anyhow. He'd be safer in the company of two.

"My lord, really, Mother will be most *vexed* if she sees me in her company," Miss Redfield whined, on the brink of panic. Justin patted the top of her hand.

Miss Mossant's gaze narrowed suspiciously as she caught sight of him approaching with Miss Redfield. Initially, he saw a hint of vulnerability behind her defiant gaze. But as she seemed to realize what he was about, it turned to relief. Too late to turn back now.

"Miss Mossant." He released Miss Redfield long enough to bow.

Grasping the skirt of her brilliant gown in one hand, the solemn lady curtsied hesitantly.

"Are you acquainted with Miss Luella Redfield? She was just now making known to me her appreciation of your dress."

Miss Redfield fidgeted for all of thirty seconds before apparently deciding she'd rather vex her mother than contradict London's newest earl. "Um, yes, Miss Mossant. No one else would ever dare appear in something so bold."

"Why, thank you, Miss Redfield. I've grown ever so bored with wearing bland pastels."

Justin smiled to himself at Miss Mossant's gentle jibe. Now that he'd located her, he was reluctant to leave her alone.

He'd make the boat ride into a threesome. But indeed, this was an ideal solution.

"Miss Mossant, you must join Miss Redfield and me for a ride around the lake." Without giving her a chance to respond, he tucked her arm into his and then winged his other toward Miss Redfield's. Again, indecision flickered over the girl's perfect features, momentarily marring her creamy complexion. She pinched her lips but slipped her hand in the crook of his elbow.

Luck was on his side, for certain. Quite pleased with himself, he assisted the ladies along the jetty toward the closest available craft. Dropping his arm, Miss Mossant stepped back while he carefully aided the other young woman aboard.

"Careful now, Miss Redfield."

She clasped his hand tightly and gingerly found her seat. Once safely aboard, she spread her gown picturesquely around herself.

Justin turned toward Miss Mossant, who surprised him with an impatient frown. "This really isn't necessary, Mr. White."

"Why do you persist in addressing him as Mister?" Miss Redfield asked from her position on the water. "Are you not aware he is an earl? Surely, you insult him, Miss Mossant."

Still scowling, Miss Mossant moved to board the craft grudgingly as Justin sidled her to the edge of the jetty.

"I take no insult, Miss Mossant," he assured her.

She tentatively placed one slippered foot onto one of the wooden seats, her hand still in his, and then lowered her other one to the bottom of the boat. Justin experienced an inkling of concern when he realized Miss Redfield was rearranging her dress once again, unbalancing the boat in the process.

And then Miss Mossant lost her footing for some unknown reason.

She fell toward and then away from him and would have gone tumbling into the water but for his hand. At that moment, the boat, secured only with a loose rope, drifted away from the wooden pier, leaving a few feet of open water between them.

Torn between releasing his hold on Miss Mossant, who by no means had found her balance, or jumping across the ever-growing expanse of water, possibly toppling all of them over in the process, Justin found himself at a complete and utter loss.

And then… the inevitable.

CHAPTER FIVE

A Hasty Escape

As MISS REDFIELD arranged herself in the boat, Rhoda hoped her mother had met with more kindly guests. Poor, dear Mr. White seemed to believe he was performing a good deed. She'd recognized the expression on his face easily as he'd steered the reluctant, but perfect looking debutante in her direction. The girl had not been happy to make Rhoda's acquaintance, let alone share her companion.

Once the confection of lace and pastel tulle had been arranged perfectly, making Miss Redfield appear like the center of a giant pink daisy, Rhoda stepped across and into the boat herself. She rather appreciated the strength of Mr. White's hand as the craft rocked slightly when she shifted her weight.

One more step, except her foot did not land on the bottom of the boat, but on the slick material of the other girl's dress. And when Miss Redfield pulled on the fabric in irritation, Rhoda shifted her weight, unsettling her already precarious balance. Without Mr. White's firm grip on her hand, she would have landed on her bottom.

And then the world seemed to shift.

Her world, anyhow.

The boat began sliding away from the jetty and what with all the helping and being gallant, Mr. White stretched himself farther from the dock than was prudent.

Rhoda wished that he had released her hand before doing so.

Regret contorted his handsome features just before he disappeared beneath the water. Regret because he obviously knew that he'd been unable to prevent a very unfortunate accident from occurring.

And he'd had the right of it for, pulled by his momentum before he'd released her hand, Rhoda dove into the water head first after him.

The water was not merely cold! It was glacial, arctic, bitterly unwelcoming. Rhoda knew better than to gasp but found it impossible when one's entire body submerged without warning. She swallowed a mouthful of water and frantically swirled about. For too many seconds, she couldn't tell which way she needed to go to reach the surface.

And then a hand appeared before her face.

Gratefully, she took hold of it and was tugged upward until breaking the surface.

Air. She took in a few gasping breaths and began shivering at the same time.

And now that she'd been tipped back to vertical, her feet found the bottom easily. Murky sludge globbed onto the bottoms of the delicate slippers Lucy had so diligently cleaned earlier.

Well, at least she wouldn't drown!

But oh, her dress had likely been ruined and her hair hung about her in long shining strands. Glancing down, she grimaced in disgust. Green slimy vegetation had attached itself to her hands and arms. Goose flesh appeared as she peeled them away.

"I'm drenched!"

Surprisingly, these words didn't emerge from Rhoda, nor even Mr. White, but from Miss Redfield, who was slowly drifting away as the rope loosely tying the boat to the jetty had come untied.

When Mr. White looked as though he might swim after her, a shout from Lord Stanton, who was rowing another lady on the water, stopped him. "We'll tow her in, Carlisle!"

Rhoda's teeth chattered, and a violent shiver rolled through her, yet she still couldn't help finding humor in Miss Redfield's plight. Other boaters hailed her to sit still, and all the while, the silly miss complained loudly that she'd been splashed when Miss Mossant jumped into the water.

"I'm going to catch my death, for certain. And even worse, my dress is ruined! And my bonnet even!" The whiney complaints decreased in volume as the craft slowly drifted away toward the center of the lake.

And then a sturdy arm dropped around Rhoda's shoulders. The warmth of Mr. White's much larger frame effectively subdued her shivers as he guided her to the bank a few feet away.

"I am so sorry, Miss Mossant. This is all my fault. I feel horrible. I imagine your gown is ruined. Oh, hell, and your shoes." His own shoes squished in the mud, but he didn't seem concerned with his condition nearly so much as with hers.

"I'll be fine." And then she deliberately added, "My lord." He was an earl now. He was no longer the humble vicar she'd met at Priory Point.

"I know this is wet," he explained, removing his jacket, "but I think it would be best to get you covered." His eyes were looking everywhere but at her.

Rhoda glanced down. Pulling her dress away from her skin, she flinched to see how transparent the material had become. Oh, yes, he had a point.

She gratefully slid her arms into his sodden jacket. "Well." She didn't know quite what to say. "That was one way to get rid of her."

Glancing up, she caught her breath. Beneath his waistcoat, his linen shirt had plastered itself to his arms and chest. His lordship, the former humble vicar, must have spent many hours laboring with his flock. Sinewy muscles showed through the material. Although Rhoda remembered considering him handsome enough, she'd not really allowed herself to consider him in that *way*. She wondered why not.

He was now an earl. Was it possible that she was so shallow as to view him differently for this? Of course, a man's status in the world mattered greatly to young ladies. It wasn't as if women could provide for themselves or a family. They'd be fools to not consider this aspect of the gentlemen they met.

And yet seeing him thus hadn't affected her mind so much as… what was he saying to her? "Pardon, my lord?"

"You don't think I would do this intentionally?" He stared at her reproachfully. His blond hair, now drenched, appeared darker.

Such brilliant blue eyes, though. She blinked in an attempt to clear her vision. Even while frowning at her, he seemed angelic somehow. Pure.

"Do you?"

"Believe you would deliberately cause such discomfort? You? Never! I was simply pointing out the silver lining to all of this." She gestured to her sodden gown.

Talking to him with his jacket draped over her shoulders, her chemise and… other things clearly visible to anyone who dared to look, Rhoda felt even more tarnished than normal.

He was watching the activity across the pond. She could tell he was fighting guilt at not hauling Miss Redfield back himself. Miss Redfield's boat no longer drifted aimlessly. The good Samaritans who'd volunteered their services were now towing her in.

"She's not in any danger. And I suppose they'll return her to dry land soon enough," he conceded with a grimace. Rhoda couldn't help but stare at his mouth. She shook her head to dismiss her surprisingly wayward thoughts.

"Miss Redfield will be fine." The dimwitted damsel. She'd likely intended for Rhoda to rip her hem.

Lord Carlisle's attention turned back to Rhoda. "We need to get you out of that dress." His ears flushed red. "I mean, you can hardly remain at the gathering looking like that." He tugged at his cravat. "Allow me, if you will, to escort you to your carriage?"

"Oh, but my mother is here… somewhere." As a breeze kicked up, she shivered.

"I'll locate her for you." He took her by the arm and began walking her to where the carriages waited. "As soon as I get you warmed up." He completely ignored the fact that he, too, was dripping wet.

"You aren't cold?" she couldn't help asking. He was just always so very *nice* to her.

She didn't deserve it.

"I'm fine." He patted her arm. She felt warmer with him beside her. And since he'd attached himself to her side, the anxiety she'd experienced earlier disappeared. Likely, he'd ignored whatever gossip had caused today's insults. Or perhaps no one had had the gall to gossip maliciously to the former vicar. He somehow didn't seem the type to allow society to dictate his actions.

Refreshing.

And yet, his attention seemed suspect somehow.

Was she his current project? But he was no longer a vicar. His vocation no longer dictated that he take pity on the wretched. Something cold curdled around her heart.

He would be at Eden's Court next week. Although she appreciated his protection, she did not appreciate his pity. She stiffened beside him.

He ought not to waste his time on her. Angelic creatures such as himself deserved to yoke themselves to somebody sweet, pure, and innocent.

Somebody like Emily.

JUSTIN COULDN'T BELIEVE he'd pulled Miss Mossant into the water after him. He'd tried releasing her hand, but she'd tightened her grip at the exact moment he'd lost his balance.

Had she been trying to save him from falling in? Good heavens. He was likely twice her weight.

Her lovely gown, the one Miss Redfield had envied so, had turned completely transparent. And although she obviously wore other garments beneath it, Justin ought not to have ever seen her… details… so vividly.

As much as he fought the urge, his gaze persisted in drinking her in.

Something about this woman seduced him.

The thought brought him up short. Did he think of her in such terms because of the rumors? He ought not.

No, that wasn't it.

The woman herself brought the notion to mind. He'd never known another lady like her. Although yet a young miss, foisted, like all the others, onto the marriage mart, her sensual essence contrasted strikingly.

She stiffened beneath his touch, as though reading his mind. She'd been standing alone when he'd located her earlier. And Miss Redfield's mother had instructed the girl to steer clear.

Likely, the other guests had been snubbing her.

Which gave him another characteristic to admire. Any other chit likely would have run away in tears.

Not Miss Mossant.

He glanced at her sideways. Even after having been dipped unceremoniously into a frigid lake, her looks moved him.

Perhaps more so, for her perfect features took prominence with her hair dripping wet and slicked down her neck and shoulders.

By now, they'd reached the drive. One of the footmen approached quickly. "Have the Mossants' carriage brought 'round, will you, sir?"

The uniformed man nodded and took off at a run.

Not often, Justin supposed, that his employer's guests departed dripping wet.

"You needn't wait with me." She went to slip his jacket off her shoulders, her lashes dropping so that she stared at the cobbled pavement. "If you'd get word to my mother, though, I'd appreciate it."

Her attempt to dismiss him was not subtle. He paused. He wasn't keen on allowing anybody else to see her in this state. "Keep the jacket. You can return it to me at Eden's Court." It was the first time either of them acknowledged the awkwardly timed house party.

He didn't wish to leave her unchaperoned either. The girl ought to know better. "I'll wait until your carriage arrives."

She frowned, staring at her hands now. "I'm looking forward to it. At first, I wasn't, but now..." The hurt in her voice revealed that she'd not been unaffected by the other guests' treatment of her today.

Justin hadn't expected her to say anything, let alone that. The smile she turned on him held a brittle quality.

"Sophia, Her Grace, I suppose I should say, has invited some of my dearest friends. Mrs. Nottingham and Miss Emily Goodnight. I believe you'll rather enjoy their company."

"I'm certain I will." A breeze stirred the trees above them and, for the first time since his dunking, he began to feel the cold.

"Your lips are turning blue. Where is *your* carriage, my lord?" She stared up at him almost accusingly as she huddled beneath his coat.

At such a question, he laughed. He'd never even owned a carriage. He'd walked.

"Don't tell me you plan on returning to Prescott House on foot."

"I've never had need of one." He shrugged along with his explanation. She faced him full on now.

"You may ride with me. We'll have the footman send word to my mother, and once home, I'll send the coach back for her."

Justin sneezed. Could he not, just once, actually save this wench?

"I refuse to allow you to walk when you're just as likely to catch a chill as I am."

The sound of horses approaching kept him from telling her that he considered her idea to be a sound one.

The coach waited, with Miss Mossant safely tucked inside, while he made arrangements for the message to be given to Mrs. Mossant. When he finally climbed into the cramped quarters, he was satisfied to see Miss Mossant had located a blanket and wrapped it around herself. His coat had been tossed on the back-facing bench.

She scooted to the far side and gestured for him to join

her. "There's only one blanket, my lord."

Justin dropped onto the bench across from her. He would have liked to take the corner of the rough wool but could not impose upon her that way. Already, his urges tempted him.

When she shivered, he couldn't help wishing he'd given in to them so that he could now tuck her up close beside him.

Necessity ought to have dictated that he impose upon her sensibilities but that he also exercise self-control. Which, of course, he would have. He simply wouldn't have slept well that night.

"Are you unhappy to leave your position as vicar? Now that you are an earl?" Her question took him by surprise.

"I need permission from the bishop, before I can officially retire. I have a worthy curate, however." He had little doubt the bishop would give his blessing. Justin had an entirely new collection of responsibilities to tend to now.

"So, you aren't reluctant? To abandon your… flock?"

An edge laced her question. As though she resented his very vocation. As though she resented the church itself. "There are indeed many families, many friends, I'll regret leaving. But I can always visit."

She nodded vaguely then folded her arms in front of her. "I imagine they'll be saddened to lose you." Again, not words he'd expected to hear.

He shrugged. "Sometimes, we don't have choices in these matters." He appreciated her interest but wanted to know more about her. He wanted to dismantle her defenses, understand why she'd so blatantly offended society.

He wanted the veil behind her eyes to lift.

If the rumors were true, hell, if St. John hadn't lied to him, she was no longer a maiden.

And yet, in her manner, in the rigidity in which she held herself, she did not invite familiarity. He'd guess that she was berating herself more than any snobbish London miss ever could.

If the rumors were true.

Seeing her like this now, he was glad her friends were watching out for her. Not many, ladies or gentlemen, could hold up against such a reception as she'd experienced today. Despite her good looks, she'd have difficulties finding a gentleman of the *ton* who would marry her. He wondered if the plans Dev's Duchess made might not all be in vain.

"Tell me about your family." He wondered if she would comply. He knew so little about this woman who had stolen into his thoughts.

Those arms remained tightly clasped in front of her. "My father is French." She didn't sound overly fond of the man. A major revelation from her. "I have two younger sisters. Coleus is seventeen and Hollyhock two years younger. And yes, my mother has a fondness for flowers."

Poor girls. Why would any parents choose to burden their daughters with such ridiculous labels?

"And they thought to name you—"

She sighed loudly. "Rhododendron."

A pink flower, from what he could recall. Hearty for landscaping. "One of my favorite flowers." He would not make a joke of it.

She chuckled. "Well done, my lord."

Could he woo this prickly young woman? As the thought crossed his mind, he brought himself up short. He was not looking for a wife. Was he? And he certainly couldn't take on a woman in her circumstances.

God, but she was a beauty though. And she tugged at him in a visceral way. His eyes searched her face; strong, high cheekbones; delicate arching brows, and lips, full, plump, the color of a pomegranate.

She watched him back warily, as though waiting for him to chastise her for such insolence. Behind her eyes lurked that combination of defiance and fear he'd begun to recognize. He quickly searched his memory for what he knew of various flowers. "The rhododendron is one of the heartiest of flowers, you know. It's from the evergreen family. Why wouldn't it be somebody's favorite?"

She looked for a moment as though she might soften, but then straightened her spine. "You haven't studied the language of flowers, have you?"

He hadn't. He'd heard of it but considered it something frivolous, suited for lovesick swains with nothing better to do with their time. "I'm afraid not. Feel free to enlighten me."

"But of course." She pinched her lips and narrowed her eyes. "The rhododendron isn't exactly a romantic flower. Whereas most flowers signify beauty, or devotion, or other such nonsense..." She bit her lip and twisted her mouth into that brittle smile once again. "The rhododendron leans more toward the macabre side of human nature. When you see a rhododendron, you ought to consider it a warning. In the language of flowers, it means caution. Beware. Danger."

"That doesn't mean it isn't beautiful." He nearly whispered the words. He'd not meant to say them out loud.

Her smile faded. He could swear her eyes welled up with tears.

And then the carriage rolled to a halt. Neither of them spoke as the driver pulled down the steps.

She blinked quickly and pursed her lips. "Good afternoon, my lord."

Justin nodded, not wanting to leave her alone, but unable to think of a single reason to remain in her company. "Good day, Miss Mossant."

CHAPTER SIX

Something's Amiss

"IT'S RUINED, MISS Rhoda," lamented the young maid shared between Rhoda and her sisters when she saw the condition of her formerly spectacular gown. "The fabric won't ever be the same." Lucy, a normally vivacious woman, had been with the Mossants for less than a year but had been as excited about the gown as Rhoda.

Rhoda stood in her chemise, goose flesh spread over her skin, awaiting assistance out of it. "It's just as well." Rhoda sighed. The afternoon had proven to be an utter catastrophe.

Not just because she'd fallen into the lake. Something was amiss. The female guests had pointedly ignored her. And the gentlemen… Well, they seemed to think they could say anything they wished to her, no matter how rude or insulting.

Except for dear, kind-hearted Mr. White—Lord Carlisle—that was. He actually seemed to *like* her. Which made no sense at all. Except that she'd never witnessed him showing anything but kindness, even to Miss Redfield.

He deserved somebody much like himself. Somebody equally good and smart. Somebody who could appreciate him for those very qualities.

Rhoda would steer him toward Emily. They would be a perfect match for one another. They were both kindhearted, pure, innocent, and undemanding. She'd do her best to help the two form an attachment next week at Eden's Court.

She'd die if Emily's mother sent her to Wales again. It was so far. And so desolate.

When Sophia had first mentioned the house party, Rhoda hadn't caught on right away as to why on earth she'd hold one. But then it had struck her. Sophia surely was hosting it so that Emily might have better luck landing a husband. Sophia had invited a handful of eligible gentlemen to come away from the throngs of debutantes in London, and since she was a duchess, they could hardly decline. Of course! That had to be Sophia's motivation all along. Nobody threw a house party at the beginning of a Season, especially when one's family was in mourning!

Leave it to Sophia to devise such a scheme.

Rhoda towel dried her arms and legs while Lucy fetched her dressing gown. Her skin felt clammy and cold.

She'd not felt chilled when Lord Carlisle watched her from across the carriage.

"Slip this on, Miss, while your hot bath is prepared." Lucy held up Rhoda's dressing gown.

Rhoda would be glad to get out of Town. Hopefully, whatever gossip was circulating about her would sort itself out after a few weeks of her absence. She hated to think Emily had heard it, or Sophia. Oh, Lord, and her mother!

"Rhoda?" Her mother stood in the open door. "Are you well? I came home as soon as John returned with the coach. What is this business I hear that you fell into the lake?"

Rhoda considered telling her mother about Miss Redfield's part in all of it but decided to keep it to herself instead. Because her mother would begin asking questions and then questioning her behavior. She only hoped her mother hadn't heard anything untoward already.

"Lord Carlisle had offered to row me about the pond and the boat moved away from the jetty before we were secured. He tumbled in as well."

"Oh, my! The Earl of Carlisle, you say?" And then a cunning spark materialized behind her eyes. "Quite an honor for you, I'd venture to say, for him to make such an offer. It's a shame you never got him alone on the water. I think an earl would make a suitable husband for you. After all, you did nearly marry a duke."

Rhoda groaned. She hated these outlandish expectations! St. John had not proposed to her. In fact…

"It sounds as if this Carlisle fellow might be interested in you. He wouldn't have made such an offer if he wasn't."

"He was being kind, Mother."

Her mother laughed. "So humble. My daughter is so humble. I was just telling Mavis how you never lorded your relationship with St. John over anybody."

Wonderful. Rhoda wondered what Mavis Torrey had had to say about that.

Her mother wandered across the room and picked up a bottle of Rhoda's perfume thoughtfully. "Mrs. Potter acted quite strangely today, though. Gave me something of a snub. I don't think I'll invite her to my next at-home. I certainly didn't appreciate her attitude."

Rhoda stilled at her mother's words. *What was being said?*

Rhoda intentionally made her voice breezy. "Perhaps she wasn't feeling well, Mother, and whatever bothered her will have passed by the time we return from the duchess's party. Think of all the morsels Mrs. Potter will be wishing to hear. Not just anybody receives an invitation to a ducal estate for two weeks."

Her mother contemplated Rhoda's words. "Hmm, I suppose. Yes. You're likely right." And then she did something quite out of character. She crossed the room and embraced Rhoda briefly. "I'm going to send Wesley up here to light a fire. I don't want you catching a chill."

Rhoda found herself blinking away tears for the second time that day. "That sounds lovely, Mother. Lucy's having a bath prepared. I think I'll take my supper in here and have an early night. If you don't mind, that is."

"Of course not, dear."

After her mother left and the fire was lit, Rhoda curled up on the comfortable chair in front of the hearth. Hugging her knees, she wondered how things might have turned out if she'd never met St. John—if Sophia had never engaged herself to Lord Harold. Would the three of them still be huddling together in the wallflower section of all the prominent balls? Would Rhoda still flirt and laugh the way she'd done before?

St. John had seemed like a dream come true. A future duke! He'd acted attentively toward not only her but her mother and Coleus and Holly as well. He'd ingratiated himself with all of them.

Rhoda had believed he loved her. He'd not ever said the words, but he'd indicated such with special looks, and... other ways.

How foolish she'd been! She should have waited. She should have followed the one rule that every girl with half a brain knew to be of utmost importance while being wooed by a gentleman. Because sure enough, after Rhoda had broken that one rule, St. John's attentions had changed. And then there'd been that awful afternoon at Priory Point.

Rhoda squeezed her eyes together tightly in an attempt to make the memory disappear.

But it never did. Surely, it would be with her forever.

THE JOURNEY TO Eden's Court didn't take more than half a day and aside from a little rain, proved uneventful. By keeping the windows open, they even managed to prevent Coleus from getting sick. Rhoda's mother hadn't mentioned her lady friend's strange behavior again and so Rhoda allowed herself something of a sigh of relief. Maybe it had all been nothing. Maybe she'd imagined it.

Rhoda had visited Eden's Court only once before, for Sophia's wedding, but she'd traveled then with Cecily and Mr. Nottingham. Today would be her mother and sisters' first visit and as they entered the long, stately drive, she enjoyed the looks of awe on their faces. "Oh, Rhoda," her mother effused. "And to think this was all nearly yours."

Argh! She needed to put a stop to this somehow. An idea struck her just then. Only one thing could change the direction of her stubborn mother's thoughts.

"Mother," she said firmly. "Every time you say something like that, every time you remind me of St. John's demise, you send me into a painful melancholy. How can I possibly consider marrying another gentleman when I am filled with such grief?"

Her mother didn't respond right away. And then, after all of thirty seconds passed, she backed herself away from the window and turned to Rhoda, her face covered in remorse. "I am so sorry. I didn't think... But of course, of course, I will do as you ask."

Rhoda almost felt guilty. "Thank you, Mother. I'd appreciate that."

Holly had been listening as well. "So, will you marry one of the gentlemen the duchess has invited to the party, then, Rho?" Rhoda couldn't help smiling at her youngest sister's naiveté. Holly, half girl, half woman at fifteen, would likely outshine both Rhoda and Coleus. Rhoda just hoped Holly didn't make the same mistake that she had.

In fact, she'd do everything she could to prevent it. Quite possibly as a ruined spinster, left on the shelf to live out her years.

Who would marry her now? Certainly not Lord Blakely, and Lord Carlisle was far too pure for her. Rhoda feigned excitement. "I'm hopeful, Holly." If such a man existed—one who didn't care about her past—were to ask, then perhaps…

They came to a stop in front of the mansion and waited for one of the grooms to set down the step. Glancing up as she climbed out, gladness filled her when she spied Sophia rushing outside toward the carriage. Cheeks flushed, she greeted them with a broad smile. Rhoda embraced Sophia as though they hadn't seen one another in months before stepping back.

Mrs. Mossant and the two younger girls dropped into curtsies.

"Are you getting used to all of this duchess business yet?" Rhoda whispered into Sophia's ear.

Sophia didn't answer her but instead laughed and then graciously invited everybody inside.

Lucy followed behind and was led upstairs by the housekeeper. Rhoda's mother and sisters were anxious to settle in and decided to follow as well. Once they'd disappeared, Sophia dragged Rhoda into a grand drawing room on the second floor.

"We arrived a few hours ago." Sophia seemed more fidgety than usual. Perhaps she felt guilty for hosting guests right now, after all. Rhoda would put her concerns to rest.

"I realized why you thought it so imperative to throw this house party. At first, I thought you'd simply gone a little batty, but I understand now."

Sophia stilled and then raised her brows. "You do?

"Emily."

"Uh..."

"The dear girl is destined to be sent to Wales with that dreadful aunt of hers again if we can't find her a husband. I'm sorry for being obtuse about this earlier. Anyhow, I know the perfect man for her!"

Rhoda pulled them both down onto the settee while Sophia stared at her in some odd sort of fascination. She seemed confused for a moment but then began nodding effusively. "Who? Have you met Lieutenant Landon before then?"

Rhoda waved a hand in the air, dismissing this Lieutenant Landon, whoever he was. "Lord Carlisle! Mr. White. He's coming this week, isn't he?" He'd mentioned that while at the garden party. Rhoda knew Sophia would never forget how Mr. White had behaved so chivalrously when Harold had met with his accident.

Sophia blinked those bright blue eyes of her. "I hadn't really considered Mr. White for *Emily*, but now that you mention it. He is such a kind man, after all, and he is an Earl now."

Rhoda held up her hand and, using her fingers, began listing all the reasons for her decision, already feeling more like herself. "Number one, he's sweet and charming. Not at all rakish. A man such as he would be tolerant and understanding of Emily's... er foibles. Number two, he's new on the marriage mart and, despite his good looks, hasn't yet become enamored with himself. Thirdly, he's good looking. Did I mention that yet? Quite dreamy, really. And fourth, but most importantly, he's *here*. And there are no other simpering debutantes to fight over him. I think with a few carefully orchestrated situations between the two of them, he'll be offering for her within the fortnight."

Sophia began nodding in agreement. "You mentioned his good looks twice."

"What?" Surely not! "No, number two was not about his looks. That was about his current mindset toward matrimony. He hasn't yet had a chance to raise his defenses, so to speak."

"Ah." Sophia bit her lip and then seemed to come to a decision. "I think it's a marvelous idea. How shall we proceed?"

Rhoda rose from the settee and began pacing back and forth. She did her best thinking while walking. Always. And it helped to focus on Emily's troubles. Give her brain a rest from her own.

"Who else is here, then?" First, she needed to understand the situation clearly.

"Lieutenant Landon, Dev's military friend, Dev, Emily, and Blakely, of course. And then there are your mother and sisters. Cecily and Mr. Nottingham won't arrive until tomorrow, and I just received a letter from her. She's persuaded her father to join them."

"So, but for my sisters, we have even numbers. We need to keep Emily separated from Coleus and Holly. If she gets caught up in their silliness, she'll do nothing to try to attract a man. After supper, Mama will send the girls to their chamber. Let's play parlor games. The interesting kind. But we'll fix the game from the beginning so as to throw Carlisle and Emily together somehow."

Rhoda stopped pacing and tapped her finger on her bottom lip.

"What about charades?" Sophia supplied.

"No, too tame." Rhoda tapped three more times and then gasped. "I've got it. Bridge of Sighs."

Sophia twisted her mouth up somewhat disapprovingly.

"The one where a lady rides around on a gentleman's back, on the floor? And then asks each of the gentlemen present for a kiss?" She sat up straight and placed her hands in her lap demurely. "I don't want Dev kissing other women, Rhoda."

Rhoda laughed. "Dev and Mr. Nottingham can kiss the ladies on their cheeks. That leaves three other bachelors who can play in earnest. We'll have Emily go first and then, after that, I'll announce that I'm exhausted and ready to retire for the evening. It will be perfect! We can see how each of the gentlemen respond to her!"

Still looking dubious, Sophia acquiesced. "Well, you might look in on her. She's having troubles with her spectacles."

Rhoda would take care of Emily's troubles. The spectacles would have to remain on Emily's dresser this evening. "She really does have fine eyes, you know, Soph?"

Sophia laughed at that. "If only she could see out of them!"

CHAPTER SEVEN

Emily's Plan

RHODA FOUND EMILY'S room easily enough, knocked on the door, and then turned the knob without awaiting an answer. Sitting in the middle of the room with clothing strewn about, Emily appeared paler than usual and somewhat distraught. "Emily, are you unwell?"

"Rhoda?" Squinting one eye, Emily stared in Rhoda's general direction. What on earth had come over the poor girl?

The room appeared to have been ransacked.

Rhoda picked her way through the discarded garments until she could examine her friend more closely. Ah, something was amiss with her spectacles. One of the glass pieces had gone missing. "What have you done to your glasses? You look strange. One eye is larger than the other."

In Emily's rather roundabout way of explaining things, she spit out that she'd dropped them in the coach during their journey and then somehow stepped on them. "And now I cannot locate my spare pair, and I've no maid to assist me with any of this!" Emily didn't become upset often. Apparently, the pressure her parents had been exerting was distressing her.

"You silly girl." Rhoda paced across the room, called for a maid, and then began scooping Emily's atrocious gowns off the floor. Browns, ugly dull green colors, and some dark lavender ones. Anybody would think the poor girl was in mourning. "What have you packed? The old usual? If you don't wish to live out the rest of your life in Wales, we'll need to come up with gowns more appealing than these."

"My predicament! What of yours? I'm so sorry Mother wouldn't allow me to attend the garden party with you. You didn't experience any... difficulties, did you?"

Rhoda froze for the slightest moment and then swallowed hard. She'd not *imagined* being shunned at the garden party. If Emily's mother heard something... Did Rhoda really wish to know? Even though her heart raced, she pretended nothing had been amiss.

"Where do you think you put the spectacles? Inside the trunk? Did you wrap them in a cloth or something? Could they be with your jewelry?"

"In a little green drawstring bag."

"Hmph." Rhoda searched around without locating anything of the like. At the same time, she pushed down the panic Emily's words invoked. What were members of the *ton* saying about her? "I don't see anything like it."

"Nothing untoward happened, did it?" Emily seemed to sense Rhoda's disquiet.

Untoward? But yes! With Lord Kensington's behavior and all the ladies not speaking to her! And of course, her dunking in the lake.

The worst by far ought to have been Flavion's advances. He'd thought he could touch her inappropriately. He'd shown her none of the respect or deference that a lady deserved.

Ironically, though, it was the gossip that troubled her now. She could not very well confront it and squash it off. At least with Lord Kensington, she could fight back. She could strike out at his attack with her knees and fists.

Unable to ignore Emily's question, Rhoda dropped into the nearest chair. "What have you heard?"

Emily's mismatched eyes widened at her question. "You mean you don't know? Sophia didn't tell you?"

"Tell me what?"

Rhoda braced herself. What were they all saying?

"Well..." The normally blunt Emily seemed to hesitate over her words. "It seems that some sort of a wager has been placed. At White's, the gentlemen's club."

"About me?" A wager? What had St. John done before having the inconsideration of dying on her? He must have told somebody about what she'd done... about what they'd done.

How many times would her poor judgment come back to haunt her? She'd hoped his feelings, his intentions toward her, had been respectable.

But she'd not acted like a respectable lady. She'd acted like little more than a light skirt.

He'd led her to believe he loved her. But he'd not come out and admitted it. Nor had he made any promises.

She'd been so foolish. She'd trusted him with more than her heart. She'd trusted him with her body!

Ice flowed through Rhoda's brain at the thought of strangers knowing. She covered her mouth with one hand, feeling the contents of her stomach lurch.

Emily rose and went to stare out the window. She waited a few seconds before turning and then dropping to her knees in front of Rhoda.

With a heavy pounding in her heart, Rhoda blinked away threatening tears.

"One of the members, one of the less reputable ones, if I don't say so myself—I thought White's was more discriminating in who they gave membership to—I can hardly fathom how such a one as whoever placed this bet has been given entry. Did you know that Lord Blakely has been denied? His father, of course."

Rhoda found herself gritting her teeth. *Get to the point already!*

"Oh, yes, the wager. Well, as I've already mentioned, it is about you." Emily frowned deeply. "Someone has spread a dreadful rumor that you, er, well, lifted your skirts for St. John before he met his end."

All the air left Rhoda's lungs, and the edges of her vision darkened.

She should have known. All those declarations of love, those whispered compliments, and avowals of devotion, had meant but naught to him.

And she'd been naïve enough to believe him!

All of that, his lies, his fake charm, were bad enough, but to then tell others what they'd done—what she'd done—she nearly choked on the bile rising from her stomach.

"Well then." Rhoda spoke evenly, ignoring the urge to sob. "How does one of these ignoble gentlemen win?"

"Amorous congress with the object of the bet. With you." Emily was not one to gloss things over. At that moment, Rhoda wasn't quite so sure she appreciated this quality.

But no. At least she knew now. It was worse than she ever might have imagined.

And then she couldn't help herself.

She gasped and slumped forward. "Men are monsters, Emily." No wonder her dance card had been filled at the Crabtrees' ball. She had known all the attention had been too good to be true. No wonder Lord Kensington had been so forward with her. That villain had simply been trying to win a bet.

A bet!

"But I have a plan."

Rhoda barely registered Emily's voice. *A plan?*

Despite feeling as though matters were beyond hopeless, she forced herself to sit up.

"Blakely's father," Emily continued, "has taken their quarrel to another level and had him blacklisted in London. Instead of bowing to his wishes, the earl wishes to thwart the duke. A perfect revenge for him is to marry somebody other than the young lady his father betrothed him to. And how perfectly delicious it would be for him to marry a lady deep in scandal herself! You! The two of you can simply dash up to Gretna Green over the next week or two and voila! Two birds with one stone!"

"Blakely?" Rhoda burst out laughing! It was either that or cry. "Blakely? He'll never marry. He's playing with you. Trust me, it's a joke to him."

Emily pushed herself up from the floor and stepped toward the window again. "Well, um, he hasn't exactly agreed to it yet, but he will. I didn't wish to present the idea to him unless I knew you would be willing." She lifted her thumb to her teeth and chewed on the nail.

Disgusting habit! Rhoda had to push her annoyance away in order to pay attention to what Emily said. Well, of course, he hadn't agreed to it. He never would.

"I realize it's quite a lot to take in right now, but you are in something of a muddle. I don't want those immoral fellows to keep saying things about you. This would quiet them for certain. What do you think?"

Emily had always been the wallflower facing the most obstacles when it came to landing a husband, the most awkward, the one who needed protecting from society's unkind assessment. And now Emily, of all people, was trying to help her.

Rhoda flinched. She wasn't prepared to face the ruinous extent of her situation. She wanted to wish it magically away.

Emily stared at her sternly. Her friend, it seemed, wasn't allowing such nonsense.

Even so..."Lord Blakely?" Rhoda doubted he'd ever come around, no matter how plausible Emily believed this plan of hers might be.

Perhaps... Rhoda may not be able to do anything about her own deplorable circumstances, but she could use this plan to gain Emily's cooperation in Rhoda's much more credible scheme.

Rhoda pushed her own troubles away, jumped up, and plucked a particularly atrocious gown from the bed. It seemed to be the color of, well, the color of—she didn't even want to think about it. "I've come to a decision." She tossed the gown aside and examined another.

"Are you still looking for my spectacles?"

"I am not." She waved one hand in the air. "However, you may tell Lord Blakely I might possibly go along with such a stratagem, but you must do something in turn for me."

"Oh, that's wonderful, Rho! I'll speak with him next time I get a chance." Of course, Rhoda expected Emily would try to ignore the stipulation.

"You need a husband as badly as I do, Emily. You, too, shall woo a gentleman to the altar over the next two weeks."

Emily frowned, temporarily losing all semblance of her brief bout of enthusiasm. "I know. I know." She squeezed her eyes together tightly and threw the broken spectacles onto the bed. "I just, I... I don't know how!" She appeared as though she might cry. She'd better not, for if she did, Rhoda would, too.

"Sit down." Rhoda steered Emily to the chair by the

window. "And listen." She rummaged around until she located some paper and a pencil and then plunked it down on her lap. "Take notes."

"Number one," Rhoda began, "Sophia will select all of your gowns for the next fourteen days. You are not to wear any of these…" Rhoda searched for an appropriate word to describe the dresses that made up Emily's wardrobe. *Oh, yes.* "…abominations. Ever again."

Emily, who'd been peering at her list from less than three inches away, glanced up from the foolscap with a scowl, but Rhoda continued without so much as an apology. "Number two." She must remain firm on this count. "You will not wear your spectacles. Men wish to see a lady's eyes, not a piece of hardware perched on your nose."

Rhoda knew this would be difficult, nearly impossible for Emily, but forced herself to remain firm at the thought of her dearest ally being sent so far away from them all.

"Number three, although you won't be able to see each gentleman clearly, I shall point you in his direction and you shall gaze longingly toward the blur, or whatever it is you see. And listen to him. Ask him questions about his childhood, about his hobbies."

Rhoda paused. Although Emily was shrewd and book smart, social affairs tended to confuse her more than anything else. Best to keep things simple.

"That's all?" Emily peered up from the paper.

A surge of warmth wrapped around Rhoda's heart. She loved Emily as though she were her very own sister. She'd do whatever she could to prevent her from being shipped off to Wales.

Not that Wales would be so bad by itself, but that aunt of hers sounded beastly!

"That's all." Rhoda would handle the other details.

"Leave the rest up to Sophia and me. We'll land you a husband first. And then." She stifled the disbelieving laughter that threatened to erupt. "Then I'll run away with Blakely… if he's willing."

Skepticism clouded Emily's eyes. "Shake on it?"

Rhoda wouldn't have to break her word. Blakely would go to his grave a bachelor. "Shake on it."

CHAPTER EIGHT

Ever the Vicar

AFTER ASSURING HERSELF Emily's appearance would be striking enough to capture even the most discerning of males, Rhoda returned to the chamber she was to share with Coleus and donned one of her own gowns. Since Lucy was busy assisting their mother, the two girls attended one another.

At ten and six, Coleus yearned heartily to make her entry into society. She'd learned all the fashionable hairstyles and had been begging their mother to take her into Madam Chantal's shop for a fitting.

"You really must marry, Rho," Coley prodded as she twisted and curled Rhoda's dark swath of hair into something supposedly stylish. "It won't be fair, you know, if I'm required to sit out another year after this one. Isn't there anybody you'd like to, well, you know?"

Rhoda met her sister's gaze in the mirror with a scowl. She most certainly didn't need to be beleaguered by an adolescent child right now. If Coleus had the slightest idea as to how Rhoda's reputation hung in peril, this very moment... She couldn't even think about it.

God help them all.

If Rhoda didn't bring matters under control, neither of her sisters would be given the benefit of the doubt either. A fine layer of perspiration broke out on her forehead.

What could she do to subdue such rumors about herself? St. John deserved to be cursed. At that moment, she imagined him baking in the depths of hell… but then her breath caught.

Likely, she'd eventually join him there.

For the first time, she had to wonder if Blakely might perhaps be amenable to Emily's outlandish idea, after all? She hadn't much choice, really. The only measure she could take to save her reputation was, indeed, to marry.

But Blakely?

She determined she'd make every effort to examine this Lieutenant Langdon fellow.

Last year, before St. John's accident, Rhoda had foolishly believed she'd all but settled her very own happily ever after. She'd believed she'd found the perfect gentleman, one whose soul melded with hers.

Now she could barely look herself in the mirror.

Coleus inserted one more pin and then stepped back. "Well, I've done my part. A work of art, if I say so myself."

Without examining her reflection, Rhoda rose and located her favorite shawl. "I'm going to explore the gardens before dinner." Lately, her lungs squeezed tighter than normal, making it almost difficult to breathe. Even within the confines of this beautiful manor, she felt stifled. Draping her shawl around her shoulders, she couldn't meet her sister's eyes.

If Rhoda couldn't squash this scandal, all of them would be ruined.

She felt Coleus's accusing stare acutely.

"You're so different now," her sister stated.

Rhoda knew she had changed. She wished she could return to her former self. "I'm sorry." She barely managed to whisper the apology.

Coleus looked at her curiously and then shrugged and sat down at the vanity herself. "Just don't get lost. Mama will have apoplexy if you don't return on time for the evening meal."

They'd be lucky if she were to disappear.

Rhoda hugged the soft wool around her shoulders and slipped out the door.

IF ANYTHING COULD soothe Rhoda, it would be this garden. Especially now, in early spring. God, her mother, the lover of all horticulture, was going to be in raptures when she discovered it.

Rhoda wandered for a few minutes and upon seeing an old wooden bench, sat down, closed her eyes, and tried to calm herself.

A bet!

About me!

God damn you, St. John!

"I'll leave you alone, if you'd prefer."

Lord Carlisle.

She didn't need to see him to identify his voice.

"No. Please stay." She opened her eyes, surprisingly eager to have her solitude interrupted.

Something about this man inherently calmed her.

"Won't you sit?" She made room for him beside her. It wasn't a large bench, but space existed enough for two.

He lowered himself and the strength of his thighs immediately pressed against hers. Rhoda chastised herself for wanting to lean into him. The wager hadn't been based upon vague rumors. They'd had St. John's word! And he'd been telling nothing more than the truth.

She was a wanton!

And now she found herself all too aware of the man

seated beside her, a man of God. Well, he had been, anyhow.

"Are you ever going to travel to your estate? Put the family out of their misery? Surely, by now, they've imagined all manner of ogres coming to banish them from their home?"

"I've written my cousins. They know they have no need to worry." His voice condemned her in the kindest of ways, for assuming he'd be one to cause anyone undue wretchedness.

"Of course, ever the vicar." She bit her lip at her unkind words. It wasn't his fault she'd ended up in such a scrape. God help her, Carlisle likely was one of the last gentlemen left who'd treat her with any manner of respect.

He leaned forward, much as he had last week, at the ball, before any of this was known. His elbows rested on his knees, and he seemed to be contemplating his loosely clasped hands. He lacked his normal peaceful countenance though.

"You are reluctant, aren't you?"

He shook his head. "You are right, I've delayed in taking on my new responsibilities. I should not have come here, to Eden's Court. It's time I looked into the circumstances of the estate."

Nothing was as simple as it seemed. Lord Carlisle might just as well have inherited a burden as an asset. "Soon enough, we'll all have to return to our troubles." The words escaped her mouth of their own accord.

"I imagine you've heard about the wager, then."

She could have groaned. His knowledge of the bet exposed her. If Carlisle, a former vicar, had heard about it, then who in heaven's name had not? In a flash of hysteria, she considered she might just as well have gone parading down Bond Street in nothing but her chemise… or less…

It seemed everyone knew something she'd considered to be the most intimate moment of her life. But that they knew the other...

She would not cry.

"Don't fancy yourself winning it." Why was she striking out at Lord Carlisle? He'd never been anything but kind to her.

"Of course not." And, of course, she had no choice but to believe him.

Rhoda barked out something between a laugh and a scoffing sound.

"That would explain Kensington's behavior last week," he pointed out softly.

Rhoda nodded. "And that of Miss Redfield's, I'd venture to guess." She could much easier think of this man as a vicar than an earl. He wasn't nearly arrogant enough.

"May I ask you a question, Miss Mossant?" His voice held no demand, only polite inquisitiveness.

She considered a snippy retort but caught herself in time. Really, he'd done nothing to merit her ill will. "You may."

She felt the air stir as he turned his head to stare at her. Rhoda shifted herself on the bench so that she could face him fully.

"What do you intend to do about it?"

Rhoda held herself stiffly. "Why would you think there was anything I could do?" Except for Emily's plan. But she wouldn't share that with him. She certainly didn't relish being laughed at.

He did not attempt to answer her rhetorical question. Instead, he merely stared at her, looking somewhat perplexed.

She'd forgotten the purity of this man's eyes. Blue like the clearest of days. When he focused so intently upon her, she could feel his gaze all the way to her toes.

"From the moment I met you, you have proven to be a woman of strength. Therefore, I simply assumed..." He tilted his head questioningly.

For a long moment, she couldn't think. He seemed to see into her very soul. Had he done that with all of his parishioners or only those of the female variety?

And if he could see into her soul, surely, he'd not be talking to her now.

She swallowed hard. "Sometimes we lose our strength."

She'd not meant to say it. Something about him drew her deepest thoughts. His quiet reassurance pulled the words from her.

"Do we lose it? Or do we relinquish it willingly?"

If she laughed at his intuition, at his astute judgment, then perhaps she wouldn't feel so compelled to examine herself to discover the answer. That would explain her unkind comments earlier. She'd known, on a deeper level somehow, that she'd best defend herself against him. Against his kindness, his purity.

"Such foolishness." She forced a harsh laugh out.

He continued staring at her, as though she'd not said a word. And then, "You can always find it again. Don't let them win, Miss Mossant."

At his words, Rhoda's laughter froze. Her lips trembled. She wanted to tell him the truth but could not form the words. As heat burned behind her eyes, Rhoda finally turned away.

For a terrifying moment, she'd had to fight the urge to bury her face in his neck, to inhale his clean masculine scent, to absorb his goodness.

And he'd probably have let her. He might be an angel, but he was also a man. He'd be susceptible to feminine allure.

But adding water to dye didn't purify the dye, it colored the water. She couldn't do that to him. She couldn't cast her sin on him.

JUSTIN HAD ASSUMED her secret was the obvious—her indiscretions with St. John. But sitting there, perceiving the torment behind her eyes, he wondered if it might be something else.

But what else could she be hiding?

He almost wished he'd never met her. Almost. If he'd never met her, he might sleep more peacefully. Dark eyes and sensual lips wouldn't taunt him in his dreams. He'd not awaken holding himself, imagining creamy thighs spread beneath him.

Her very essence tempted him. He had a desire to protect her but more than that. He wanted to possess her, in all the ways a man ever could.

God help him, but he wanted to take her into his arms. He wanted to stop her lips from trembling by covering them with his own.

He'd found other women attractive; he hadn't lived a chaste life, as many chose to believe. But his feelings for Miss Rhododendron Mossant nearly overwhelmed him. Since the day he'd met her.

And he didn't understand exactly why.

She tore her gaze from his and stared across the garden. Such perfection, he thought as he studied her profile. And yet, her beauty was only part of it.

"I'm going to disappoint everyone," she stated with far too much conviction.

He could not help himself. Lifting one hand, he turned

her chin so that she had no choice but to meet his gaze again, thankful he'd left off his gloves this evening. The tips of his fingers registered skin as soft as a butterfly.

"Is there something else?" he had to ask. Her lashes fluttered as she seemingly blinked away tears but shook her head nonetheless. There *was* something else. "I want to help you, if you'll allow me."

She shot off the bench. "I... I..." Looking everywhere but at him, she could not hide her distress. "There's no need. You cannot! Won't you let me alone, please? You're no longer a vicar, are you? It's not necessary for you to seek out my confession."

Justin simply watched her. Dear Lord but something tormented this woman. "I won't seek it out." His voice halted her. "But I'm here... if you change your mind."

She shook her head again, hesitantly this time though, and then made her escape.

Justin's gaze fixed on the path she'd taken long after she disappeared.

When he'd first met her, at Priory Point, just before Harold's death, she'd been a vibrant, carefree woman. His attraction to her had been instantaneous. Watching Miss Mossant back then, he'd been forced to suppress the desire to request permission to court her. He'd not had any choice. St. John had been squiring her around town for over a month by then. A gentleman simply did not pay his addresses to his cousin's... lady friend.

Justin had been plagued with irritation at his cousin, for he'd known that, as a marquess, St. John merely toyed with her. Luke's intentions toward her had been dishonorable from the beginning.

If only he'd died without blathering of his conquest first. Miss Mossant and her family could have moved forward, grieving, of course, but all the better for their loss.

Less than a year had passed since the tragic accident that had claimed three lives, the former duke, the duke's brother, and his heir, leaving Prescott to pick up the pieces. The duchess had suffered greatly—as had Sophia and Dev. At least they'd found solace in each other.

Justin rose from the bench and strode toward the house. With St. John gone, he'd have thought Miss Mossant might be somewhat approachable. He'd hoped to have the freedom at last to follow his urges. He'd have liked to take her driving, woo her… And despite his physical needs, he fully intended to act honorably.

With every attempt to gain her attention, she'd thwarted him.

In fact, she seemed more unattainable than ever.

CHAPTER NINE

Evening Entertainment

"LET'S PLAY A parlor game!" The resplendent meal had passed uneventfully and after biding half an hour over their port, the gentlemen had finally deigned to rejoin the ladies.

Rhoda and Sophia had decided that Emily was going to need some pushing in order to land herself a husband. She only hoped all of this didn't have the opposite effect. Sophia met her gaze from across the room with a spark of mischief behind her own.

"But not Charades," Rhoda returned, playing her part. "Something new! Something fast!" Her mother and Hollyhock had retired for the evening, leaving Emily, Sophia, Rhoda, and Coleus downstairs with Prescott and three equally available bachelors.

Rhoda had been more than a little amazed to see that Emily had actually upheld her promise to leave off her spectacles. Although not a raving beauty, Emily looked sweet and inviting and... pretty tonight. And, when she smiled, as she was doing now—Rhoda swallowed hard—she *did* look beautiful. Of course, Rhoda had known all along how truly wonderfully gorgeous her bluestocking of a friend could be. She delighted in the fact that the gentlemen seated beside her seemed to see it as well.

Even if one of them did happen to be her earl—scratch that, *not* her earl—the Earl of Carlisle.

Emily deserved to marry somebody wholesome and good. She most definitely did not deserve the fate her mother promised if she failed to become betrothed.

But if Emily did somehow manage to land a husband then… Rhoda glanced toward Marcus Roberts, the Earl of Blakely. Such a smug, self-satisfied man. Yes, precisely what she herself deserved.

Rhoda wondered if Emily had spoken with him yet about *the plan*.

Just then, he caught her watching him and a slow, sinister-looking grin spread across his handsome face.

Pox on it, *he knew*!

Her cheeks warmed.

"I know of just the game." Sophia had risen to her feet to stand beside her husband. The duke absolutely doted on her. She could ask him for a star, and he'd likely find a way to bring it back to earth. "Cecily wrote me of a parlor game some ladies in her neighborhood played last winter. It's called Beast of Burden." She then went on to explain the rules and how it was played.

Carlisle looked skeptical, whereas the other gentlemen grinned stupidly.

"So, if I'm to understand correctly," Lieutenant Langdon said, "the gentleman crawls around on the floor carrying the lady on his back so that other gentlemen might kiss her?" He gave a bark of laughter. "I'm game if the ladies are."

Coleus grinned stupidly while Emily scowled outright. Rhoda ought to have insisted her sister retire.

Rhoda moved across the room, sat down beside Emily, and then squeezed her hand. "We'll play, won't we, Em?"

Emily squinted at some unknown object in the distance. A twinge of guilt pricked Rhoda at how lost her friend seemed without her spectacles. But a vulnerable side to her showed, soft and feminine. "I, er, suppose?" Emily answered uneasily.

Prescott's scowl rivaled Emily's. "I can't abide my wife kissing anyone other than myself."

Scrunching up her nose, Sophia placed her hand on the duke's arm. "The kiss can be either on the cheek or the lips. Like brothers and sisters."

Even so, Prescott's arm pulled Sophia close to him. "As long as my objections are known." The glint in his eye warned the other gentlemen present, however. Any fellow choosing to attempt more than a buss on the cheek with his wife would find himself in hot water.

"One more thing," Rhoda added. "Everyone is blindfolded but the maiden and the beast."

Sophia smiled secretly upon hearing this. It was not a part of the rules, but she and Rhoda had decided earlier that it could possibly make things more… interesting.

Sophia called for a maid to fetch scarfs for blindfolds while the gentlemen moved the furniture, placing eight chairs in a circle.

The scarves were handed out and everyone was instructed to sit gentleman-lady-gentleman-lady. Blakely grumbled, and Carlisle looked resigned. Always the peacemaker.

Sophia had put everyone's names in two different bowls to decide who was to go first. "Emily," she announced. Then she drew from the other bowl. "Blakely, you're to be the beast."

Unanimous laughter erupted. What with Lord Blakely's reputation, even he could agree with being deemed a beast. Rhoda crossed her fingers for her friend as the earl removed his jacket and then got down on hands and knees. Emily glared in Rhoda's direction and sat upon his back.

"Now we all put our blindfolds on," Sophia directed.

The room went silent, except for a few hushed murmurs as the group donned their blindfolds. Rhoda sat between Prescott and Lord Carlisle and waited impatiently. It was up to Emily to guide Blakely toward the man she'd like to kiss her. This game was beyond risqué and if her mother discovered them, they'd all be in heaps of trouble. Her mother might even insist they return to London.

Rhoda listened, listened… heard some ruffling and then, far too quickly… "Blindfolds off!" This from Emily.

Her face had blushed beet red. Sophia and Rhoda met one another's eyes meaningfully. Had she gotten a kiss out of Lord Carlisle? She certainly looked as though something had ruffled her feathers.

Glancing toward Lord Carlisle, though, one would think nothing untoward had occurred. Unexpected relief swept through Rhoda at his practical and calm demeanor.

"Rhoda is next," Sophia announced, enjoying their game more than she ought.

Presumably, Rhoda resigned that she ought to steer her beast toward Blakely. If she intended to snag him, even for very unromantic purposes, it might be wise to make some sort of overture. "And the beast is Lord Carlisle."

For some reason, this caused her heart to skip a beat.

Nerves she'd not expected kicked into gear as he removed his jacket. Without the heavy wool coat, his waistcoat, and cambric shirt revealed his lean but muscular build. Rhoda's mouth went dry when she remembered how he'd looked after they'd had their dunking.

He efficiently rolled up his sleeves and then dropped to his knees. "Miss Mossant." His brilliant blue gaze bore right through her. Was he mocking her? Judging her? What could that look be all about?

Rhoda rose and, feeling unusually timid, crossed to where he awaited her.

"Blindfolds on!" Sophia announced.

Lowering herself onto his warm back, the intimacy of riding atop a gentleman returned to bite her. No wonder Emily had been blushing!

Trying to act as though nothing was amiss, Rhoda placed one hand on his shoulder and scooted her bottom onto the arch of his back. He felt warm and solid beneath her.

Now, without talking, she was supposed to guide him toward Lord Blakely. But how to guide him?

Twisting sideways, she grasped both of his shoulders and pressed down on the side she wished him to go.

Rocking slowly as he moved, he turned them in the opposite direction. "No!" she said aloud.

"You're not supposed to talk," Emily chided.

"Oh, yeah. Sorry." Drat this man. Rhoda pushed and then tugged harder.

Lord Carlisle continued in the wrong direction. Oh, well, she'd simply allow him to make the full circle and then she'd get to her destination anyhow.

Except before he reached Blakely, he stopped at an empty chair.

His!

She smacked the top of his head. Why was he being so difficult?

She went to smack him again, but her hand didn't quite obey her brain. Instead, it remained on his head, enjoying the feel of his hair.

Mesmerized by her own audacity, she watched her fingers thread downward toward his neck. Heat crawled through her arms and into her legs. She clenched her thighs in reflex to the liquid warmth that pooled between them.

What would it feel like to sit on him in a very different way? To touch his skin, instead of the fabric of his clothing. He seemed stronger than St. John had been.

Would his skin feel smooth to the touch? Would the hair on his legs be brittle or soft? Her fingers trailed around his neck to his jaw. The day's growth of beard scratched against her fingertips.

And then one hand grasped her wrist tightly.

What was he doing?

She tugged, in order to escape, but he refused to budge. In fact, he was slowly pulling her down.

As he did so, her face hovered just behind his neck.

A spice, bergamot? The clean scent of soap tickled her senses as she inhaled, inches from his hair.

He turned his head so that she could see the outline of his face. And then he released her hand and tapped his cheek.

He wanted her to kiss him.

He was only playing the game! And all he asked for was a kiss on the cheek. Not on the lips. Was he doing this to keep her out of trouble? Was this his way of trying to protect her from her wanton ways?

Red clouded her vision. His attempt to manipulate her was misguided indeed!

How dare he!

Allowing the frustration of the day to vent itself, Rhoda did not think about what she was doing. She relaxed her head, opened her mouth, and placed it on the side of his neck. She'd show him! He thought he was protecting her! He wanted to control her!

With the taste of his skin on her lips, however, she forgot quite what she'd intended. Sensing his racing pulse, Rhoda nipped at, and then swirled her tongue along the taut skin.

He gripped her hand again.

Locating his earlobe, Rhoda bit down, ever so gently.

"This is becoming rather boring," the lieutenant complained from across the room. "Is anything happening?"

Rhoda lurched from atop Carlisle's back and made a mad dash for her chair.

"Blindfolds off." Her voice came out lower than she expected.

As everyone slipped the silk from their faces, Rhoda couldn't help but look over to the man she'd been licking like one of Gunter's Ices. Kneeling now, he met her gaze squarely.

He gave nothing away. What was he thinking? Was he angry? Disappointed in her? Shocked? The man possessed an uncanny ability to conceal thoughts and emotions.

But then her eyes dropped to his hands, casually clasped together on his lap. There was one thing he wasn't quite so talented at concealing.

JUSTIN HAD BEEN a rule follower for most of his life. Rules existed to maintain order. Order protected the fabric of society. Society, well, society didn't always conform to rules or order.

So, when he'd listened to the rules of the game, and then later been selected to act as beast to Miss Rhoda Mossant, he'd already worked out the notion that the person did not need to be sitting in his chair to demand the maiden's kiss.

He could reveal something of his feelings, in a most respectful manner, by requesting the maiden's kiss for himself.

Which was exactly what he did.

Except that he'd angered her somehow. He'd seen it on her face just after making his request.

Had she wanted to kiss Blakely so badly? Was that it?

He'd known that was her direction when she'd placed those cool, feminine fingers upon his shoulders.

But he'd already decided upon his course of action.

When those same fingers began dragging sensually through his hair, he'd found himself tempted to…

He couldn't even think about it.

At this moment, he needed to focus on anything but Miss Mossant's attributes.

He reached up and tugged at his earlobe. By God, she'd bitten him.

She'd not drawn blood, of course, but she'd…

Think of something else, anything else. Kneeling, he could rest one arm across the front of himself, but if he were to stand right now, it could be rather embarrassing. A cold swim. Dead fish. The sickly-sweet flavor of Ratafia… But Ratafia was often a dark red, much like the lips of the woman who'd recently sat atop him.

Much like the lips of the lady eyeing him suspiciously.

"My duchess and I had best retire. Our little lady Harriette tends to make the nights rather short on occasion." Prescott rose, his hand firmly clasping that of his duchess.

Babies.

Clouts.

There we go. Justin planted one foot on the carpet and pushed himself to stand.

"Oh, but we haven't all had turns yet," said young Miss Coleus Mossant.

Her older sister shushed her. "It's been a long day. We'll play games again, I'm quite certain of it."

What kind of games? Justin casually sauntered over to the bowl in which the duchess had placed all the folded-up pieces of paper to draw from. Picking one of them up, he was not surprised in the least.

Blank.

CHAPTER TEN

I Did It

RHODA STEPPED OUT of Emily's chamber and closed the door. She pressed her back against the heavy oak and closed her eyes.

It was unbelievable, really.

Emily had asserted most adamantly that Lord Blakely was willing to marry her! He would elope with her—as a twisted form of revenge against his father.

What had her life fallen to?

Marcus Roberts, the Earl of Blakely, wished to marry her for the soul purpose of *punishing* somebody.

Sweat broke out on her forehead, and her heartbeats sounded loudly in her own head. After counting to ten, she lifted one hand to her chest. There wasn't enough air in here. Dragging in shallow breaths, all she could hear was the pounding of her heart.

I've become a punishment.

When she opened her eyes, the hallway appeared as an endless corridor.

On legs much weaker than they'd been only moments before, she forced herself to walk toward the staircase. She needed to be outside.

Who had she become?

Locating the banister, she carefully made her way down the stairs and outside.

The air chilled her bare skin, but it was not so cold that

she needed a wrap. Where could she go? She needed somewhere to hide. She needed to hide from herself, from the past that would haunt her forever.

"Are you running away, Miss Mossant?"

How did he do that?

Rhoda jerked her head around to see Lord Carlisle leaning against one of the brick walls that divided the terrace.

But then he pushed himself away from it and approached her. "I was only joking. Are you unwell?"

Where had her voice gone? She sensed something horrible chasing her. Gripped in inexplicable terror, her mouth refused to form any words and then the lawn, the walls, the trees were spinning out of control.

She shook her head in confusion.

In the next instant, strong arms tightened around her, pressing the side of her face against the wool of his jacket. "Shh… It's all right. Take deep breaths." His voice soothed, as did the motions of his hand stroking her hair and back.

She rested against his strength, eventually absorbing his warmth but still unable to make her voice work. She wanted to apologize, to step away from him but her body refused to obey.

After what could have been hours or mere seconds, he finally steered her toward a conveniently placed lawn chair.

Sitting unaided, now, she should feel better, not leaning against him, clinging to him. Instead, she acutely bemoaned the loss of his touch.

He'd located another chair for himself.

"I remember the first time my mother brought me to Eden's Court. Surely, I felt it must belong to the king himself."

Rhoda's heart slowed a little at his words. Even though

they seemed to come from far away, they summoned her back to the present.

"I was all of eleven years old. The duchess invited us for the summer. My mother was ecstatic! And how could I complain? There were even other boys my age."

"Harold? St. John?" Ah, her voice worked once again.

"And Dev."

"How exactly are you related to them?" She'd never really asked him about himself. The sound of her heart-beats no longer echoed as loudly. The air she breathed in actually filled her lungs now.

He seemed to make himself more comfortable before answering. "My mother is a distant cousin to the dowager, *very* distant."

"So, you inherited your title through your father?"

"Ah, yes." But he didn't say anything more on that. Suddenly, curiosity prodded her.

"How long ago did your father die?" She was being nosey now. Would he mind?

"My father went to war shortly after he and my mother married." The steady tone of his voice showed no irritation at her questions. "He didn't make it back. I never knew him."

"Your mother never remarried?"

He took a deep breath. "I think she wanted to. I think she would have... at first. But my father failed to provide for her, and she fell on hard times. She lacked... protection. She's never told me, but I've since deduced that her family opposed their marriage. And she was too proud to return to them upon his death. We lived in a small village not far from Bath. The men who wooed my mother never followed through with any sort of respectable offer."

Rhoda swallowed hard as the reality of his childhood dawned upon her. "You were poor?"

He nodded. "We were."

"But I've met your mother, on a few occasions. She's a beautiful woman. She mingles in the *ton*." Her statement was a question.

"I'm not sure who wrote who first, but the duchess and my mother began corresponding at some point. My mother told me we were only coming to Eden's Court for a short visit." He smiled ruefully. "We never really left. I was sent off to attend school along with the heirs to a dukedom. The duchess never made us feel as though we were an imposition. She insisted we were family. Family took care of one another."

"So… you were close to all of them." He'd been close to the family that had been decimated by tragedy last year. She remembered how he'd nearly jumped off the cliff after Lord Harold's fall. He'd persisted more adamantly than St. John that they bring in rescue efforts.

He nodded. "Not so much the duke, himself. But to Harold and Dev." He met her eyes candidly. "And yes, to St. John."

The honesty of his gaze caused her to look away and, staring across the lawn, she spoke without thinking. "I thought that I loved him. I thought that he loved me." What was it about this man that invited her confessions?

He didn't respond to her declaration, just sat calmly as a gentle breeze swirled across the terrace. When she shivered, he rose, removed his jacket, and dropped it on her shoulders. She huddled in his leftover warmth and watched him take his seat again.

"I did it." She spoke the words aloud. "I lay with him." A small portion of the weight she'd been carrying lifted from her chest. "I assumed he'd visit my father shortly after, but he didn't. In fact, I saw less of him afterward. He ceased singling me out." She swallowed the sob that threatened to follow her admission. She'd not said the words aloud to anyone.

She'd been so hopeful. So damnably proud.

She'd imagined how pleased her father would be. She'd thought it might change things for their family, for her father…

St. John's touch had felt like love, like a promise.

She'd tried to forget, but the memory remained as vivid as ever. He'd collected her from her parents' home, and they'd ridden the short distance on his high flyer. "He invited me to visit Prescott House." She laughed at herself. "I felt so honored. He wouldn't bring me to his home if his intentions weren't honorable! Would he? Of course not! I ignored every piece of advice I'd ever been given. Even so, I should have suspected something when no one else was about. It was a few days after Sophia and Harold's wedding, just before we were to leave for Priory Point." God, she'd been so excited. "I was such a fool!"

Lord Carlisle still hadn't spoken.

"He wanted to give me a tour, he said. He showed me the gallery, the gardens, and then, of course, the tour would not be complete unless I saw his chamber."

"But you trusted him." These were the first words he'd spoken since she began her confession.

"Yes." A sudden lump formed in her throat. She had. She'd trusted him. He'd treated her as though she were special. As though he *cared* for her.

"At some point, I stopped thinking of him as a marquess, and I began to see him as the man, St. John. Lucas. Was all of it a ruse? I was so easily deceived."

Lord Carlisle leaned forward, that thinking position of his that was becoming all too familiar. He loosely clasped his hands together, staring at the ground. "I don't think St. John would have feigned affection. Not that I'm defending him, mind you. You must understand, he was always set apart from the rest of us. Duty to his legacy came first. We went to school, and he had a tutor. We played games while he sat at his father's feet." His voice broke.

"And it was all for nothing." Miss Mossant spoke the words he couldn't quite bring himself to say aloud.

"All the training, the grooming, destroyed in the blink of an eye against the side of a rocky cliff." Justin cleared his throat. "What I'm trying to say, what I'm doing a poor job of saying, is that I don't believe St. John did *not* love you. I simply believe there were limits to what he could give."

"You don't seem shocked." She stared at him, her gaze cool and collected once again. She'd scared him earlier. Her face had turned white as a sheet and she'd nearly fainted dead away. She seemed better now. He only wished she didn't find it necessary to rebuild all her defenses.

He shrugged. "Let he without sin cast the first stone."

She laughed at that. He hated when she did that. He ought to leave Eden's Court tomorrow. Purge this woman from his blood. He had responsibilities at Carlisle House.

"I'm sorry." She'd stopped laughing, and some warmth entered her expression. "You don't deserve my acid tongue." At the mention of her tongue, he couldn't help but recall how she'd used it earlier that night. She avoided meeting his eyes. Perhaps she, too, was remembering.

He wouldn't leave yet. He had to see this through.

He clenched his fists and took a deep breath. "I wish to court you." He was not a person to play games. He would be up front about his intentions.

"No!" she nearly shouted as she sprang out of her chair. "No! No... You mustn't say that." Her eyes had grown wide, and a flush tinged her cheeks now.

He didn't appreciate the sting of rejection he felt at her adamant response. Damn his eyes, but this woman tied him up in knots. "Are you repulsed by me, then? Is that it?" He knew she was not.

Her eyes remained wide as she shook her head adamantly. "You don't understand. You don't know anything!" She held his jacket out for him to take.

But he knew she had some other secret. She loathed herself right now. And by God, he wanted to fix all of it and bring her into his bed. Into his life.

She attempted to turn away, but he caught her arm. "I'll escort you to your chamber." He'd not have her wandering the halls alone at this time of night. She ought to be safe here, but…

He opened the door and followed her inside.

"I'm to marry Blakely." The words hit him from out of the darkness.

Had he heard correctly? "Blakely?"

Lord Blakely had shown her no favor since they'd arrived. He'd seemed inordinately distracted, as a matter of fact. Was she now lying to him? Was this an attempt on her part to repel his attention?

She held her head high, answering his question with a barely imperceptible nod.

Needing to retreat, to rethink his course of actions, Justin escorted her upstairs, deep in thought. He avoided watching the line of her back as she walked in front of him. He would not allow his gaze to linger on the sensual curve of her spine and derriere.

"This is my chamber, here." She halted. She probably regretted telling him the truth about St. John.

"I've not heard anything about an engagement." Disappointment warred with anger at himself for not moving more quickly. "Has there been an announcement yet?"

She fiddled with the door handle and bit her lip. After all of thirty seconds, she finally said, "It's complicated."

She opened the door and slipped inside.

Well, then.

CHAPTER ELEVEN

New Arrivals

RHODA WISHED SHE could simply enjoy the company of her closest friends. She wished she could tell them everything. Be carefree as she'd been in the past.

Just be herself.

Sophia had canceled the picnic she'd planned the following day upon the arrival of Cecily and her husband, Mr. Stephen Nottingham, a day early. Surprisingly enough, Cecily's father had accompanied them as well. Apparently, he and Mr. Nottingham were merging their two companies, creating an importing and exporting business that would only be rivaled by the East India Company itself. Cecily apologized, not that he'd come along, but that he intended to iron out many of the details with Mr. Nottingham while here.

"Think nothing of it." Sophia waved off the apology as the good friends settled into her favorite drawing room. The last time the four of them had come together had been for Sophia and Prescott's wedding. And although they'd all come for the ceremony, the gathering had been brief. Nothing had been the same since Cecily married.

"Flavion is in London. Did you know that?" Cecily didn't waste time with platitudes, instead making her announcement before Sophia could finish pouring hot water into the cups for tea.

Rhoda stiffened. Yes, she was aware the earl had returned to London.

"Can you believe you were actually married to the lout for nearly six months?" Emily tucked her feet beneath her and shook her head. "Thank heavens things turned out the way they did."

"I was lucky, indeed," Cecily agreed, a mysterious smile flitting over her mouth. "And I'll freely admit that I far prefer his cousin."

"You do seem happy now," Sophia asked. "And we didn't even need to kill him."

At these words, a concerned frown replaced Cecily's smile. "He's up to his old tricks again, though."

"Flavion?" Sophia confirmed.

"Yes."

Emily became engrossed in her sewing while Sophia handed out plates for scones. The atmosphere had turned decidedly… uncomfortable.

Cecily turned a sympathetic gaze toward Rhoda. "You are aware of the wager by now, aren't you?"

Emily glanced up with a grimace, and Sophia took her seat gingerly.

Rhoda's stomach lurched. Even the mention of it… "I am."

"Mr. Nottingham and I stayed over in London a few days before coming here. I was lucky enough to get an earful from Mrs. Worthington at the Winters' Gala Saturday night.

"Of course, she had nothing flattering to say." Rhoda sipped her tea and took a deep breath as she contemplated the mean-spirited gossip spreading amongst the *ton* in London right now.

About her.

Rhoda caught a meaningful glance exchanged between Sophia and Cecily. "Don't hide the details from me." As much as all of this hurt, she'd rather know the truth than remain in the dark.

"Since you've left town, so many gentlemen have entered the bet that the stakes have risen considerably." Cecily picked up an embroidery circle and stabbed the needle into the cloth quite viciously. "The would-be winner, if, and of course, I say 'if' because I know there never will be one, but *if* there were to be one, he stands to win over fifty thousand pounds." She completed her stitch and then added, "And the amount continues to rise."

Rhoda's jaw dropped.

"If I could bet, I'd put all my money on Rhoda," Emily said.

"Well, of course," Sophia agreed. "But what does Flavion have to do with any of this?"

"Rumor is that the bastard has healed."

"Healed?" Did she mean…?

"Yes, he's regained the ability to—"

"His *mentula* works again?" Emily sat up straight and frowned. "Of all the rotten luck."

Mentula? What in the world? But then understanding struck and Rhoda raised her brows. Oh…

"My sentiments exactly. But that's not the worst of it." Cecily sounded apologetic. "He's bragging to everyone that he came close to winning the wager at the Crabtrees' ball. Of course, he is lying."

"Of course," Rhoda echoed through suddenly dry lips.

Cecily studied her a moment. "Since Stephen's put a steward in charge of the Kensington funds, Flavion's spending has been limited. He's determined to lay claim to the winnings."

"And we all know the lengths he'll go to for money," Emily interjected.

Yes, yes, they all did.

"How could he substantiate something like that, to prove he'd won? Wouldn't he need some sort of incontrovertible evidence? What would prevent any one of them laying claim to the winnings with a lie?" Emily asked, ever the logical one.

But Rhoda knew. "He must provide a witness." She shivered at the memory of that evening.

"Yes," Cecily confirmed.

Rhoda had been such a fool that night, thinking she looked prettier for some reason. Or had been more charming than usual. She'd imagined herself somebody special. Why else would so many gentlemen reserve a set with her?

Of course, someone must have been in the garden watching that night. If Lord Carlisle hadn't come along when he did... Yes, she'd managed to disarm Flavion, but what if his *witness* had made himself known? She'd never have been capable of fighting off two of them.

"I'm so glad we got you out of London." Sophia looked terrified for her.

"I thought this house party was for Emily." Rhoda glanced around the room. She hated that her friends must all pity her right now. At the same time, she didn't know what she'd do without them. "But, of course..."

"She'll be completely safe, soon enough." Emily met Rhoda's gaze, and Rhoda nodded. "Blakely's going to marry her. The two of them have plans to run away to Gretna Green. She'll be protected then. And since Blakely's blacklisted, they'll not have much reason to even *be* in London.

"What?" The word exploded in unison from both Cecily and Sophia's mouths.

"You and Blakely are engaged?" Cecily's brows rose almost to her hairline.

"And you didn't tell me? When did this happen?" Sophia looked hurt.

"Emily brokered the entire thing." Rhoda didn't *feel* engaged. "It happened rather suddenly."

"Just last night," Emily concurred. "He's going to marry her to get back at his father."

Rhoda's hands felt cold and clammy again. Would she ever come to terms with the notion that her bridegroom's sole purpose for marrying her was revenge?

The remainder of her life would be based on hatred. And fear.

The room fell silent.

"When?" Sophia asked the pertinent question.

"Blakely's flexible but Rhoda insists she won't leave until *I* am betrothed." Emily wrinkled her nose, making her spectacles bounce a little. She obviously didn't appreciate Rhoda's stipulation.

"Have the two of you gone completely mad?" Cecily no longer made any pretense of embroidering, setting her circle on the table beside her. "Emily isn't even close to being betrothed!" And then, questioning her own statement, she turned her gaze upon Emily. "*Are you*?"

But Cecily didn't understand how cruel Emily's aunt could be! Nothing would be worse for her friend than to be sent away to that woman!

"I'm determined she should marry Lord Carlisle," Rhoda interjected before Emily could respond.

"What about Lieutenant Langdon?" Sophia looked doubtful.

Emily scrunched up her nose again, but before she could answer, Rhoda responded, "Carlisle is perfect for her."

Cecily narrowed her eyes and turned to Emily. "Do *you want* to marry Lord Carlisle?" Before Rhoda could speak,

Cecily held up a halting hand. "And hush, Rhoda, I'm asking Emily."

Hush? Of course, Rhoda would allow Emily to answer for herself.

Emily set her tea aside and then shrugged. "He seems tolerable enough."

At this, Cecily threw up her hands in repugnance, and Sophia burst from her chair.

"*Tolerable*?" Cecily's tone carried disgust.

"If she doesn't marry, she'll be sent to Wales. Her aunt requires a companion, and her mother is hell-bent upon Emily filling the role," Sophia replied.

"So, you see?" Rhoda glared at Cecily, daring her to hush her once again. "Emily's situation is nearly as urgent as mine."

"I'm not so certain of that." Cecily shook her head. "Marriage is forever. She could always leave off her aunt. It's far more difficult to leave off a husband."

"Except you did," Emily said.

Rhoda nearly chimed in that Sophia had as well, except that would be rather insensitive, in light of the circumstances. Although Rhoda would always be of the mindset that Sophia had been in love with Devlin at the time she married Harold.

"Only by the grace of God," Cecily insisted.

"And Flavion's treachery," Sophia added.

"What I'm *trying* to get all three of you to consider is that Emily ought to find her future husband more than simply *tolerable.*"

Emily sighed loudly. "We cannot all marry for love, Cecily. Rhoda isn't, and I hardly expect to. But Lord Carlisle is a good sort of man and quite handsome to boot. Good heavens, and he's an earl now! I'd have been satisfied with him even if he were still a vicar."

Cecily moaned and shook her head. "You've all gone mad. Surely, you don't support this tomfoolery, do you, Soph?"

"It isn't really up to us, Cece. Lord Carlisle *was* quite attentive to Emily at dinner last night. And he truly is one of the finest gentlemen I've ever met." Sophia blushed. "Aside from Dev, of course."

"And very good looking," Rhoda added.

Cecily eyed her suspiciously. "Indeed..."

JUSTIN NODDED, PLEASED when his ball dropped into the pocket on the opposite end of the table. Taking a sip of fine scotch, he contemplated the remaining configuration. Prescott leaned against the back of one of the settees, holding his own cue, while Blakely, Lieutenant Langdon, Mr. Stephen Nottingham, and his father-in-law, Mr. Thomas Findlay, lounged on the other side of the room.

The gentlemen had been abandoned for the afternoon while the ladies locked themselves away in one of the drawing rooms together. They'd considered going riding, but ominous weather lingered on the horizon and none of them fancied getting drenched.

Apparently, Blakely and Nottingham knew one another from their various travels.

"You realize my cousin has returned to London." Nottingham strolled across the room to address Prescott.

Dev nodded, still studying the table. "He showed up at White's before we left."

Justin missed his shot and stepped back. Nottingham, the Earl of Kensington. He'd not forget the name of the man who'd attempted to force himself upon Miss Mossant barely one week ago.

Oh, hell. How had he not connected the names before now? "He is a relation of yours?" Justin asked the gentleman who'd only just arrived today.

"My cousin," Mr. Nottingham replied. Looking at him now, Justin was surprised he'd not made the connection immediately. There existed an almost uncanny likeness between the two men—physically, anyhow. Both were fair-haired and blue-eyed. Except this gentleman wasn't a dandy like his titled cousin. His eyes possessed an intelligence the earl lacked. And his build and complexion reflected years of physical labor.

"Did you speak with him?" Dev asked Nottingham.

Mr. Nottingham ran one hand through his hair. "I did. Dammit, but I wish he'd remained in the country with Daphne."

"Daphne?" Justin hadn't listened to gossip enough to stay abreast of all this.

Nottingham glanced his way. "His wife."

Devlin sank his shot and then gave the subject his full attention. The other gentlemen had struck up a game of cards and paid little heed. Dev spoke softly though. "He's intent upon making matters difficult for Miss Mossant."

Nottingham nodded. "That doesn't surprise me. When we had drinks, Flave said he blamed Miss Mossant for most of what he went through last year."

"How would that be her fault?" Justin would have clarification on such a statement.

"He thinks she informed the chit's father... the one who sliced through one of his bollocks with his sword. Ridiculous, of course. Everyone knew what he was up to. He's always brought these calamities upon himself." Such relations certainly couldn't be an enviable situation for Stephen Nottingham.

Devlin then went on to relay an almost unbelievable sequence of events involving Mr. and Mrs. Nottingham and his cousin, Kensington.

Miss Mossant, Mrs. Nottingham, the duchess, and Miss Goodnight all had good reason to mistrust the earl. Justin was surprised Miss Mossant had consented to partner Kensington for that one dance.

"So, is it true then, that the incident rendered him… impotent?" The bastard hadn't appeared to be when he'd come across them.

"Initially." Mr. Nottingham grimaced. "But apparently, his virility has been restored. More compelling, however, is his lack of funds. He's torn through his allowance and although I've increased it and set up advances for him, he cannot, to save his life, stay out of debt." Stephen Nottingham pinched the bridge of his nose. "Since returning most of Cecily's dowry to Findlay, I've poured a considerable amount of my own funds into the estates. I simply cannot continue doing so."

"So, Kensington sees his only hope to fill his pockets is the wager. What are the estimated winnings up to now?"

"Sixty-two thousand pounds the last I checked."

Dev let out a low whistle. "That amount is unreal. I'll need to inform Sophia."

Mr. Nottingham nodded. "It's a deuced fortune. A fortune Flave sees as the answer to all his woes. I don't trust him. He disappointed me last year. I have a feeling he figures he has nothing to lose."

Dev nodded.

Justin glanced across the room. Shouldn't Blakely be included in this conversation? If he was to become her protector? Were Prescott and the duchess aware of Miss Mossant's engagement? Hell, *was Blakely*? He certainly didn't act like it.

For all of one second, he considered revealing what Kensington had attempted at the Crabtree Ball. But he did not. Miss Mossant already seemed shaken by the rumors and the wager. Nothing in her life was private anymore. She'd certainly not appreciate him exposing the events of that evening.

"Join us for a hand!" Lieutenant Langdon beckoned from across the room. "You gents are far too serious for a house party. Put down the cues and place your bets."

Justin grimaced. Not his cup of tea.

Watching the first hand being dealt, anger roiled beneath his calm. Anger at Kensington, at St. John, and surprisingly, at Miss Mossant herself.

Was she lying to him about Lord Blakely? Did she so adamantly oppose his suit that she'd make up a fake betrothal?

A manservant entered to have a word with Prescott. The duke nodded and folded his hand. "It seems little Harriette is in need of her mother. I'm afraid I'll have to interrupt the ladies."

Justin wished to contemplate his next move. His conscience already berated him for ignoring his inheritance. But he could not drop this business with Miss Mossant.

Damned if he knew why.

She was not his concern. He ought to abandon her protection to her fiancé. At that moment, Blakely punched his fist in the air and then gathered his winnings from the table.

The man certainly didn't appear to have any worries.

Justin couldn't bring himself to depart for Carlisle house just yet.

He excused himself and stepped out the door.

CHAPTER TWELVE

Emily Takes Action

AS THE HOUSE party guests exited the manor for an afternoon walk in the rain, Rhoda was beginning to wish she could run away from *herself*. She'd argued with Cecily this afternoon, bullied dearest Emily, and last night, she'd snapped at Lord Carlisle, when all he'd ever done was show her kindness.

She wished the last year had never happened!

Lord Carlisle wanted to *court* her!

Despite the wager!

Despite the scandal that would follow her until the end of her days.

He wanted to court her!

Even after she'd admitted that she'd willingly given her virtue to St. John!

The walk outdoors today ought to have been calming, but all sorts of tension hung over the party.

Cecily had been disapproving, Sophia hurt, and Emily disappeared with Blakely. A roaring filled Rhoda's ears when she assumed they'd likely be discussing more of the details for the elopement.

For *her* elopement.

And Lord Carlisle had kept his distance, choosing instead to escort both Coleus and Hollyhock. She didn't blame him but…

She walked behind, on Lieutenant Langdon's arm,

forced to make meaningless conversation. Well, it wasn't meaningless to him. He spoke of a few exploits at war, and admittedly, Rhoda encouraged him.

All the while, she watched the tall man walking between her two obnoxious but lovable sisters. He'd bend his head toward one of them, making her giggle, and then dipped his head toward the other.

Their mother strolled on Mr. Findlay's arm a short distance ahead, and the other two couples made up the rear.

Rhoda felt horrible. She'd upset both Cecily and Sophia, and she had done nothing but pressure poor Emily since they'd arrived. At least Emily had located a spare pair of spectacles today. It hadn't been fair of Rhoda to insist she go without.

She'd treated her dear friends atrociously. What on earth was the matter with her?

Even now, she illogically resented her sisters for basking in Lord Carlisle's attention.

She released a sigh.

He wants to court me.

"I must admit, you seem a trifle distracted this afternoon, Miss Mossant." The lieutenant's kindly words pricked her conscience yet again.

She turned to look up at him. The man's appearance was unique in that she'd never seen such bright orange hair on a person before. "Please forgive me, sir." He also had brilliant blue eyes and an easy smile. An abundance of freckles blended in with his weathered complexion. "I haven't slept well," she added, which was surprisingly true.

He patted her hand where it sat on his arm. "Perhaps the walk today can rectify that. I've always found the outdoors a good antidote to sleeplessness."

"Do you experience difficulties sleeping?" A mild curiosity surprised her.

For the first time since meeting him, she saw something other than kind pleasantness cross his features. Ah, the haunted look of a man who'd been to war. This time, she patted his arm comfortingly.

"On occasion," he said.

Perhaps Rhoda had overlooked this gentleman too easily as a prospective husband for Emily. She needed to reconsider.

Certain misgivings had formed at the thought of Emily marrying Lord Carlisle, bearing his children. Unease settled in her gut. She didn't wish to see Justin White with Emily but didn't examine too closely why.

She set out to discover more about the military man while they meandered through the garden. Yes, perhaps the red-haired man would be a better match indeed.

Throughout dinner, Rhoda attempted to ease the awkwardness that had been stirred up earlier that day. She asked about Little Finn and Lady Harriette but even so, a tension had developed between Cecily and herself.

She hated it. She hated that her miserable outlook on life affected the friendships she held dearer than anything else in the world.

When the ladies removed themselves to the large drawing room, Rhoda drew Cecily aside, so the others could go before them. After they'd passed, the two strolled at a more leisurely pace.

"I'm sorry. I hate when we are out of sorts. I'm consumed with worry over—" She shook her head, utterly overwhelmed. She didn't even know what to call all of it. "Can you forgive me?" Rhoda genuinely needed to repair the rift that had arisen between them.

Cecily nodded, but her expression held concern. "I hate being at odds with you as well. I feel as though I've been away from all of you for so long that we no longer truly know one another." She glanced down at her fingernails. "You didn't return any of my letters."

More guilt. "I'm sorry." Rhoda didn't know what else she could say. She'd so wanted to confide her worries and fears to Cecily but dared not. "I'll do better in the future. It's just that..."

Cecily sighed. "I know. Well, I don't really know, but I can only imagine some of what you went through with St. John's death. I just wish you'd talk to all of us about it. About your feelings. We love you, you know. Nothing you've done can ever change that." And then she stopped and took Rhoda in her arms. "Don't shut us out," she whispered.

Rhoda squeezed Cecily tightly, doing her best to hold back tears. "I'm trying not to. And I love all of you, too. I'll do better with my correspondence in the future. I promise."

Both girls held on for a few more moments before Cecily stepped back and dabbed at her lashes. "I have a better idea than that. Why don't you return with Stephen and me to Southampton? If you're with us, you won't need to deal with all of this betting and whatnot in London. You won't have to do anything rash."

Rhoda hadn't considered simply not returning to London. But even as she felt tempted, the thought of her two younger sisters and mother came to mind. She couldn't allow them to be exposed to the scandal alone. Not after she'd run away.

And her mother was going to insist upon returning to London once the house party wrapped up.

"Coleus, Hollyhock, and your mother are welcome as well," Cecily added, as though reading her mind.

Only her mother would never abide missing the entire Season.

"I'll think about it." Rhoda offered in light of their new understanding.

THE GENTLEMEN DIDN'T spend much time over port, instead choosing to join the ladies after less than half an hour. When they strolled in, Coleus began plucking away at the pianoforte, causing Sophia to stand up and suggest, "Let's play Sardines!"

Rhoda wasn't really in the mood for games, but it wouldn't be fair for her to not show any enthusiasm. After all, she'd helped Sophia cook this scheme up.

Emily played Sardines unusually well, and if she could get a particular gentleman alone for a short while, in a confined space, hope was that she could bring him closer to some sort of an offer.

The plan had been for her to get Lord Carlisle alone.

But would Emily really do it? Could she?

Did Rhoda want her to?

Truth be told… She did not.

I do not!

Emily nodded firmly. "Splendid idea, Soph."

Coleus stopped her atrocious playing and rose excitedly. Oh, yes, dear Coleus would find this all very intriguing.

Lord Carlisle shook his head but then met Rhoda's eyes and smiled. Warmth spread through her limbs at the thought that he was no longer angry with her.

Had he felt her watching him all day? When he held her gaze, she did not look away. She wanted to tell him… everything. She wanted to apologize.

She'd hurt him. She knew and felt sorry. But courting led to offers and offers led to marriage. Surely, he'd not wish to be tied to her and all her scandals!

A niggling voice taunted her though... *What if he does?*

"Just so everyone knows the rules. One person hides. After the others count to one hundred, they seek the original sardine out. When they find him or her, they take cover as well. The last person to find the packed in sardines is the loser," Sophia explained for those who hadn't played since they were children. Which would likely be most of them.

"Any rules about where a person can hide, Soph?" Emily perked up. The house was massive. This game could go on for hours.

"Er..." Sophia puckered up her mouth thoughtfully. "Bedchambers are off limits, and the nursery, of course."

"Of course," Cecily agreed although she appeared less than enthusiastic.

"Very well. Who shall be the first person to hide?" Coleus rubbed her hands together.

"I'll think of a number between one and twenty. Whoever comes the closest wins." Sophia winked at Emily. Alarm bells went off in Rhoda's head. Sophia and Emily were going to cheat! A wave of misgivings attacked her. What would Emily do? Why was Emily looking so determined?

Rhoda hadn't spoken with her about pursuing Lieutenant Langdon instead. Panic set in. Everything was moving far too quickly now.

Sophia made an elaborate production of asking everyone for a number and then shaking her head until it was time for Lord Carlisle to guess.

Of course, he chose correctly.

Rhoda's heart skipped a beat. Emily had the same look on her face that she'd had while devising methods for Cecily to kill her first husband.

Not Lord Carlisle! Rhoda had changed her mind!

The earl smiled obligingly and rose. "No bedchambers and avoid the nursery then." At Sophia's nod, he walked toward the door.

"Everybody close their eyes now." Rhoda pretended to close her eyes but could see just enough to catch sight of Emily tiptoeing out of the room and Sophia waving her along.

No! Should she cry foul? But she could not!

Should she chase after Emily? Bring her back and avoid embarrassment for them all?

Just when Rhoda could hardly stand in a second longer, Emily slipped back into the room. Maybe she hadn't found him yet.

"Ninety-six, ninety-seven, ninety-eight, ninety-nine, one hundred!" Everyone opened their eyes.

Emily looked more than a little out of breath.

"Good Lord, Sophia," Coleus complained. "You're the slowest counter I've ever played with!"

Rhoda followed Emily into the foyer. She'd stick to her like glue, if necessary. "I thought I heard him heading toward the attic." Emily sounded quite convincing, but Rhoda knew better.

Most of the party took off toward the stairs. Sophia smiled wickedly. "I'd imagine he'd head for the kitchens." Sophia grabbed Rhoda by the wrist and dragged her halfway down the hall. Cecily followed at a slower pace.

Rhoda tried to resist but aside from wrestling her friend to the ground, she could not manage to get herself free. When had Sophia become so strong?

Where had Emily gone?

"What's going on?" Rhoda whispered to Sophia. "Let me go, will you?"

Sophia just grinned.

No! No! No!

Rhoda broke free and took off at a sprint in the opposite direction. Rounding the corner, she nearly slammed into her mother, who was just peeking inside one of the large coat closets, illuminating the inhabitants with what seemed to be an amazingly brilliant candle.

Her mother's loud shriek echoed in the corridor. "Miss Goodnight!"

Such a reaction was not without merit. Along with her mother, Rhoda clearly identified her dearest and most innocent friend pressed intimately against Lord Carlisle's chiseled form.

Lord Carlisle's arms were wrapped around Emily's tiny little waist. He'd been kissing her as though a man possessed.

"Lord Carlisle?" She couldn't help the betrayal she felt. Not twenty-four hours ago, he'd admitted to wanting to court her! And already he could kiss her best friend?

"Good God, Justin!" Prescott, who'd silently appeared behind her, sounded nearly as shocked as her mother.

Rhoda couldn't help feeling betrayed by the last man in the world whom she'd trusted. Upon catching sight of her, Carlisle's brows furrowed. He glanced down at Emily and shook his head in a daze. "But I thought…" His voice trailed off.

And then Rhoda's gaze met Emily's.

Good God, what had she done?

CHAPTER THIRTEEN

Compromised

SCARED TO DEATH at what would assuredly happen next, Rhoda reached inside of the closet and dragged Emily out. She refused to meet Carlisle's gaze. She couldn't. *How could he?*

Chaos had erupted in the foyer, everyone arriving to see what all the outbursts were about.

She couldn't look at him. She wouldn't cry. She didn't know why she even felt like doing so.

Lost in her own vortex of despair, Rhoda just barely listened as her mother chastised the couple and then addressed Prescott.

"Your Grace, I expect you'll have a word with the earl. This is quite unacceptable! Something must be done to remedy this! Otherwise, it will reflect upon all of my girls!"

Rhoda could not remain to listen to her mother's complaints. Instead, she dragged Emily upstairs to her chamber. The poor girl hardly needed to be dragged.

She'd gone rather pale herself.

Rhoda's mother was going to insist Carlisle make an offer.

Emily had landed herself a husband after all! Lord Carlisle! Rhoda couldn't erase the image of his arms around her dearest friend, his mouth on Emily's.

On Emily's mouth! Kissing her!

As they practically ran upstairs, Rhoda couldn't help

thinking she deserved this. She deserved all of this. Once inside Emily's chamber, she covered her face with her hands and moaned. When she peeked between her fingers, she saw Emily looking quite confused.

Dear sweet Emily, who'd done nothing more than what she'd been instructed to do.

Rhoda shook her head. "I can't believe you did it! I can't believe he did it! I'd thought he wasn't the type. Why are all men destined to turn out to be disappointments?" She dropped into a chair in resignation.

"He'll make an offer, won't he?" Emily's expression went from confusion, to concern, and then accusation. "Why didn't you tell me that you'd told Lord Carlisle about your engagement to Blakely?"

Lord Carlisle had discussed her engagement to Blakely with *Emily*? Not that it mattered, but couldn't anybody keep a secret anymore?

"He *told* you?" How dare he share something she'd told him in confidence! In her mind, she imagined Carlisle and Emily talking about Blakely's plan to use her for revenge. Had he laughed over it? Had they decided together that it was the only way she could be redeemed? "Quite the little tête-à-tête the two of you shared."

Oh, God! Rhoda was *jealous!*

Emily twisted up her lips into a grimace. "Lord Carlisle thought I was you."

"That's ridiculous." Likely excuse. "I'm at least six inches taller and—"

"I was standing on a box. And I'm wearing your perfume, remember?" Was it possible? "Rhoda, do you, are you—?"

"No!"

She couldn't be. And besides, it was too late now! "I mean, he's been a friend to me. But I... I'm not at all..."

And then she realized how much courage Emily had shown. "You did it. You actually did it."

"Well, you said you wouldn't leave with Blakely until I did. Figured I'd best get it over with." Oh, God! Blakely! She was going to have to marry Blakely now! She'd promised Emily! And truth be told… she didn't have a choice.

A knock sounded at the door and, without waiting for an answer, Cecily stepped in.

She regarded them both with a murderous light behind her eyes. "You two deserve to be thrashed! Did you plan this together?" She glared in Rhoda's direction. "I've no doubt this was your idea."

She must think Rhoda had been hiding this scheme from her earlier. But she hadn't!

Cecily turned to Emily. "But you cheated, I'd venture to guess, at the game. And now! Now there is a kind gentleman sitting in the duke's study who's going to be forced into offering for you. He's going to sacrifice his freedom due to no fault of his own. What you've done is utterly reprehensible!" She paced back and forth, waving her hands in the air. "How could you? Both of you? How could you?"

Rhoda couldn't allow Cecily to blame Emily for this. Rhoda had pushed her. If only she hadn't made that blasted pact earlier this week. She'd only done in it an effort to spur Emily to make more efforts at flirting. "You don't understand, Cecily." Oh, what a mess she'd made. With everything. "And you never will."

"Why don't you explain it to me then?" Cecily sat down beside Emily. "You've been secretive for months now. We're your friends, aren't we? Tell us what's wrong. I mean, besides the obvious. Besides the fact that St. John took advantage of you and then died. What else is bothering you?"

Rhoda didn't know what to say. She couldn't tell them everything! She couldn't!

"None of us are perfect. You know this! I made a horrible decision when I married Flavion, but all of you stood beside me. And then I committed adultery. *Adultery,* Rhoda. Whether it fits the legal definition or not, I lay with a man who was not the man I'd married. What can you have possibly done that is any worse than that?" Cecily cried.

Rhoda couldn't tell them. She just couldn't. She squeezed her eyes together.

"Why are you blaming Rhoda?" Emily demanded.

Oh, Emily!

Now *Emily* and Cecily would be at odds with one another.

"She had nothing to do with it. I compromised Lord Carlisle. I am the person responsible for that poor dear man sitting with Prescott now. And I'm glad." Emily jumped up and strode across the rug to wear Rhoda sat. "Now Rhoda is free to marry Blakely, without worrying about me. And she won't have to worry about any stupid wagers, or insincere praise… or worse! Now, if both of you will excuse me, I have some business to attend to."

Where could she possibly be going off to right now?

"What business?" Rhoda demanded.

"I'm to schedule your elopement."

Oh, hell.

JUSTIN COULD NOT believe his own stupidity and utter lack of self-restraint. He sat in Prescott's study, stunned, berating himself in a thousand different ways for his behavior.

When she'd first stepped inside, he'd thought she was Miss Goodnight. He'd even said her name, hadn't he? But then the scent of her perfume had made him think she was her friend.

He'd been keenly aware of Miss Mossant all day. In fact, he'd done nothing but think of her lately. Perhaps if he'd not been so besotted, he wouldn't have accosted her friend.

He ought to have known.

But he'd... wanted it to be Miss Mossant. He'd wanted Miss Mossant to purposely find him, and then press herself against him, reach her arms up around his neck.

"Damn, Justin, I never thought I'd see the day." Prescott sat on the corner of his desk.

Justin wondered if Dev would, in fact, read him the riot act for compromising a young woman under his protection or if this was merely a formality in order to placate the irate Mrs. Mossant.

Justin ran one hand through his hair. "I..." He shook his head, dumbfounded. Had Miss Goodnight initiated all of it? It was so completely beyond her character. He must be at fault! The lust he'd experienced lately had obviously gotten the better of him. "I can hardly believe it myself," he finally answered.

"You'll offer for her, of course." Dev sounded a trifle more dukeish than he had a moment ago.

But, of course, he would. He had no choice. But Miss Goodnight? How on earth? "Of course," he responded.

"Although, knowing Miss Goodnight, it's quite possible she'll decline. She's an odd sort. I'll admit, I've never really understood some of Sophia's friends."

If Miss Goodnight declined, Justin would simply have

to convince her. He could not allow a young woman's reputation to be besmirched due to his own animalistic behavior.

But had she placed her arms on him first?

She would not have. The woman could barely meet his eyes on most occasions.

"It's no matter. She won't have a choice. I'll go to her parents if necessary. By, *God*, Dev, who *are* her parents? And why do they unleash their daughter on the world in this manner?"

He had all due respect for women, for their intelligence, their wit, and even their strength, after seeing Miss Mossant handle Lord Kensington so handily, but the men in their lives had a responsibility to protect them. From themselves as well as the less reputable gentlemen circling in the *ton*.

Of which class, he apparently belonged. He'd compromised a woman less than one week after inheriting his title.

Justin rose wearily. "I'll meet you here early tomorrow morning, then." He'd seen this situation before, just never imagined himself playing this part. "In order to offer for her."

He tried to picture himself going down on one knee in Dev's study. Asking Miss Emily Goodnight to be his wife. As much as he tried to, he couldn't shake Miss Mossant's face from his imaginings. What a mess.

Dev simply nodded.

Without another word to his cousin, Justin exited to the foyer and wandered aimlessly until he located an outer door. He ought to pray. He ought to be begging forgiveness.

The moon shone brightly tonight, making the landscape appear brighter than the sconces did inside. Damn, but he out to have left for Carlisle House two days ago. He'd sensed trouble ahead but couldn't bring himself to leave because of one woman.

Because of unbridled lust.

Feeling the need for solace, peace, he knew where he must go. He crossed the lawn and followed the dirt road along the forest. Less light shone through the trees, but he didn't care. He knew this route like the back of his hand.

Luckily, he still had his key.

The chapel, which was built in a rectangular shape, had never been ornate. It dated back to the thirteenth century. There was only one entrance, but tall windows lined both sides, rising above the pews somewhat majestically. When Justin entered, he inhaled and the peace that had eluded him all day finally came.

He allowed the door to close behind him, shutting out the turmoil of the last week. He'd missed this. His time with God.

Moonbeams filtered into the building. He'd not need to light a flint. He strolled down the aisle toward the altar and then took a seat in the front pew. He's spent many hours in this place, both as a child and later performing services. He'd been honored to marry the duke and duchess last winter.

Dropping to his knees, he bowed his head. He did not close his eyes though, choosing instead to watch the shadows cast by trees outside as they danced eerily on the stone floor.

He'd thought he was better than that, than *this*.

"Dear God, forgive me." The words left him on an exhale. "Forgive me." His God was the embodiment of grace. Justin had heard many a hell and brimstone sermon, but the New Testament spoke to him.

Would Miss Goodnight ever forgive him? And Miss Mossant? When he'd peered out of the dark closet, her eyes had stared in accusingly. She'd been confused. Shocked even.

Almost as shocked as he'd been to realize it was Miss Goodnight he'd been kissing and not Miss Rhododendron Mossant.

Fathomless coffee colored eyes brimmed with tears. He'd hurt her.

All during the course of a game. A parlor game. Good God, a child's game. He tilted his head back as though the answers he sought could be read upon the ceiling of the chapel.

And then a breeze swept through.

Turning toward the entrance, he wondered if his eyes deceived him.

Surely not.

This time, he made no mistake.

The woman who'd taken up permanent residence in his thoughts had slipped inside and was kneeling in the back row. Her presence sent a buzzing through his limbs. The air itself came to life, charging the chapel with an energy it had lacked only moments before.

He froze. She'd not seen him. He swallowed hard and just as he would make himself known, a gut-wrenching moan echoed off the ancient stone.

"I'm sorry, God, I'm so sorry. I don't know what to do. I didn't mean to do it." Her forehead dropped onto the pew in front of her and great sobs shook her shoulders. "But I can't go on this way, God, I can't."

CHAPTER FOURTEEN

Confession

SHE NEEDED TO repent. She needed to confess, if only to an empty church in the middle of the night.

"I'm sorry, God, I'm so sorry. I don't know what to do. I didn't mean to do it." Once she allowed the tears to flow, she couldn't rein them in. "But I can't go on this way, God, I can't." The thought of taking her own life beckoned, but she pushed it away. But what could she do? She faced hopelessness at every turn.

"Rhoda."

The sound of her name echoed from near the altar.

She froze. God didn't just speak to people like that. Did he? She reared back and peered farther into the chapel. Sitting in the very first pew, she eyed a masculine silhouette. "Who's there?"

He rose and stepped into the aisle.

Carlisle.

This man evoked a tumult of confusion inside her. Sometimes, he gave her peace; other times, he'd stirred up want. Tonight, she ought to be angry with him.

No, that wasn't fair. He owed her nothing.

Despite that she'd felt betrayed earlier. And if he'd truly thought Emily was *her*, well…

Had he really thought she was Emily? Emily would not lie about such a thing.

"What are you doing here? Do you come here every

night? Is that what vicars do?" She sniffed and wiped at her eyes. She hated that he'd heard her crying. She'd sounded like a wounded animal, for heaven's sake.

As he approached, she made room for him to sit in the pew beside her.

"Sometimes. When I feel the need." He sighed deeply. "I could use some clarity tonight."

And then she remembered. He'd been backed into a corner, by Emily—practically at her will. She had encouraged Emily to do whatever might be necessary.

"Did you really think it was me?" The words escaped her mouth before she could think better of them. She had to know. Would it change anything? Likely not, but she wanted, no, she *needed* to know.

"Of course, I thought it was you!" Affront and disgust laced his voice in his abrupt response. Irritation etched lines in his forehead. His countenance carried a darkness she'd not think he could summon.

He'd thought Emily had been her.

Warmth spread through her. He'd been sincere in his declaration. He really had wanted to court her. Only none of that mattered now.

Would he feel the same if he knew everything though? Her conniving? Her manipulating?

What she'd done to Dudley Scofield, to Sophia's stepbrother?

That burning sensation crushed her lungs at the thought of revealing her sin. And yet. She could trust him. She *knew* she could trust him.

No matter what transpired after this. She'd know how special of a person he was.

"You will ask for her?" Of course, he would. She'd hate him if he didn't. And then she'd hate him after he did.

No, she would not. How could she ever hate such a

man?

He nodded. "I will. In the cloakroom. I thought it was her at first, but then I thought it was you. The perfume." He held her gaze. "It was the same. I thought you'd come to me..."

Rhoda nearly stopped breathing at the thought of what could have been. If she'd gone to him, if she'd discovered him in the closet instead of Emily.

"You touched her," she reminded him. "And you didn't know the difference." She didn't mean to sound accusatory, but she wondered. Did all women feel the same to a man? Could *she* identify *him* by touch alone? Would she notice the strength of his jaw? The muscled cords of his neck?

He shook his head. "I wanted it to be you. I think perhaps I'd fooled myself into believing what I wanted."

He leaned forward, resting his arms on his knees. That thoughtful position she'd seen him in so many times. And now, here they sat. Alone, in a darkened church.

Perhaps Emily and Lord Carlisle would be happy together. Her eyes burned at the thought. She loved Emily. She wanted nothing more than for her to find contentment in marriage.

He glanced over his shoulder, a self-deprecating expression twisting his beautiful face.

Rhoda leaned forward slowly. As she did so, his throat worked, as though he had to swallow hard. Mere inches separated their lips. She wanted to kiss him. The truth was that she'd wanted to kiss him for a very long time.

Why had she ignored this?

She didn't deserve him. He'd never be hers. But at that moment, she didn't care. Lifting her hand, she trailed her fingertips along the line of his jaw.

He closed his eyes, and a tremor vibrated through him.

He'd declared that he wanted to court her, and she'd blurted out that she was to marry Blakely, ignoring the longing she'd seen in his eyes so many times.

She'd hurt him.

Unable to deny him now, unable to deny herself, she inched closer until her lips barely skimmed the corner of his mouth. "Justin," she whispered.

Her heart nearly melted at such nearness. This man, he'd absorbed her pain since the day of Harold's death. He'd absorbed the pain of others, too. For how long, she wondered? Had he done it all his life?

She adjusted herself to align their mouths better and then placed her hands on both sides of his face. Without thinking, her fingertips caressed the bristly texture of beard that had appeared since earlier that morning. His jaw, his neck. As she did so, the pulse fluttering in his throat quickened.

This man.

"Justin," she whispered again. He opened his eyes and, even in the darkness, she wanted to drown in his blue depths. He held himself like a statue, not resisting nor responding.

Leaning forward, testing, she pressed her mouth against the tender skin of his lips. Her kiss was an apology, a need, a question. It would say all the words she'd kept inside.

"Justin," she whispered again. "I'm so sorry. So very, very sorry." She spoke her heartfelt apology against his mouth.

And then he grasped her wrists and groaned.

Desperate hands moved to her hair.

"My fault," he whispered back.

Opening his mouth beneath hers, finally, his hunger unleashed. Lifting her onto his lap, his body cradled hers, effortlessly, all without breaking the kiss. His hands traveled from her cheek, to her chin, her neck, and shoulders. He held her as though she might evaporate any moment. So much tenderness she thought she'd melt. A whisper of a touch here. A sigh of a kiss, a murmur of affection. Surely, this was what if felt to be kissed by an angel.

Of course, he blamed himself for what happened tonight with Emily. Rhoda couldn't allow it.

He cared for her.

She craved him. She ached for him. But…

She buried her face against his throat. "I can't. I can't allow you to think you know me. You don't. It's not just about St. John." She squeezed her eyes shut, holding back the tears this time. She'd own up to what she did. He'd be glad to walk away from her after knowing.

She moved her lips, but no sound escaped.

Again, and nothing. Her blood might as well have turned to ice. All she knew was his touch.

And fear.

Terror.

"It's all right. Take all the time you need. I'm here." Those tender hands touched her hair and back soothingly. "You are safe. I'm right here."

She shook her head side to side and then inhaled deeply.

And then, after nearly a year of locking it away, she spoke the words of her nightmares. "I killed a man." They scraped past her throat, a ragged whisper. She cleared her throat. "I killed a man."

His motions stilled for the briefest of moments before starting up again. His throat moved against her forehead. "Tell me."

He hadn't pushed her off him yet.

Later, when all of this was over, she'd allow the numbness to take over her heart forever. She'd accept her fate. Her punishment.

She pulled away and met his gaze. "The day Harold fell." God, she'd never forgotten that day. Likely, he wouldn't either. "Later, I went to Sophia's room, and she wasn't alone. I found her with her brother, her stepbrother. Dudley Scofield."

Justin shook his head. "I was unaware that Her Grace *had* a brother."

She did.

She *had.*

A stepbrother. A horrible, horrible man. A person who ought to have been her protector, her champion, who'd instead tormented dear Sophia.

"He hadn't arrived until later that day. And when I found him in her room, he was… harassing her." Rhoda couldn't go into the details of what Dudley had done to Sophia. That was Sophia's secret alone. "I offered to escort him to the rescue efforts. And, of course, he couldn't very well refuse, could he?"

Rhoda remembered the late afternoon sunlight clearly. Long shadows and the slightest hint of a breeze. That unique hint of seawater had been in the wind. Every muscle in her had ached at the time from weeping over Lord Harold. But she'd needed to go to Sophia. She'd needed to see for herself that Sophia was going to make it through the horrible accident. She needed to hold her friend. She'd wanted to comfort her. And when she'd entered Sophia's chamber…

"I don't suppose he could," Lord Carlisle affirmed. And then he waited for her to go on.

She had to continue. She had to tell him. She had to tell *someone*! Surely, if she kept this inside much longer, like a poison, it would eat her alive.

Rhoda had manipulated Dudley Scofield into coming outside with her, so that he could work with the rest of the search party. But by the time they'd exited the castle and worked their way along the path, the sun was already setting. "When we reached the cliff, the search effort had been called off."

"St. John and Dev feared the cliff posed too much danger for the rescuers. The tide had come in… without the sunlight…"

Justin's finger threaded through her hair. She felt his lips against her forehead.

"Mr. Scofield accused me of bringing him outside for some other purpose. And then he… grabbed at me." She remembered Dudley's sinister snarl. His breath had reeked of decay and cheap wine.

His hands had squeezed at her breasts and then violently sought the crease between her legs.

"I pushed him."

She'd said it. She finally told somebody.

"You pushed him? Away from you?" Justin's voice sounded so reasonable, so matter of fact.

"We were at the edge of the cliff. The ground was muddy from the rescue efforts. I pushed him, and he lost his footing. And then he fell. Off the cliff." She needed him to understand. So many times since, she'd wished it had been her who'd fallen into the sea. But no.

The memory of that moment haunted her. She'd dropped to the ground but been afraid to crawl to the edge, to look over. Afraid he'd climb back up and attack her again but also afraid that he wouldn't.

The mud. So much mud. And the wind. She never wanted to breathe in salty air again.

"What did you do after?"

She'd been horrified, but a part of her had been glad!

That horrid, horrid man had hurt Sophia badly. He'd caused her to live in continuous fear. Yes, Rhoda had pushed him… and then she'd done nothing afterward. And she'd told no one. Perhaps if she had … But, no. Such thinking was of no use.

She'd run in the opposite direction. "I ran."

Justin sat calmly but then nodded. "So, you did not see where he landed? You did not ever see him flailing in the water or broken on the rocks below?"

Rhoda shook her head side to side. "But it was a cliff! The same cliff that killed Lord Harold."

Justin pulled away from her. "Look at me, Rhododendron."

The sound of her name on his lips sent warmth traveling through her veins. "I spent hours on that cliff, and just below it. There were several places where a person could have caught themselves, stopped themselves from falling, depending upon where they went over."

Rhoda wasn't sure what he was saying. "But he disappeared afterward. He never returned to the castle."

Justin tilted his head. "I've heard nothing of another body being discovered. Dev would have been informed if Mr. Scofield's remains turned up on his estate. Have you ever asked him?"

Surely, he could guess the answer to that.

What was he saying?

"You think he might have survived?" She shook her head. The cliffs near Priory Point were treacherous.

But Rhoda felt a glimmer of hope. A flicker so tenuous she feared to acknowledge it. Could he be right? Was it really possible that Dudley hadn't died that day?

"But…" She had to challenge this new hypothesis. "Why would he not go back to the castle? Why would he simply disappear?"

"Perhaps he had debts. Perhaps he feared exposure." Justin squeezed her tight. "A body would have eventually washed up, and it would have become public knowledge."

"Prescott would know," she said in a daze.

At that moment, she felt something she'd not felt in nearly a year.

Hope.

It might be fleeting. Likely, she only invited further disappointment, but she would allow it to wash over her broken soul for now.

She wished she could stay in his arms forever.

But she also had a sudden urgent need to seek out Prescott. "Do you think it possible he's still awake?" She sat up straight, one arm still draped around Justin's shoulders.

She saw a flash of his white even teeth when he smiled. "Only one way to find out."

CHAPTER FIFTEEN

Coming Clean

LORD CARLISLE LOCKED the chapel doors behind them and then offered his arm as they turned to walk toward the house.

"What if they did?" she couldn't help but ask. Terror gripped her. "What if they did find his body?" She shivered, and he pulled her closer.

He did not answer right away. She liked that he would give her question due consideration. So much might be at stake!

"You led this Scofield fellow away from the duchess because he harassed her?" he asked.

Rhoda remembered when Sophia had finally admitted what Scofield had done to her. Sophia had *apologized* while regaling the mistreatment she'd received at the hand of her stepbrother. *She'd apologized!* She'd believed she had been to blame.

"He'd done it before," Rhoda answered. When she'd discovered Dudley in Sophia's room, she'd known she had to do something to get him away from her. Sophia had been distraught and sleepy from laudanum.

Dudley Scofield had been something of a monster to Sophia.

Had been. In her heart, Rhoda believed he must be dead. Surely, he would have come out of hiding if he were alive.

"So, you put yourself in danger to protect your friend?" He squeezed her hand, bringing her back to the present.

"I did what was needed." She dismissed her action as something anyone would have done. For a friend. For somebody she loved dearly. And then a low moan escaped her for the second time in his presence. "What if a body was found? What if he is dead?"

Was it possible Dudley had lived? Something in the pit of her stomach insisted that he had not. She'd shoved. He'd stumbled and then disappeared. So different from earlier that day but with the same result. He'd died. Her breaths grew shallow. She tried to wish her fears away but could not.

"Wait." Her feet couldn't move. "I can't breathe," she gasped.

Dudley's body would have been found. The magistrate would want to speak with her. And she couldn't lie after confessing to Justin. She couldn't lie after confessing to the duke and to Sophia. Her heart pounded in her ears. How was her heart pounding when she couldn't breathe?

Justin's mouth was near her ear, and he was whispering something. She tried to focus on his words. "Trust me." A soothing hand rubbed her back. "I won't let anyone hurt you. Shh…" She nodded as air seemed to enter her lungs again.

Lord Carlisle did not attempt to pull her along right away. When she was breathing normally again, he drew back a few inches and bent down so he could peer into her face.

"Dev is a fair-minded person. Beyond that, you need to remember Sophia is his wife. If this Scofield fellow harmed the duchess at one time, and then threatened you…" His voice trailed off. He did not make a move to drag her farther along the path. He would allow her to make the decision regarding her confession. A cold wind swept through the trees and drew a shiver from her.

His warmth protected her from the brunt of it.

She leaned inward, her forehead dropping onto his shoulder.

"Yes." She wanted to trust him. She wanted so badly to believe his words. To believe that everything would be all right... but it seemed like a fairy tale.

She curled herself against him. In another life, she'd stay here forever. Just like this, with the wind whipping around them, holding one another for warmth. She'd never have to face her mother with this. She'd never see the disappointment on her sisters' faces.

When she finally stepped away from him, he took hold of her hands. "All right? You're ready?" He looked so earnest, so dependable.

She nodded, and they continued on their way. The terrifying thoughts threatened once again when the manor came into sight. And again, when he opened the large front door. She stepped inside, hoping against hope the duke and Sophia had retired for the evening.

She needed answers though, didn't she? Was knowing better than not knowing? With one hand protectively guiding her from behind, Justin's other hand gripped hers supportively.

They approached the duke's study, and Justin knocked loudly.

Rhoda's heart fell into her shoes as Sophia called out, "Come in."

They hadn't yet retired for the night.

Stepping in, Rhoda took in the brocaded walls, the heavy wooden desk, and a few paintings hanging behind it. She recognized one as the previous duke and the dowager.

She shivered. Could her secrets be contained within this

room?

Justin steered her inside, their hands clasped together but hidden in the folds of her gown.

The duke had been carrying Sophia and was just setting her down as they entered.

"If we've come at a bad time…" Rhoda shook herself free of Justin and attempted to back out of the room. They wouldn't want to discuss this now. They would wait until morning.

"No, it's fine." Sophia looked curious. Of course, she would. Sophia always looked curious. "Sit down. Dev, let's sit by the fire, shall we?" Half the candles had been doused. Sophia moved the screen to one side of the hearth and then gestured for the duke to join her on one of the sofas.

That left a second loveseat for Rhoda and Lord Carlisle.

By the time they all made themselves comfortable, Rhoda's mouth had gone completely dry. She sat primly, ankles together and back straight. Justin leaned forward and rested his elbows on his knees.

As the clock ticked loudly, the awkwardness of the situation grew.

"Um, would you care for something to drink, Rhoda, my lord?" Sophia went to stand but when both of them shook their head, she dropped back onto the cushioned sofa beside Prescott.

"Last summer," Lord Carlisle began.

These words captured the duke's attention. "Yes?"

Sophia straightened her spine.

"Other than Lord Harold's, have any remains been discovered?" The question sounded so very non-incriminating. Rhoda wished she'd not released his hand. Did he never need anyone else's strength?

"Of course, a few weeks later." Prescott seemed to

phrase his answer cautiously. "When the carriage was recovered following the mudslide. My uncle's, St. John's." He swallowed hard. "And my father's."

Lord Carlisle nodded solemnly but then clarified, "Not near the road. On the beach."

Sophia turned wide eyes toward Prescott. Oh, dear God, there had been. Rhoda's breath caught in her throat.

"Why would you think there might have been?" the duke asked.

Justin stared at his elegant hands thoughtfully. "Your Grace." He looked up and addressed Sophia. "It was a horrible day for everyone, but no one more so than you. But I must ask. Do you remember your stepbrother, that is, Dudley Scofield, arriving at Priory Point? Do you remember Miss Mossant interrupting him in your chamber that evening?"

Rhoda waited for her to confirm this.

"No." Sophia shook her head. "I don't remember that at all. I'd been given something to calm my nerves. I remember falling asleep."

Prescott seemed to be watching Sophia *very carefully*. When he spoke, his voice sent a chill down Rhoda's spine. "If that bastard saw fit for any reason to enter my wife's suite, then, or ever again, he'd not live to tell about it."

The meaning of his words washed over Rhoda and then Justin spoke up again. "So, no second body was ever found on the beach, washed up from the cove? No one who might have been identified as Mr. Scofield?"

Sophia shook her head adamantly.

Dev leveled his gaze upon Rhoda. "I can assure you. In fact, I give you my word. Only one body has ever been recovered from those cliffs. And that man is now buried on these grounds beneath Lord Harold's tombstone."

Rhoda could hardly believe it. It was as though the vise

that had been squeezing her chest for nearly a year loosened slightly.

"He went to your room, Sophia." She couldn't keep it in a second longer. "He was up to his old tricks, so I offered to take him to join the rescue effort. But when we got there, everyone had left. Oh, Sophia, I pushed him away from me! I pushed him, and he fell! I thought he'd fallen off the cliff, the same as Lord Harold, but Lord Carlisle suggested he may have survived his fall and then run away. I've felt horrible. I think I might have killed him." Her eyes filled with tears, and Sophia burst from her chair.

"Oh, Rhoda, no, dear." Sophia's arms wrapped tightly around her. This embrace felt like a benediction. They clung to one another in the center of the room, both of them weeping and laughing. Rhoda could hardly believe it!

"I thought I killed him," she repeated again, but Sophia shushed her.

"And that's why you've been so changed! Oh, Rhoda, I wish you'd told me! But no worries! You have nothing to worry about!"

Rhoda sniffed a few times, suddenly feeling quite ridiculous for making so much of this. She'd been so certain though…

The duke had risen and placed one arm around Sophia. "If it's quite all right, I think it's time my duchess and I check in on our daughter." He met Justin's gaze. "We'll see you in the morning then?"

He would make his offer to Emily! He had no choice.

Justin nodded. The mood of the room changing from a giddy relief to that of somber determination. "Take your time in here, if you'd like." Sophia gestured toward the liquor cabinet. "I'm certain some sherry wouldn't be out of order."

"Or something stronger," the duke added.

Justin nodded again. When the door closed behind them, Rhoda couldn't help but meet his gaze.

"You were right!" She had a wobbly smile left inside of her. She'd been so stupid. So foolish!

How had he come to mean so much to her? And now he would offer for Emily, one of her best friends. Somebody she loved like a sister. How could she stand by and watch them wed? Watch Emily grow large with his child?

She was such an idiot!

THE DUKE AND duchess, God bless their souls, were hiding something. Rhododendron hadn't caught on but there'd been something in the way they glanced between one another. Justin shook it off. He didn't care what, and he didn't care why. Only one body had been discovered, and it was buried now. Of that, he had no doubt. Prescott spoke the truth.

She was free. He'd known she had a secret, but God, he couldn't have guessed in a thousand years.

From the look on Dev's face, the duchess's brother wouldn't have lived long anyway.

Or wouldn't live much longer, anyhow, if he were to make a reappearance.

Justin opened the door to the duke's liquor cabinet and poured two snifters of brandy. Rhoda would need something to calm her nerves. What a night!

She'd kissed him.

He'd thought he'd died and gone to heaven when she'd placed her fingers along his face. She'd touched him in wonder, almost. And then he had, in fact, experienced heaven on earth when those soft lips of hers settled upon his. Lips he'd longed to taste for months now.

She'd come to him. She'd trusted him. And God help him, she'd wanted him. For a moment, she'd wanted him and needed him the way he'd wanted her since the moment they met.

And he was beholden to offer for Miss Goodnight in the morning.

What a mess. What a sodding blasted mess.

His hand brushed hers as she took the snifter from him.

"Have you tasted brandy before?" Somehow, he thought that she had.

She smiled secretly over the glass as she tilted it to take a sip. She had. Of course, she had. God, this woman...

He took his seat beside her again, close enough so that they touched, through his breaches, through her skirts. Her aura tugged at him. Could he consider himself free for a few more hours? He might be, but that didn't mean he was free to compromise another woman.

"Tell me about this betrothal of yours, with Blakely. Explain to me why it's so complicated. Surely, it isn't more complicated than this?" He waved a hand between the two of them. Perhaps if she spoke of her upcoming marriage to another man he'd stop focusing on the warmth of her thigh. Perhaps if she told him the details of her planned elopement, he'd stop leaning closer to capture the scent of her perfume.

It wasn't the same on Miss Goodnight. He should have known. The scent was different on Rhoda. It was spicier, warmer.

She cringed. By God, she cringed. "I imagine we'll be leaving soon. Now that Emily's future is settled."

"Excuse me?"

"I told her I wouldn't elope until she..." As though

suddenly realizing who she was talking to, she trailed off, looking ashamed.

At her words, his heart dropped. Had Rhoda conspired with Miss Goodnight? Had Miss Goodnight worn the perfume intentionally?

The look on her face confirmed his suspicions. Hadn't Blakely warned him about marriage-minded misses? He ought to have listened to the man. Except... "Did the two of you conspire against Blakely as well?"

A cold black sensation gripped his heart.

Miss Mossant's gaze dropped to her lap. He nearly felt ill. Justin had all but fallen in love with a conniving liar. Ironic that he could ignore what she'd done with St. John, believe the best of her where a man's death was concerned, but for her to have lied to him... For her to have conspired with her friend against him...

He rose from his seat tiredly. "I'll escort you to your chamber then." She glanced up with apologetic eyes. God, those eyes. The depths of her gaze nearly overwhelmed the disappointment running through his veins.

She stood, and he gestured for her to precede him out the door. He didn't want her to take his arm. He didn't want to touch her. It bothered him that his body craved her despite what he'd learned. Even now, his eyes devoured the delicate curve of her shoulders, her slim waist, and flared hips. And now that he'd held her in his arms, tasted her kiss, he burned for more.

CHAPTER SIXTEEN

Change in Plans

DESPITE BEING RELIEVED of her guilt over Dudley Scofield, Rhoda climbed into bed sick at heart.

She'd kissed him. He'd held her in his arms as she'd told him everything. He'd seen reason where she never had. And Prescott said they'd never recovered a body.

But then she'd gone and admitted the plan she and Emily had devised. Even though Rhoda hadn't come up with the specific details for Emily to compromise Lord Carlisle, she'd certainly pushed her in that direction.

He'd looked at her differently the moment he learned the truth. He'd pulled away and then addressed her formally once again.

As though they'd never been together in the chapel.

Rhoda buried her head in her pillow.

Tomorrow, he would offer for Emily. He'd offer because of his honor. Because he was that sort of man. Perhaps it was best that he hate her.

Would he forgive Emily? Could they ever find peace together? Contentment?

Cecily had been right.

"Mama wants to depart for London in the morning," Coleus whispered from her side of the bed.

"I thought you were asleep." Rhoda turned over to address her sister. Of course, mother wouldn't wish to stay on after what had transpired tonight. Hell and tarnation, if her mother knew the half of it, Rhoda would never see the light of day again.

But they couldn't return to London yet! Her mother would learn of the wager. Rhoda wouldn't care nearly so much for herself, but this would be ruinous for Coleus and Hollyhock.

"Coleus, I need you to do something for me." Ah, more lies.

"What?"

A great deal of convincing was not going to be required. Coleus likely didn't want to return to London either. "You need to tell Mama you're sick tomorrow. We need to stay one more day."

Coleus yawned. "How come?"

Hmm… she couldn't very well confide that she intended to run away with Lord Blakely. "Er, well, we have to be here to support Emily! I can hardly leave on the day my best friend becomes betrothed, now, can I? Will you, Cole? Please?"

"That will mean I have to spend the entire day abed."

"Once matters are settled, I think Mama might change her mind about leaving. You don't really want to go back to London before the party is over, do you?"

Coleus plumped her pillow. "No. I'll tell Mama I'm too sick to travel. But you need to bring me some sweets from the kitchen, okay?"

Of course, Coleus wouldn't allow Rhoda to get away without some sort of exchange. She was her sister, after all. "I promise." Rhoda sighed and lay back against her own pillow, watching shadows from outside dance on the ceiling.

Where would she be tomorrow night? Would she be in a carriage, in route to Gretna Green with Lord Blakely?

That stupid wager! Stupid Flavion Nottingham! He'd

brought all of them nothing but trouble. She had been so reckless, so incredibly careless to go walking with him at the Crabtree Ball. How many times would she berate herself for being stupid before learning her lesson? The lesson to… not be stupid?

She'd barely dozed off before soft but persistent knocking on the door woke her up. Despite the sun filtering through the curtained windows, Coleus slept like the dead. Rhoda slid out of bed silently. It likely would be Emily, having second thoughts… contemplating declining the earl's offer.

A lump formed in her throat at the thought.

She tiptoed to the door and pulled it open. Not Emily.

Sophia stood outside, wringing her hands in front of her. "Emily's gone!" She bit her lip.

"What do you mean, Emily's gone?" Rhoda ran a hand through her hair, stepped into the corridor and pulled the door closed. She didn't want Coleus to overhear something she'd gladly share with Holly all too gleefully.

"She's gone. She left with… Blakely last night!" Sophia's gaze shifted to the end of the foyer. When Rhoda didn't respond right away, she grimaced. "Are you angry?"

Rhoda could have been knocked over with a feather. It would have been easier to believe Emily had sprouted wings and taken flight. But was she angry? "No… But why? When? Are you certain?"

Sophia's eyes shifted again. "I need you to tell Carlisle. He's in Dev's study now."

"Me?" Rhoda squealed and was immediately shushed by Sophia. "Me?" she whispered. "Why me?"

"I, er, well… Perhaps he'll be less upset hearing it from you." But Sophia would not meet her gaze.

"What have you done?" Rhoda smelled a rat.

"It's just that you didn't seem all that enthusiastic

about Blakely. And Emily, well, I rather think she's taken a shine to him…"

"What did you do?" And she'd thought *she'd* been the manipulative one!

Sophia handed her a folded piece of paper. *Have Rhoda meet Blakely behind the mews at three in the morning. A readied traveling coach would be greatly appreciated.*

"When did you receive this? Did you have this when we met last night?" She could hardly believe Sophia had the audacity to take such matters into her own hands. Sophia didn't need to answer. Rhoda could read the answer merely by the look on her face.

"You must get dressed. Come into your dressing room, and I'll assist you." Sophia turned to open the door, but Rhoda grabbed her arm.

"I can't see him. I can't be the one to tell him."

But Sophia was shaking her head. "Well, I cannot tell him! What kind of a hostess would I be if he found out I'd sent his intended away to elope with another gentleman?" Her blue eyes looked mortified at such a thought. "If your mother found out, she'd tell everybody!"

"Why don't we tell him the truth? Or some version of it anyhow? But wait! Just because I didn't show, what makes you think Emily is eloping with Blakely?" No answer. "Oh, good Lord, Sophia! What else have you done?"

"I might have ordered the coachmen not to stop until he absolutely had to. But she got into the carriage. I think it's something she wanted all along."

Rhoda wanted to pound her forehead against the wall. This! *This* was what lying and manipulations led to! No wonder Justin hated her now. "I will go to him. I will tell him."

"Not everything? Not my part in all of this?" Sophia pleaded.

"I will tell him… I will tell him that…" More lies? Must she lie to him some more? And furthermore, did she betray Sophia, or did she betray Emily?

"Simply tell him Emily left. If he happens to learn that Blakely's gone as well, then he can surmise his own opinion from that." Sophia led them through the chamber to a small dressing room and then pulled out one of Rhoda's favorite day dresses. "Hurry now, he's already waiting."

RHODA STILL HADN'T decided exactly what she would tell Justin by the time Sophia led her to Prescott's study. She paused, intending to knock, but Sophia simply opened the door and pushed her from behind.

Sophia would pay for this! But Rhoda loved her. They would get through this somehow. God only knew how, but they would.

He looked even more angelic today, staring out the window, the early morning sunlight glinting off his golden hair. He turned to glance over his shoulder when the door clicked shut. Upon seeing her, confusion showed on his handsome features.

And then his mouth twisted in derision. "Is this another joke? I was under the impression I'd be offering for Miss Goodnight."

She hated that he looked at her that way. As though he despised her.

I've given Justin White reason to feel hatred for another human being!

She swallowed hard and blinked away the burning sensation behind her eyes. "No more scheming. I'm simply a messenger." Taking a few hesitant steps, she moved farther into the room. He was not going to make this easy.

He'd turned to gaze out the window again, his feet shoulder-width apart, hands clasped behind his back.

And then she knew what she must do. "Emily has left with Blakely for Gretna Green. It was supposed to be me. I was supposed to meet Blakely early this morning, but I never got the message. I was… I was with… you."

He didn't move at first. He didn't even blink. After what felt like a lifetime, he finally shook his head. "Miss Goodnight and Blakely?" At last, he turned to face her. Although his expression still revealed contempt, Rhoda spied a trace of something else. Was it surprise? Disappointment? Pleasure? She couldn't tell. It was as though he'd turned off his emotions.

He no longer trusted her.

Rightfully so.

Rhoda nodded and then shrugged. "To be perfectly honest, I don't understand it myself. But Sophia asked me to tell you. And we… I… wish to apologize for the trouble we've put you through. The duchess and Prescott knew nothing about it." Ah, so she would lie. "It was mostly me and Emily. I'm sorry." She didn't know what else she could say. *Please don't hate me?* He'd come to be one of the few people in the world whose opinion of her truly mattered. She cared what he thought of her.

He ran a hand through that beautiful hair of his and then turned to stare out the window again. "So, what will you do then?" he asked with his back to her, as though he'd rather not ask such a question.

Rhoda dropped into the nearest chair. What *was* she going to do? Without the specter of Dudley Scofield hanging over her, she faced the horror of her situation clearly for the first time. The wager. The blasted bet would ruin her forever.

And she was not the only person who would be affected.

Coleus would be. As would Hollyhock. She raised trembling fingers to her lips and shook her head. Had she been hoping the reality of the wager would simply disappear?

No, she'd been imagining herself hanging from the gallows. She'd imagined herself in hell for all of eternity.

"I… I… don't know," she answered honestly.

Upon returning to London, it wouldn't be long before her mother found out about it. She needn't worry about her father.

Carlisle exhaled loudly and then turned and pinned her with his gaze. "Were you in love with him?"

She wanted to rail at him for asking such a question. Had she not been kissing him less than twelve hours ago? But oh, no, her reputation preceded her. Even Lord Carlisle now would question her morals. Was she to forever be branded a woman of easy virtue?

Except that she had been.

So, instead of releasing a stream of venom, she shook her head. "Of course not." But she could not help adding, "How can you ask me that after…?" She held his gaze defiantly. Those blue eyes that had always been so tender and understanding now chilled her to the core.

"But you'd promised yourself to him, had you not? Did he hold you in affection? Have you broken his heart by failing to meet him?"

"*I never got the message*!" she defended herself, unable to remain meek for any longer. She spoke through gritted teeth. "*I was with you*!" But she couldn't help wondering what would have happened if she *had* received the message. Would she have followed through with it?

At last, Justin's shoulders seemed to relax ever so slightly. "Well then, I hazard to say Miss Goodnight is no longer expecting an offer?" His chuckle rang cynically.

Rhoda stared down at her hands. "She is not."

When she finally peered up through her lashes again, she found him studying her, a serious expression on his face.

"What will you do now? About the wager? Do you have some other gentleman lined up to marry you?" His words were hurtful, but his tone was not.

She merely shook her head. "I don't know. There is no one else."

He raised one fist to his mouth, deep in thought. Should she leave him alone now? He didn't seem overly upset about Emily's defection. Rhoda had not truly believed that he would be.

"Your sisters will be ruined as well," he spoke just as she'd decided she would remove herself.

She slumped into her chair again. "Yes."

"I'd prefer to speak to your father first. Is he in London?" It took a moment for her mind to wrap itself around what he was saying. So now, he'd martyr himself for her. He'd marry her despite all that had happened?

"You don't have to do that."

"Is he in London?" he persisted.

And she had to catch herself from refusing again. Because this wasn't just about her. Her mind conjured up Coleus, trying on dresses and simply dying to make her come out. And Hollyhock, who already was showing signs of the beauty she'd become. "Father never resides in the same place as my mother. So, no. He isn't in London. He's at Pebbles Gate, near Oxford."

"I will meet with him, then and return. It shouldn't take me more than a few days." His words were firm. Not much enthusiasm but neither did he sound overly reluctant.

"My mother is in a hurry to return to London. I doubt I can keep her here more than another day." Coleus would play ill for one day but no more than that. And besides... Rhoda was tired of the deceit.

"Very well, then." He strode toward her, hitched his trousers at the top of his thighs, and then dropped down onto one knee.

In any other situation, she'd be giddy with delight at the sight of such a handsome gentleman, an earl no less, preparing to make her such an offer. Would she always remember this moment? For the rest of her life? The way the sun slanted in upon the carpet; the sound of the clock as it ticked upon the mantle; the aroma of lemon oil and leather, and now, with his nearness, the scent of his soap and cologne.

He lifted one of her hands in his, and she couldn't help noticing how comforted she felt, hers small and fragile tucked into his strong tanned grasp.

And yet it was wrong.

"Miss Mossant." His voice sounded gravelly, as though the momentousness of the occasion had suddenly struck him as well. She glanced from their hands to peer into his eyes once again. She willed his blue depths not to be cold any longer. She wanted, she *needed* to see a hint of the warmth they'd held last night before... before he'd realized the extent of her conniving.

Perhaps he'd seen the pleading look in hers, for they lost the iciness from earlier but remained guarded. "Will you honor me by consenting to be my wife? Will you marry me?"

She couldn't help but remember all the times he'd shown her kindness. At the Crabtrees' ball, after they'd fallen into the lake together, when she'd gone walking in the garden, and then last night. He'd freed her from a lifetime of guilt with his reason and insight.

She owed him so much already. A steely determination came over her. She'd make this man happy. If it took a lifetime, she'd somehow repay him. And although she had no idea what this would require, she nodded. "I will," she answered.

JUSTIN HAD NEVER imagined such a scenario would present itself. Especially after last night, after learning she and Miss Goodnight had conspired to trap him into a marriage with not Rhoda but with the other woman.

She likely would have preferred Blakely. Blakely, although considered a womanizer, had been considered the most sought after, although most unattainable, bachelor in London for nearly a decade. Why wouldn't she have preferred Blakely to himself, a former vicar?

But now here he was, kneeling before her in Prescott's study, holding her hand, and she'd consented to marry him.

Although something in his heart thrilled at her response, another part was terrified. Had he just doomed himself to a lifetime of pain? Would she stray? After last night, he knew she was attracted to him but once that passed, would she move on to another? Would she replace him with more sophisticated lovers?

He wanted to believe she was the woman he'd first imagined but the lies perpetrated by her and Miss Goodnight left him with doubts.

And yet, she gazed into his eyes with a determined glint he'd not expected. He swallowed hard and then raised her fingertips to his lips. Closing his eyes, he sent up a prayer as he kissed her soft, fragrant skin.

"Thank you." And although he knew she believed he was doing this as an act of kindness, he meant the words wholeheartedly. "But no more lies." If they were to stand a chance at happiness, he needed to be able to trust her.

She nodded.

"I will speak with your mother and then depart shortly afterward. If your father has no objections, we can begin having the banns read this Sunday and you can plan for a ceremony in London. I don't think we should delay any longer than necessary."

And then he supposed he'd be obliged to introduce her to his cousins at Carlisle House. Hell, he'd be obliged to introduce himself. If he'd ever met any of them before, he couldn't remember now.

Her eyes flew open wide. "But I'd thought… I expected you'd want to simply elope." Fear entered her eyes. "Or can we simply marry here? I can't return to London until everything is settled. Can't we just get the ceremony out of the way and *then* return to London?"

"We will not simply *get the ceremony out of the way.*" He ground the words out. Obviously, she didn't realize what it was going to take to restore her reputation. As her intended, he needed to address the wager at White's in his own way. Marrying, by itself, would not be enough. Had she simply eloped with Blakely, it would have taken years for her to be able to return to the *ton.* And even then, he doubted she'd be afforded any respect.

No, he had work to do. Dropping her hands, he pushed himself up from the floor. He then strode across the room and opened the door. Not surprisingly, Her Grace was pacing just beyond it. "Will you have Mrs. Mossant summoned?" He didn't mean for the words to sound as demanding as they had. "If you please, Your Grace?" he added.

She nodded and scurried away.

CHAPTER SEVENTEEN

His Way

"BUT I WAS under the impression you were going to offer for Miss Goodnight." Mrs. Mossant sat stiffly on the long leather settee in Prescott's study. Sophia, Prescott, Cecily, and Mr. Nottingham were present as well.

Justin had declared all would be aboveboard from this point forward.

Rhoda tried not to bristle at Carlisle's high handedness. He'd refused even to contemplate the notion of an elopement and when she'd tried to suggest he obtain a special license, he'd denied that request as well. When had he become so very overbearing?

"Mama, Emily is eloping with *Lord Blakely*." Rhoda didn't know how much she ought to confess to her mother about all of this.

"Not that I'm opposed to Lord Carlisle." Her mother sent a meaningful glance toward the earl.

Toward her daughter's fiancé.

Of course not! Her mother expected Rhoda to marry no less than an earl after having been squired about by St. John! "But I admit to being confused. And a little concerned. My Lord," she addressed Carlisle. "Forgive me for asking, but how can you turn your affections so easily? Just last night, you were, ah, rather… exhibiting a great deal of it toward Miss Goodnight. And now, you are offering for *my* daughter?"

These questions surprised Rhoda. She'd expected her mother to do no less than express glee at the engagement of her oldest daughter.

"I understand your concerns, Mrs. Mossant." Justin resembled the former vicar right now more than the high-handed earl Rhoda had become engaged to. "To be perfectly honest with you, I had thought Miss Goodnight *was* your daughter. I've carried my affection for Miss Mossant for several months now. Since last summer's unfortunate event, in fact, at Priory Point."

Rhoda watched him speak. He'd told her there would be no more lies.

Upon his words, her mama brightened. "Ah, well then. Of course, I give you my blessing."

"Thank you, ma'am." His expression had turned inscrutable, once again. "There is something else, though, that I feel you must be made aware of."

Rhoda's insides flipped in her stomach. Laying all of this bare before her mother left her feeling rather naked. Sophia and Cecily knew of it, of course. But she squirmed in her seat that it was to be discussed with their husbands present.

Her mother appeared mildly curious but simply nodded, giving him permission to continue.

"The gentlemen of the *ton* have instigated some egregious behavior toward your daughter."

Her mama lowered her brows and frowned.

"There is a wager, at White's. Rumors spread by the late Marquess of St. John have done considerable damage to her reputation."

"What kind of rumors?" her mama asked. But then she held up a hand. "No. I do not wish to hear them." But her face had turned a reddish hue. She pulled a handkerchief out of her sleeve and dabbed at one eye. Had her mother, in fact, heard about the rumor? Did she suspect Rhoda had been indiscreet with St. John? The thought made her cringe inside.

"I wish to reassure you that I intend to restore your daughter's reputation completely." He didn't go into any further detail, but he sounded so confident that Rhoda almost believed it. "You have no need to worry for your other daughters' opportunities, but I'd request, please, that you remain at Eden's Court for at least four more days. By that time, I'll have settled matters in London and can meet you there."

Her mother nodded eagerly. "Of course, my lord." And it was as simple as that.

"I will be leaving for Pebble's Gate shortly, in order to obtain your husband's consent, of course. And as long as he has no objections, I'll then go to London to order the banns read and deal with these other matters."

Rhoda met her mother's gaze knowingly. Both knew how little her father cared to involve himself in his daughters' affairs. Rhoda raised her brows and her mother shrugged.

"I'm certain that will prove to be an... interesting visit," her mother responded.

Lord Carlisle apparently hadn't noticed their exchange. For he'd already risen and seemed anxious to end their meeting. "Please, feel free to begin any planning necessary and of course, have the expenses billed to me."

Rhoda rose, as did her mother, Sophia, Cecily, Mr. Nottingham, and Prescott.

"Are you sure you don't want me to accompany you, Justin?" Prescott had offered earlier, Rhoda knew, but he'd declined.

"I need to do this alone, Dev." And then she glimpsed a part of him she'd not seen before. Vulnerability. And uncertainty. But also, a steely glint of resolve. Something about this caused a frisson of fear to crawl through her. She suddenly wanted to insist he take the duke along, or to take her with him but knew he'd not appreciate this.

Rhoda hugged herself and shivered. She wished he'd taken her in his arms after his proposal. She wanted to touch him, to seal her commitment with more than just words. "Will you take luncheon with us, before you leave?" she couldn't help but ask.

But he was already shaking his head. "I don't want to waste any more daylight." He would be riding alone.

Something in her tone must have alerted Sophia to Rhoda's need. "Mrs. Mossant, Cecily. I have some new fashion magazines in the drawing room. There's no harm in leaving these two alone for a few minutes before Lord Carlisle takes his leave, is there?" This, she said to the duke.

He smiled dotingly at his wife. "I don't believe so." And then he ushered both Rhoda's mother and Sophia out the door. Cecily and her husband followed. "I'll meet you in the stables in half an hour." Mr. Nottingham spoke over his shoulder. And then he closed the door quietly behind him.

Rhoda had the feeling Lord Carlisle would have avoided being alone with her again. But she'd made herself a promise. She stepped forward tentatively and then took his hands in hers.

She closed her eyes and searched for the right words. "I believe I'm coming to know you a little..." She squeezed his hands even though his own remained lax. "And so, I'm not going to thank you for this. You wouldn't do it unless you wanted to." He'd told her mother he'd had feelings for her since *last summer*. "Don't do anything rash for me in London. And if you do, please, have a care."

His larger fingers finally curled around hers gently. She couldn't help it. She leaned forward and rested her forehead against his chest. "I couldn't live with myself if something happened to you."

He released her hands and his arms came around her. Rhoda refused to cry. She refused to allow him to leave believing she wasn't strong enough to handle what lay ahead. But she felt his lips on her head. And then his hands were on her neck, her chin, lifting her lips to meet his.

Last night, she'd initiated their kiss, and he'd held a part of himself back. This kiss today.

This kiss was all him.

His mouth claimed hers, his tongue sliding through the seam of her lips, inciting her heart to race. With a tilt of his head, still holding her face, he delved even deeper. Rhoda clutched at his wrists. A roaring filled her ears, flashes of light burned in her brain and she came alive. "Justin." With a heavy ache settling between her legs and in her breasts, she wanted to beg him to stay. But before she could do any of this, he released her and took a step back.

"I'll see you in four days' time." The intensity of his gaze shook her. And then he smiled. It wasn't much, just the tiniest tug at the corner of his lips. "Don't do anything stupid," he said almost teasingly. "No more plans. No more schemes. No more switching of perfumes or cheating at games. In fact, no parlor games. I absolutely forbid you to play any parlor games while I'm gone. And stay put. Don't even think of coming to London any earlier."

She nearly wept at his words. "You silly man," she said instead. She would either burst into tears or hysterical laughter. "Take care of my vicar."

He nodded. Looking as though he might sweep her up again, he hesitated. She couldn't stand it if he did. *God, please take care of him.* He stood tall; he was fit, firm, and agile. She remembered the risks he'd taken last summer attempting to save Lord Harold. He'd climbed down the cliff as far as possible. He'd done so when St. John, Lord Harold's own brother, would not.

This man had an abundance of courage.

But he was only a man. As had been Lord Harold. As had been St. John.

The moment passed, and he nodded again. "No games," he ordered again.

And then he was gone.

Rhoda dropped to the sofa and covered her face. *Breathe. He'll return. He isn't St. John.*

Good Lord, he was only going to visit her father, for heaven's sake.

And then onward to London. How did he intend to put an end to the wager? Was it even possible? She remembered the desperation she'd seen on Flavion's face when he'd attacked her. At the time, she'd thought he'd been overcome with wanting her. But now, upon hearing the staggering amount the winnings had grown to… So utterly ridiculous! Was there a man alive who would allow the opportunity to win such a windfall slip away so easily?

She touched her lips.

Lord Carlisle. Justin White.

Her betrothed.

He'd ordered her to stay put. He'd asked her to do something no one had ever done before. He expected her to leave matters up to him.

She shook her head in disbelief. He'd told her to wait. She was expected to do naught but look through fashion magazines, decide upon flowers and a menu. Where would they hold the wedding breakfast? Ought they to have a pre-wedding ball? She steeled herself to avoid trying to think of ways to put an end to the bet.

She needed to leave it up to him.

To a man.

Gah! These four days might prove to be the longest of her life.

JUSTIN DIDN'T KNOW very much about Rhoda's father. In fact, he couldn't recall ever crossing paths with the man in London or elsewhere. As he rode toward Bristol, the thought struck him that if the man had joined his wife and daughter in London to begin with, then perhaps this wager wouldn't have gotten so out of hand.

A man ought to protect and defend his daughter. As Justin rode along, he pondered how little he knew about these devilish debutantes. One glaringly obvious fact, however, was that their fathers needed to further invest themselves in their daughters' affairs.

No wonder they found it necessary to arrange their own and the lives of those around them. No one had ever done much to guide them in their own.

This thought brought to mind his own mother. Her own father had failed her, and then she'd lost her husband shortly after. She'd done what was necessary in order to survive.

A woman couldn't sail the seas in search of treasure. She couldn't invest, buy land, or learn a trade. Oh, yes, she could teach, or she could be a companion, but that left her at the mercy of others.

A woman had her family and friends, her wits, and her body. And even then, she didn't have complete ownership of herself.

He remembered clearly the day he'd discovered how his

mother provided food and shelter for the two of them. He'd been at school. Two rowdy, raucous boys had demanded Justin hand over his lunch. When Justin refused, they'd taunted him. They'd told him both their fathers had likely paid for it. They'd made crude remarks about his mother.

Justin had fought back, violently overcome by the need to defend her honor. And he'd paid dearly. He hadn't been a weakling. He'd done his fair share of chores around their house, but without brothers, or a father, or any man really to test his metal on, he'd failed to learn even the most basic techniques of fighting.

He had not returned to the schoolroom that afternoon. With an injured foot and two black eyes, he'd practically crawled home.

And then taken another blow, not a physical one this time, but something even worse. Upon entering, he could still remember the shame he'd felt when he'd crept into his mother's room and discovered Kent Crane's father with his dear sweet mum.

On top of his dear sweet mum. Grateful his presence had gone unnoticed, he'd backed out of the room in mortification.

Justin hated that memory.

He'd wanted to lash out again but had been physically powerless to do so. He'd been powerless in all of it.

He'd wanted to scream at his mother and protect her at the same time, but he'd not been too young to notice the extra chickens in their yard later that night. He'd felt sick at heart, angry, trapped, and frustrated, but he'd also seen his mother for what she was.

A survivor.

He'd not liked it. He'd not been happy about it. But he'd understood.

Riding along the highway alone left him with far too much time to think.

Just a few weeks ago, he'd felt a similar sensation when he'd watched Rhoda fight off the blighter, the Earl of Kensington.

And then again, when she'd told him she was marrying Blakely.

He'd not liked it. He'd hated it, in fact. But he'd understood.

And although his vocation had taught him otherwise, that women needed to rely upon the men in their lives, Justin had respected his mother. He'd even respected Miss Mossant.

Rhoda.

His fiancée.

Because somehow, God had decided to give him the desire of his heart. Not the way he'd imagined it, and not without nearly insurmountable challenges, but he was being given a chance.

He'd promised her mother he'd deal with the wager. Put it to rest. But damned if he knew how to go about doing so. Perhaps her father would step up and assist him. Perhaps declaring his intent to wed her would dissolve it. These men valued honor on some level. He hoped their honor was worth seventy-five thousand pounds or so…

Justin stretched and rubbed the back of his neck.

He'd been on the road for two long days. After staying the night in a local inn, he'd cleaned up this morning to meet with Mr. Mossant. When he'd asked for directions, the innkeeper had given him an odd glance. Everyone knew where Pebble's Gate was. Less than half an hour from town.

Except, surely, there must be some mistake? He'd expected a small country estate, under no misconceptions that Rhododendron was any sort of heiress.

But the home ahead looked to be something of a mansion. A large iron gate displaying the name of the estate proved he was in the right place. Justin gazed about in awe as he traveled the length of the drive. The mansion didn't sit in a yard; it had been built in nothing less than a park.

A groom exited the large front doors in the distance, but just as quickly disappeared upon catching sight of an approaching guest.

Why had he expected that Rhoda's family lacked funds? But yes, he'd heard mention of a small dowry. The grounds, although vast, were in disrepair, and as he neared the home, he could see it was in need of maintenance. Justin dismounted and loosely tethered his horse to a railing.

With a tug at his cravat, he knocked loudly once, twice… after the third time, finally heard movement from within. A tall, haggard-looking butler opened the door and stared down a rather crooked nose at him suspiciously. "Do you have your invitation, sir?"

Justin noted that the servant's scarlet uniform was stained darker in places, and the shirt he wore beneath it appeared yellowed.

He answered with a shake of his head. "I have no invitation. I am here to meet with Mr. Mossant." At the butler's narrowed eyes, Justin added, "I have important business with him, sir."

The servant's brows rose. "Your name?"

Out of habit, Justin nearly answered Mr. White, but caught himself. "The Earl of Carlisle."

The servant eyed him suspiciously. "And business, you say?"

Justin nodded. "Indeed."

The butler sighed tiredly before answering, "Follow me, my lord." He led Justin to what once must have been an elegant drawing room. "Wait here."

Justin tried to imagine his fiancé and her sisters living here. The hair stood up on the back of his neck. This place hardly felt like a home. It seemed... off.

Although the property seemed to be eroding, it also appeared to encompass a vast amount of land. Surely, her father could have done better for them?

Justin didn't sit while he waited. He'd sat too much in the last few days and nervous energy coursed through him. Instead, he paced back and forth across the room. Inadvertently, he noticed the wear on the furnishings and the tapestries as well as a few noticeably empty spaces on the wall where artwork had once hung. Although perhaps cash poor, the family possessed assets.

Or they had, rather.

"The master will see you, my lord." Holding the door, the butler indicated Justin follow.

Justin had never been suspicious, and despite his lifelong vocation, he'd eschewed making judgments, but the only word he could summon at the ambiance of the house was evil. Pure and simple evil.

Perhaps he'd spent too much time alone with his horse.

They climbed one side of a U-shaped staircase and then strode along a carpeted corridor. Several paintings hung along the walls, but where pedestals stood, statues were noticeably absent.

When Justin neared a set of large double doors, a sweet acrid scent assaulted his nostrils.

His gut clenched when he stepped inside. Six or seven

gentlemen lay about the room and nearly a dozen ladies draped themselves around them.

Except they were not ladies, with their nipples pushed up and out of their corsets, and a few skirts lifted to expose their nether regions; they were obviously prostitutes. His gaze passed over entangled limbs, gaping mouths, and listless eyes as he searched for the man he'd come to speak with.

"My butler says you've come to speak business with me." A sardonic voice drew Justin's attention to the settee near the hearth. The jaundiced looking fellow most certainly was Rhoda's father. Same hair coloring. Same eyes. He lounged sideways, a plump woman beside him, her eyes closed, head tilted back, and legs spread. Mr. Mossant casually combed his fingers through the curly hair she displayed.

Justin made a quick bow. "Mr. Mossant." He returned to his full height but declined to offer his hand. A cloud of smoke hung in the air. "I'd like to speak to you about your daughter, Miss Mossant."

"Rhododendron?" Mr. Mossant furrowed his brows. "I thought you came to look at the art. You're not here to purchase from my collection?" The man's English was perfect but for a slight French accent.

Justin cleared his throat. He'd heard of these sorts of parties but never witnessed one in person. Upon the rustling of clothing, Justin turned and inadvertently witnessed one of the ladies straddling the gentleman behind him.

"Yes. The eldest Miss Mossant. I'm here to ask for her hand," he clarified. His heart raced. He clenched his fists.

Had the Mossant women known what he'd find here? Had Mr. Mossant exposed his daughters to such despicable behavior? Bile churned in his gut.

Until that moment, he'd not realized the respect due to Rhoda's mother. She'd removed her girls from their father's influence.

Justin suppressed the urge to pummel his future in-law into a speck of dust.

"Bah!" Mr. Mossant lifted the woman's leg off of him and slapped her dimpled bottom. She slid to the floor as he pushed himself off the settee. "I've made it clear from the beginning. Her dowry is two thousand pounds. Not a farthing more. All you nabobs come looking to take what's mine. Well, take the girl, but don't get ideas about anything else."

The man swayed as he rose to his full height. At that moment, he remembered the enigmatic glance he'd seen pass between Rhoda and her mother. Yes, they'd known. They'd known what he would find.

Justin ran a hand through his hair and then thrummed his fingertips against the top of his thighs. This man was Rhoda's father.

This *disgusting piece of vermin* was Rhoda's father.

Justin reached inside his coat and extracted the contracts he'd obtained from his solicitors while passing through London. With steady hands, he opened them up on a nearby table. "I'll have your permission in writing then."

Mr. Mossant stumbled across the room, located a pair of spectacles, and amazingly enough began reading through the legal document. "Blah, blah blah." His fingers skimmed the lines. "Very well, so she told you of the two thousand pounds." He looked at him sideways. "Fucking hell. You bastard. You're doing it to win the wager, aren't you?" He reached for a pen, dipped it in ink, and then drew a line through the dowry amount. "You won't be needing this once you've collected. Wiley bloke to come up with the idea. Taking a risk, though, aren't you, leaving her in

London while you come all this way to speak to me? Knowing that someone's likely to beat you to the winnings in the time it's taken you to come after a mere two thousand pounds."

Red clouded Justin's vision.

"You know of the wager? You know what's being said about your own flesh and blood, your daughter, and yet you remain here doing nothing to defend her honor?" This villain didn't deserve to have daughters.

Justin nodded. "Remove the dowry then. This has nothing to do with the wager and everything to do with protecting not only Miss Mossant, but your other daughters and your wife as well! Good God, man, don't you realize they're about to be chased out of London, out of the *ton* forever? You'd simply sit by and watch that happen without doing anything to help them?"

"I could care less what happens to them." Mr. Mossant finished perusing the document and then signed with a flourish. "You see all that I have here?" He gestured to the room, the house. "It will all go to my brother's sickly scamp. A good for nothing whiny rat. Time after time, my wife presented me with only daughters. And simply because she had some difficulties birthing, she refuses me. She's taken the girls and run off. They are not my problem. Let them rot in the gutters for all I care." And then he reached for a long thin pipe and inhaled deeply.

Justin wanted to lay the man out flat. No, he wanted to shake him first, give him a piece of his mind, and then lay him out flat.

Instead, he took up the signed document and blew on it to be certain the ink had dried. Satisfied it wouldn't smear, he folded it neatly and returned it to his pocket. "Good day. I'll find my own way out."

AN HOUR LATER, Justin returned to the village and located an out of the way table at the local pub for something to eat and drink. He didn't wish to speak to anybody. He needed to think.

The meeting with Miss Mossant's father had left him more than a little unsettled.

"You look hungry, my lord." A pretty barmaid leaned over the table to get his attention, her ample bosom level with his gaze. How would she know to 'my lord' him? He shook his head in disgust.

"An ale and stew, if you have it."

Women didn't normally act so brazenly around him. Ah, but he'd not worn his collar today.

She winked and flipped her hair. "Anything for one so fine as you. Will you be needing a room for the night?"

Justin grimaced.

What he needed to do was meet with the solicitors regarding his financial situation. This was the niggling that bothered him.

He took a swig of the bitter ale and pulled the contract out of his pocket.

No dowry.

It shouldn't trouble him, the lack of dowry, but guilt pricked his conscience.

Others depended upon him now. Not for spiritual guidance, but for shelter, food, security. And he imagined a great deal of other vital necessities required by ladies of qualities who now fell within his care.

And his fiancée.

And possibly her sisters and mother.

"I'd be happy to share mine with you."

He'd forgotten the barmaid's question. Meeting her pretty gaze, he shook his head. "Not tonight, Miss."

She pursed her lips into a sultry pout at his words.

He'd make a stop at Carlisle Manor before returning to London. It wasn't too far out of the way, and upon doing so, he could at least know what he was dealing with.

CHAPTER EIGHTEEN

One Small Obstacle...

"BUT OF COURSE, under normal circumstances, we'd be more than happy to host a pre-wedding ball at Prescott House." Sophia's mother-in-law had made one of her rare appearances at the main manor that morning to add her two pence to the wedding plans. "But it hasn't yet been a year."

"Of course, Your Grace," Rhoda's mother chimed in.

Sophia's gaze met Rhoda's apologetically.

"We really needn't have a pre-wedding ball," Rhoda insisted. She wished Carlisle had not been so adamant about a London wedding. Lucky Emily!

She missed Emily and hoped she and Blakely returned before her mother dragged her back to London.

Just the thought of facing the ladies who'd ignored her at the garden party, even worse the gentlemen who had not, sent her innards flip-flopping.

She was engaged now, though. Surely, that ought to put a stop to all that nonsense.

"My father's house in Town has a good-sized ballroom. We could host it there," Cecily suggested.

Rhoda's mother's grimaced.

Cecily's father, although immensely wealthy, wasn't *ton*.

"Or not," Cecily muttered.

"Doesn't Carlisle's new estate come with some sort of

property in Town? It's an earldom, for heaven's sake. Surely, the former earl would have maintained a residence for when Parliament is in session?"

Sophia wasn't usually the practical one, but Mrs. Mossant apparently saw this as a viable option.

"But of course, he must have!" she exclaimed. She turned to Rhoda. "As soon as we are back, you must have your betrothed take you to examine the residence. See if it is large enough."

Ah, large enough. Her mother had drawn up a guest list of over three hundred people and this was just for the ball. She wished to invite close to five hundred of her dearest friends to the wedding breakfast.

Rhoda hadn't realized her mother even *knew* five hundred people.

"It will be the first thing I ask when I see him again," Rhoda said with an expressionless face.

Cecily lifted a hand to cover a choked laugh.

"I do wish he hadn't asked us to wait here," Rhoda's mother complained. "Not that we don't appreciate your hospitality, Your Grace," she said apologetically to Sophia's mother-in-law. "It's just that there is so much to do."

"What kind of flowers will you have, Rho? Not rhododendrons." Leave it to Coleus to make such a ridiculous suggestion. Rhoda could have knocked her upside the head. Instead, she glared ominously in the younger girl's direction.

"Of course, she'll have rhododendrons." Mrs. Mossant frowned at her middle daughter.

"It's not very romantic, Mother." They'd had this argument before. "For heaven's sake, it's practically a bush! And it means 'danger' of all things!"

"A warning for your groom," Coleus teased. "Beware

of your future bride." She sent herself into a fit of giggles.

"It's a beautiful flower," her mother insisted. "And I've imagined decorating your wedding with them since the day you were born."

"You know," the older duchess spoke up again. "I believe there are several growing on the grounds at Prescott House. What a charming idea."

It seemed Rhoda was to have no part in the planning of her wedding ceremony.

"Now, for your dress, something pink, I think, to match the flowers."

"Not pink!" Rhoda hated pink. "Green. I want an emerald green." She'd assert herself on something, anyhow.

"I do wish I could come to London with you." Sophia and Prescott were going to wait at Eden's Court for Emily and Blakely's return, as were Cecily and Mr. Nottingham.

"I wish you could, too."

And Emily. Rhoda missed Emily more than she would have thought.

Was Emily already married? They'd left three days ago. They likely were already on the road back.

"We'll come to London in a few weeks' time," Cecily assured her. "You won't be alone for long."

Rhoda wanted to ask Cecily if she thought it would be safe yet, if she thought the wager would be canceled with news of her betrothal, but she didn't wish to have that conversation in front of the duchess, her mother, and her sisters.

"Don't take any longer than necessary." She winced.

Already she wondered if Lord Carlisle regretted his proposal. He'd have met with her father by now.

Sitting in the lovely drawing room discussing the exciting details of her own wedding, Rhoda wanted nothing more than to escape. Her wedding day was growing into some horrific spectacle. Normally, she would have welcomed it, but not now... not after having all of the *ton* judging her most personal of affairs.

She could do nothing to stop them. They would gleefully examine her every move. Believe what they wanted and then repeat it to another.

Her chest tightened as if an elephant had sat down on top of her.

She'd control the only thing she could.

"Just not pink," she murmured. "I refuse to wear pink."

THEY'D MADE THE journey to London the day before and it had barely taken more than four hours. Not knowing what she would face had tied her nerves into knots. She'd almost wished the journey had been a longer one.

Her mother had gone to visit a close friend and taken Coleus and Hollyhock with her.

It had been five days now since she'd bid Lord Carlisle farewell. He'd promised to call upon her when he arrived back in London.

Rhoda glanced over at the clock. Nearly noon. She and her mother had an appointment that afternoon with Madam Chantal. Normally thrilled at the opportunity to be fitted for a new dress, Rhoda wished she could remain hidden inside today instead.

She was afraid.

And she hated it. She absolutely hated being afraid.

All year, ever since pushing Dudley off that blasted cliff last summer, she'd been afraid of the truth. She'd finally faced that and now she was afraid to face a handful of supercilious debutantes, their mothers, and a bunch of dandies.

The men of the *ton* were bored, vile, and cruel. They were ridiculous creatures.

They considered their pranks harmless, but a man might just as well send a woman to a nunnery as cast aspersions upon her reputation.

Rhoda wasn't ready for that.

The trouble was, she wasn't certain as to what exactly she would face when going out. Would she be given the cut direct? Would gentlemen persist in harassing her?

"Miss Mossant, a visitor."

Rhoda spun around. She hadn't heard the butler slip into the room.

Lord Carlisle stood behind him. Really, what was Leo thinking? Presenting a gentleman to her without warning?

Rhoda touched her hair and smoothed her dress, feeling suddenly self-conscious. She'd donned one of her prettier gowns this morning, assuming he might make an appearance, but even so, would have appreciated a moment to prepare herself.

He looked as though he'd come straight to her from his travels, his blond wavy hair tousled, and his clothing wrinkled.

"My lord." She dipped into a stilted curtsey. He'd kissed her five days ago as if he'd been leaving for the battlefield. At the time, she'd felt as though their souls were one. Today he appeared as though a stranger.

"Miss Mossant." He bowed.

When she finally met his eyes, she immediately saw regret. Her heart sank. He'd changed his mind. He didn't want to marry her after all. And yet, she knew that he would never cry off. He was far too honorable for that.

The hope she'd allowed to flicker disappeared, leaving

a trail of smoke.

She gestured for him to sit upon the loveseat and lowered herself onto a stiff-backed chair facing him.

"I take it you've met with Father, then?" She would not make niceties with so much at stake.

Those blue eyes of his stared at her intently. He shifted forward and clasped his hands together, dangling between his knees. "I did." Of course, he wouldn't smile upon such an admission. Her father wasn't exactly a person who inspired fond memories. "I also journeyed to Carlisle Manor, since it wasn't far out of my way."

He'd been dealt some sort of blow. Something had gone terribly wrong, and for the first time in ages, Rhoda didn't think she was to blame.

"What is it? Are your cousins unwell?"

He shook his head and stared at the floor. "I'm afraid I..."

She could not remember any occasion when he'd been at a loss for words. Rhoda shifted uncomfortably in her seat and remained quiet.

He was going to call off. He would break their betrothal for some unknown reason and then forever carry the guilt of it.

"I was rather hasty in accepting your proposal." She blurted the words out before he could say anything more. What was she doing? Her mother was going to kill her. She swallowed hard and ignored the regret squeezing her insides.

It wasn't as though she loved him.

She hardly knew him.

But he'd glanced up sharply at her words. "You were what?" The sadness she felt mirrored the hurt in his eyes.

Now it was her turn to stare at the floor. "You were rather cornered by my situation—compelled to ask out of a misplaced sense of compassion and..."

"I did not ask to marry you out of compassion." He spoke the words without delay and quite clearly.

Her head jerked up.

"You do not wish to cry off?" She studied him carefully. If she saw any doubts, she needed to release him. Cecily had been right to warn her and Emily against a hasty marriage. It was forever, regardless of the fact that Cecily had escaped hers.

Trapping oneself was one thing. Trapping another human being, quite another.

He was shaking his head. "I do not wish to cry off." Except... She did see something in his gaze. Something unsettling.

"Did my father say something to you? Is that what has brought on your reserve?"

She'd not seen this side of him before. From the moment she'd first met him, he'd been uplifting, encouraging.

Strong. Dependable.

She remembered he'd gently chastised her for her hopelessness when he'd sat beside her at the Crabtree Ball.

Had that only been a few weeks ago? So much had changed!

Emily was married, happily, she hoped.

The wager would go away, upon her own marriage, she hoped.

And this matter with Dudley Scofield, well, it suddenly lacked the power to haunt her every second. She no longer woke up in a cold sweat from nightmares where a rope was dropped over her head. She'd stopped imagining herself swinging from the gallows.

Everything had changed because of him.

He rose from his chair and paced toward the window. Staring outside for a few moments, he almost seemed to have forgotten she was there.

"I'm broke." He wasn't facing her when he murmured the words. She barely heard them, in fact.

If he was broke, then surely marrying her might, in fact, have some benefit. Her dowry had never been large, but it would be something...

"I do have a small dowry."

"Your father has withdrawn it."

He did what? Rhoda took a few deep breaths to keep herself from exploding in outrage at her father's selfish and disgusting lifestyle.

"Your inheritance?"

"Amounts to naught more than a mountain of burdens and debts." He held his shoulders stiffly. He'd yet to turn around again to face her.

He'd apparently been unaware of the conditions of his inheritance when he'd proposed. He must have believed it had come with some sort of income.

As he'd believed she'd come with some monetary relief as well.

Unfortunately, neither were the case.

Rhoda understood the responsibilities and demands of running an estate all too well, having seen her own father ignore them for years now.

This man she'd been fretting over for nearly a week now, who'd brought so much hope into her life, finally turned to face her, those beautiful blue eyes shuttered. "I visited Carlisle House before returning. It is why I did not come to you yesterday. I apologize for the delay, but after meeting with your father, I felt compelled to ascertain the condition of the Carlisle coffers." He ran one hand through his hair, distracting her for a moment with the glints of gold reflecting the sunlight from behind him.

"The estate itself is in dire need of repairs. Tenant

payments have been neglected, as have their living conditions. And my dear cousin mortgaged himself up to his eyeballs before having the inconsideration of dying."

Rhoda bit her lip. For him to take on a wife right now, he needed one who would come along with the added bonus of a dowry.

A significant one.

It was, in truth, the only acceptable manner in which he could address his new situation.

But Rhoda wanted to keep him! There had to be a way.

The honorable thing would likely be for her to break their betrothal.

She shook her head. She couldn't!

She had to marry him! And then it donned on her! Her mother was, this very moment, telling all the world that she had become engaged. She'd be ruined forever if she cried off now.

They'd all be ruined.

THE TRICKY THING was, Justin *wanted* to marry Miss Rhododendron Mossant.

He'd only been away from her all of five days and he'd missed her.

Dark circles shadowed her eyes but did nothing to diminish her beauty. She'd obviously not rested well in his absence.

A war raged within him.

"I have a small savings," she offered. "I've held back from spending much of my allowance."

He had savings as well. Not nearly enough to satisfy the Carlisle estate's creditors, let alone begin repairs. He was a fool to delay the inevitable.

Furthermore, he could never keep her in the manner in which she'd grown accustomed. And what of her sisters and mother? And his cousins? The situation was impossible. He swallowed hard before squashing her suggestion.

But just as he went to speak, his breath caught.

Light, unlike anything he'd seen in her eyes before, glowed up at him.

Hope.

Along with rose-tinged cheeks and a certain breathlessness...

She burst out of her chair. "I could talk with Mother. I'm uncertain as to the details but I know she has oversight of some of the household funds. Perhaps she could..."

She'd told him that hope could only lead to disappointment. Justin moved to be closer to her. She tugged at him more than ever in that visceral way, like a whirlpool, a vortex.

Or gravity.

He couldn't disappoint her now. He didn't know the answer, if one existed, and yet he couldn't be the one to douse her hope. Not when she'd known despair for so long.

He caught a whiff of her perfume. Standing before her now, he refused to give up.

He wasn't ready to let her go yet.

Maybe Dev would have some ideas.

Justin could not—would not—take charity from his cousin, but he'd certainly be open to advice. There had to be a way.

"No need to be hasty." He licked his lips and placed one hand upon her waist.

Just then footsteps sounded, increasing in volume. Feminine footsteps,

Matronly footsteps.

"Lord Carlisle! I trust your journey was successful?" Mrs. Mossant entered the room unapologetically, casting a disapproving glance in their direction.

Justin stumbled backward. "It was." He bowed over Mrs. Mossant's hand. It wouldn't do to sour her mother on their upcoming nuptials.

They needed all the support she could provide.

Mrs. Mossant stood with shoulders back. He'd not once seen the woman act in an undignified manner, quite the opposite of her husband.

He wondered at Rhoda's mother's strength, her independence, and the hardship she faced being bound to the bastard he'd met at Pebble's Gate.

"And Mr. Mossant." She narrowed her gaze upon him. "Was he… amenable?"

"He—"

"Father is withholding my dowry!" Rhoda paced across the room quite suddenly.

"It is of no—" he attempted.

"Oh, dear." This time, Mrs. Mossant interrupted him. "Not well done of him at all."

"He has no right!"

"That wouldn't stop him, you know that." And then seeming to realize they were discussing a highly personal matter in front of him, the older woman pinched her lips together tightly. "My apologies, my lord." The smile she summoned seemed more than a little forced.

"Was he in his right mind when you spoke with him?" This from his fiancée. Her anger had flushed her cheeks with a rosy hue and her eyes sparkled in anger. Her hopeful energy lit something inside of him. Caused his heart to skip a beat and speed up at the same time.

What had she asked him?

Justin reached into his pocket to retrieve the contract.

"Despite the, er, goings on around him, I do believe he was in his right mind."

He handed the contract over so both of the women could peruse it. Mrs. Mossant nodded, and his betrothed let out a low moan.

Good lord, but it sent a surge of lust through him.

He cleared his throat. "I have business to attend to." Such as checking the balance of his savings, reexamining the estate books, and asking his solicitors about investments.

Perhaps while walking over to their offices, he might stumble upon twenty thousand pounds or so miraculously.

A prayer or two couldn't hurt. He glanced across the room and studied his betrothed. A determined glint had appeared in her eyes, one he barely remembered seeing before the tragedies last summer.

He couldn't give up yet.

Definitely, prayer was in order.

"If you're amenable, I will return this afternoon to take you driving in the park?" He wanted more time alone with her, regardless of what the future held.

She met his gaze fiercely. "I look forward to it."

CHAPTER NINETEEN

Thinking Outside the Box

RHODA'S MOTHER'S TIMING could not have been worse.

"Let's not be hasty," he'd said. He'd been about to kiss her. He'd reached out to pull her in his arms. And she'd been about to swoon in his direction.

She'd wanted his mouth on hers. She needed it. His head had tilted forward.

But, of course, her blasted mother had chosen such a romantic moment to come barging in!

A frustrated huff escaped Rhoda's lips.

And now he was gone again.

He still wanted to marry her, but *did* he really? A small savings, even her small dowry, would have done little to bolster an estate.

But he hadn't cried off. Perhaps he felt sorry for her and was delaying the inevitable. She imagined she'd find out this afternoon, when he collected her for their drive in the park.

It would be her first time in society since leaving London last week. Would she be received?

"I have a little money set aside, dear. I thought something like this might happen. My grandmother gave it to me, and now I can give some of it to you. I cannot give all of it to you, of course. But if the only obstacle to your happiness comes down to the matter of a dowry... You needn't be denied. I need to save some for Coleus and

Hollyhock's come out, of course. If your father had known the funds existed, they'd be long gone."

What was her mother going on about? "You kept money from Father?" Rhoda wrinkled her brow. Perhaps there was more to her mother than Rhoda had given her credit for.

"I can give you one thousand pounds. I expect you to invest it wisely, in case your husband is unable to provide for you properly."

Who was this woman and what had happened to her mother?

"I… um. Mother. I don't know what to say."

Her mother met her gaze and smiled wisely. "We women, even ladies of the *ton*, have to take care of ourselves."

At that moment, Rhoda studied the starburst of wrinkles around the corners of her mother's eyes, and the lines at the corners of her mouth from smiling too much. Her mother, more than anybody in the world, ought to have frowned more than most.

There had been times when Rhoda thought her mother laughed too often, too loudly. When she'd been embarrassed by her.

Now, reflecting on her father's behavior, she wondered how her mother had ever laughed at all.

"How did you do it, Mama? How did you cope with such a husband?" She'd never asked her mother anything like this before.

Her mother turned her head to stare out the window, the same as Lord Carlisle had a few minutes ago.

And then she exhaled loudly. "We do what we need to do, Rhododendron. Our decisions won't always be popular. People will not always appreciate us for them. But we survive." She glanced over her shoulder and winked. "And if we're lucky, we thrive."

This explained why Emily had cheated at Sardines and perhaps why she'd ridden off to Gretna Green with Lord Blakely. She wanted some independence in life. She did not wish to live her life as her aunt's servant.

The desire to thrive explained why Cecily had fought to escape her bitter union with Lord Kensington and why Sophia had married so quickly again after the death of Lord Harold.

And it explained the strength inside her mother, a woman with three daughters and an unfaithful spendthrift of a husband.

Thriving and surviving.

Except a thousand pounds would not be enough for her and Carlisle to be prosperous. It likely wasn't even enough for them to survive. Not with a failing estate.

Rhoda wanted to *thrive*! She was so tired of feeling guilty. Of feeling ashamed! And now she had to cope with that idiotic wager. Last she'd heard, a winner, depending upon who they bet on, could walk away with close to seventy thousand pounds.

An astronomical amount of money! Of course, she'd make certain that there would never be a winner.

She'd never allow it.

But a bet on a long shot could win one person seventy thousand pounds! What would a gentleman do for seventy thousand pounds? The memory of what Lord Kensington had attempted illustrated the answer quite adamantly.

A shiver of fear nearly made her hands numb.

Seventy thousand pounds, and she, Rhododendron Mossant, was the key.

I am the key!

Surely, the answer couldn't be as easy as that? The seed of an idea took root.

Lord Carlisle needed to wager upon himself.

But would he? The notion quite went against everything such a gentleman represented. Could she even bring the subject up with him? He'd already become angry with her once for being manipulative. And he certainly must doubt her integrity after everything she'd told him.

But seventy thousand pounds! Lord Carlisle could take care of his new estate. His new wife.

Her sisters and mother would never be dependent upon Father again.

But how? Oh, she wished her friends were here. Even Cecily would likely go along with such a scheme.

"Rhoda?" Her mother's voice drew her back into the present.

Rhoda jumped. "Um. Yes?"

"I'm quite certain I don't like the look on your face. I've known you too long to misread it. It portends trouble."

Emily was not here. Nor was Cecily or Sophia.

Her mother *was*, however. And her mother had just revealed an entirely different dimension of herself.

"Women ought to thrive?" She tested the waters.

Her mother narrowed her eyes but nodded slowly.

"A thousand pounds isn't nearly enough. He has an entire estate to care for, not to mention his cousins, *female relatives*. But I have an idea." Rhoda bit her lip. "This wager, Mother. It's grown to more money than I ever would have imagined!"

"How much?"

"Last I heard, over seventy thousand pounds."

At the amount, her mother's eyebrows rose nearly into her hairline.

This was the tricky part. "If a wager was somehow made, in Lord Carlisle's name. And if he were to win." She bit her lip, her face burning. "If he could provide some sort of proof. Mother, *I* have the power to make him the winner!" The words sounded so much worse out loud than they had in her head.

Because both of them could only imagine what sort of proof she'd have to provide. Surely, her testimony would be enough?

"I could come forth and announce that..." She cringed, unable to go on.

Her mother had seemed to be listening with an open mind, but at Rhoda's last words she began shaking her head. "No. Absolutely not. It is an outrageous amount of money but absolutely not. I cannot fathom the scandal if you were caught placing such a wager. Which is what you have in mind, I suppose. Oh, good heavens! And your poor sisters would suffer as well!"

Her mother twisted her mouth in thought. "This wager, I imagine. It is much like a horse race? The 'suitors' are the horses and the finish line..." She shook her head adamantly. "I forbid you to participate in something so outrageous. Put it out of your head completely." Her mother's gaze turned distracted for a moment but then she dropped onto the settee and began fussing with her writing desk. "Seventy thousand pounds," she mumbled.

Her mother continued shaking her head adamantly. "It's likely illegal. None of us could ever appear in society again. Think about your sisters, Rhoda."

"But I am!"

"It's not worth the risk." Her mother began writing something out but then glanced up again. She tapped her lip thoughtfully with the blunt end of her pen. "And it's best you not appear in public with him. It's possible that being seen with you could ruin his chances with another. And that poor man, he deserves to marry money."

What on earth? "Another?"

"Another debutante, Rhododendron. Another debutante with a much larger dowry. We need to end this betrothal."

"What? But, you just said—"

"Break it off, dear. I no longer support the idea."

Had her mother knocked herself on the head that morning? And even though Rhoda herself knew Lord Carlisle's interests would be served best if she were to release him from their agreement, she hated that her mother now demanded it. "It's a feasible plan, Mother, the betrothal, if not the wager!"

"Call off the betrothal, Rhododendron. The poor man deserves to be free of all this."

"I thought it was me that you cared about! And Coleus! And Holly!"

"Well. Yes. Of course. Trust me, darling. Best he court another. He'd resent you for certain when he's taken off to debtor's prison."

Something stabbed at Rhoda's heart. And yet, her mother was likely right. Many a heiress would most certainly be amenable to marrying an earl, Rhoda had no doubt, regardless of how empty his pockets were. In fact, the emptier his pockets, the better!

Rhoda did not appreciate the image of Lord Carlisle marrying another, even less so now that he'd escaped a betrothal to Emily.

"But I like him."

Her mother grimaced. "You'll come to like another."

Rhoda bit her lip. "He's returning to take me for a drive in the park."

"Not the park. Have him take you somewhere the two of you will not be seen. Better to break it off in private, anyhow," her mother added.

Again, that painful sensation.

"Madam. Miss." Leo appeared at the door. At least

Rhoda believed the man beneath the gigantic bouquet of flowers was their butler. "There have been several deliveries for you. Er, rather, for Miss Mossant."

"Oh, dear!" Her mother crossed the room to examine the various flowers in the arrangement. She plucked and picked at the blooms without considering that Leo's arms were likely growing fatigued from holding the massive vase. "You say several deliveries have arrived?"

"Indeed," Leo answered and then spit one of the leaves out of his mouth. "At least seven others, a few larger than this one. Where would you like me to put them?"

"With the rubbish," Rhoda answered firmly, before her mother could speak. The jackals had discovered she'd returned to London. "Or toss them back into the street. I really don't care."

As she swept out of the room, her mother's voice followed her. "Is there anything here that is edible? I suppose we could use them in a stew…"

JUSTIN KICKED A rock as he hiked aimlessly along the sidewalks that lined Bond Street. How had he managed to find himself in this predicament? Had it only been two weeks since the course of his life so drastically changed?

He counted back the days. Indeed. Just eleven days prior, his greatest concern had been the contents of his next sermon. He'd gotten word of Percival's death, his inherited title, traveled to London, and by pure happenstance, come across Rhododendron Mossant again.

She'd not ever truly been far from his thoughts. He'd found himself besotted with the dark-haired beauty from the first time he'd laid eyes upon her at Harold's nuptials.

And then later at Priory Point. Where she'd transformed into a woman of character as well as beauty.

But St. John had staked his claim on her, even if it was not an honorable one.

So much had changed since then!

In a farcical turn of events, he'd nearly found himself betrothed to Miss Emily Goodnight but fortuitously managed to become betrothed to Miss Mossant instead.

It seemed all his prayers had been answered.

Which was when God decided to make matters interesting. Of course, nothing worthwhile could be come by easily.

The back of his neck itched. He hadn't worried about finances since his mother moved them to Eden's Court. Since he'd been a lad.

But he remembered the sensation. He remembered evenings when his mother had served them soup so watered down he'd been tempted to add grass. He remembered huddling in the dark, even a few candles beyond their means.

And he remembered all too well the manner in which his mother had originally resolved the situation.

He glanced at his watch, having just met with his man of business to no avail. He'd already wasted most of the afternoon. It was time he collected the vehicle he was borrowing from Prescott House if he was not to keep Miss Mossant waiting.

Rhododendron Mossant. *His betrothed.* Because damned if he was willing to lose her so easily.

He changed direction and increased his pace.

The day the Duchess of Prescott had sent her missive inviting his mother and him to come and 'visit' had been a blessed one indeed. Justin had not been close to her. Neither had Dev nor St. John, but perhaps she'd been closest to Harold.

Not a demonstrative person, in the least, she'd seemed too proud for affection.

But he'd be grateful to her until his dying day.

And he'd never, not in a million years, deign to put a woman in the same situation his father had done to his mother. He'd not put his cousins, his betrothed, nor his betrothed's sisters and mother in such a situation.

Damn his eyes.

Just when he thought perhaps she might be within his reach, the expanse between them seemed to widen.

His pace quickened. Perhaps it was just as well. She'd created nothing but chaos in his life.

Chaos, passion, lust…

The memory of that kiss in the chapel nearly caused him to stumble.

He'd not known such excitement, such completion before.

He unhitched the large iron latch and opened the gate that protected the Prescott grounds from passersby. The manor set back from the street, the grounds something of a park unto themselves.

He'd been privileged to be brought up with this family. He'd known they allowed them to be there on charity, but they'd never spoken of it.

He'd been duty bound to serve the church. And he'd done so willingly. He'd found peace there.

Acceptance.

Purpose.

And now all of that had been flipped upside down.

Mr. Evans opened the door before Justin could even knock.

"My lord." The longtime retainer bowed. Even this irritated Justin today. The butler had never bowed to him before. He'd always simply been plain old Mr. White. Or Vicar White.

Justin tugged at his cravat, feeling the absence of his collar acutely. "Just stopping for a moment. I'm borrowing one of the vehicles from the mews."

Mr. Evan's eyebrows rose. "You did not wish to see His Grace?"

Dev was here?

"As a matter of fact, I would. Is he available?" He and Sophia must have only recently arrived. That meant Lord Blakely and Miss Goodnight would have returned to Eden's Court, or sent word.

"Right this way." Mr. Evans led him upstairs and then, with more pomp and circumstance than ever before, opened the door to the study wide.

Dev, wearing traveling clothes, was propped against the sturdy desk perusing one of the letters in the mountain of mail that awaited him.

He glanced up from his reading. "How fares your future father-in-law?" Never a man to beat around the bush, he was even less so now that he'd become Prescott.

Justin hardly knew where to begin.

He did not want charity from the Prescott coffers.

"He didn't kick me off the property," he hedged. "Nor did he invite me to supper." None of which mattered, in fact. "I stopped over at Carlisle House."

Dev paused and then nodded slowly. "I see."

But did he?

"I'm broke. Not only broke but in debt up to my eyeballs."

Dev winced. "I'd heard rumors about the Carlisle coffers."

"I suspected myself. Just didn't realize it was this bad." Justin attempted to stifle the frustration eating away at his heart. "Why now? Damn and blast, but why now?"

Another sympathetic look from his cousin. "Sophia would kill me if she knew I even suggested such a thing, but has your betrothal to Miss Mossant been made official? I've yet to read any announcement, and I'm quite certain there is more than one heiress out there who would be more than happy to marry you."

"The betrothal is set." Justin had expected to receive this course of advice, just not from Dev. "I wanted to ask you about investments. I have a small savings. Nearly a thousand pounds. I need to turn it into twenty."

"I knew you were a man of faith, but I didn't realize you actually believed in miracles." Dev laughed, angering him further.

"I'm quite serious, Dev." Justin ran one hand through his hair and paced across the floor to the window. "I need to bolster my new damned estate. And I need funds to support a wife."

"You know you needn't come up with this yourself. I—"

Justin held up one hand, effectively cutting off the offer Dev was about to make. "I've already accepted far too much generosity from your family." Even his mother yet depended on the Prescott coffers.

Justin had his own responsibilities now. He needed to devise his own means.

"Well," Dev hedged. "There's always—"

"The wager."

There. He'd said it. He'd voiced the thought that had taunted him all afternoon.

The first time the idea niggled at him, he'd just begun reading over the Carlisle estate books two days ago. And as the extent of his predecessor's debts grew in his mind, so did the idea.

He hated that he'd entertain such a notion nearly as

much as he hated the debts themselves.

Justin paced across the room again. He would not take more charity.

If he won the despicable wager, he would be protecting his betrothed from all those other cads with their eye on such a large pot. He'd then be able to provide for her, for her family, for his cousins. He could bolster his new estate.

Each time he considered it, he wanted to vomit.

"I'm a blasted vicar, Dev! What kind of an example would this set?" Justin rubbed the muscles at the back of his neck, knowing his cousin watched him closely. Was even Dev judging him this very moment?

Dev didn't answer, rather watched patiently as Justin crossed the room again.

"But the wager is a danger to her as well," Justin defended the idea. "You're more familiar with the so-called gentlemen involved. Will they call it off if she marries?"

Dev grimaced. "For seventy thousand pounds? I doubt it."

Justin wanted to punch something. He had never been a violent man, but this afternoon he'd gladly pound the bastard who'd initiated it into the ground.

Except he didn't know who that was. It didn't matter at this point anyhow. The person who most likely deserved a facer was dead.

St. John. For leading her on. For taking advantage of her affection. And then for not keeping the information to himself.

"I ought to do it then." Except participating in this damnable wager went against everything he'd ever stood for.

"Will you tell her?"

Tell her? And then take her virtue? Or what was left of it?

God, the mere thought of exposing such intimate information about her… Justin shook his head. "I don't know."

"You don't know if you'll tell her, or you don't know if you'll participate in the wager yourself?" Dev understood him all too well.

"Neither." Justin scrubbed a hand through his hair again. "Both."

Dev lifted a decanter from the corner of his desk. "A drink then?"

Justin was about to take him up on the offer when the sounds of horses on the pavement outside reminded him why he'd come in the first place. "I'm to take her for a drive this afternoon." With a glance at the clock, he moved toward the door. "I'm late already."

"Justin." Dev's voice gave him pause. "I'd avoid the park."

"Hell and damnation," Justin spoke the words on a harsh exhale. He could only imagine what Miss Mossant faced next time she stepped out in society. "My thanks for the reminder."

CHAPTER TWENTY

To Be Betrothed or Not To Be Betrothed

DESPITE THE TURMOIL rolling around inside him, Justin couldn't deny the anticipation he felt at seeing Rhoda again.

His heart jumped at the thought of hearing her voice, at watching the shifting emotions behind her brandy-colored gaze. His eyes hungered to drink in the curve of her neck and shoulders and hips. He cleared his throat self-consciously as he waited in the foyer of her mother's house.

The butler had assured him she'd only be a moment.

Rustling at the top of the stairs drew his immediate attention. She'd changed out of the gown she'd had on this morning. She'd been wearing maroon then, but this afternoon, she was a blaze of gold.

Earlier, her hair had been drawn back into a tight chignon at the nape of her neck. She'd appeared stern, almost like a teacher or a governess.

Since then, she'd pinned it up loosely, allowing curling tendrils to caress her cheeks and jaw.

Justin swallowed hard.

He couldn't let her go.

He couldn't.

"Lord Carlisle." Her voice echoed in the high-ceilinged foyer. "I was beginning to think you'd forgotten our appointment."

She referred to it as an appointment. He considered

himself to be courting.

Did one court a lady who already had accepted him?

If she'd give him the chance, he believed he'd court her for the remainder of his days.

"Prescott and the duchess have returned to London." He didn't want to discuss his meeting with Dev.

He didn't even wish to think about it.

"Sophia is here?" Her eyes flew open with something between relief and joy. But then she seemed to check herself. She smoothed a non-existent wrinkle from her gown and began descending the steps.

Justin could only watch her move, fully appreciating one of God's finest creations.

Woman.

This woman.

"They arrived today," he answered vaguely, his gaze settling on her delicate hands as she tied the bow of her bonnet. When she finished donning her gloves, he offered his elbow. "Shall we?"

Tucking her hand into the crook of his arm felt right. Familiar and yet exciting. He breathed in her scent, appreciating her nearness all the more for his fear he might not be able to keep her.

Neither of them spoke as he assisted her onto the high-perched seat and then went around to climb aboard himself. No room for a maid, nor a groom.

With a flick of his hands, Justin steered the horses into the street and at the jerking motion, she clutched his arm again. Her continued silence gradually became somewhat uncomfortable and that was when he realized… "This was St. John's Phaeton," he stated baldly.

He glanced sideways in time to see her nod. "It was."

Justin inhaled deeply. "Do you think of him often?" He'd wondered this on more than one occasion. Did she compare every gentleman she met with St. John? Did she compare *Justin* with St. John?

They drove past the entrance to the park. Justin turned in the opposite direction. "At first," she finally answered. "I fooled myself into believing I'd lost the love of my life."

Justin clenched his jaw.

"But now," she added, shaking her head. "I realize he cannot have felt the same. I was a toy."

Justin covered her gloved hand.

"Tell me about these Carlisle sisters, your unmarried cousins. Are they elderly? Are they your wards now?"

He appreciated her change of subject. "Definitely not elderly." And they were not his wards either but still his responsibility. "The eldest, I believe, is thirty. The youngest twenty-one." He'd only met the eldest of the women, the other three having been out during his short visit.

"Did the former earl give them the benefit of a Season?"

He'd not thought of that. He'd barely had time to inquire about their health. "I have no idea."

"Are they pretty?"

Justin raised his brows. Again, he had no idea. The oldest was not an antidote, but he'd not really paid much mind to her looks. In answer, he merely shrugged.

And then that bell-like laughter he'd not heard nearly enough of rang out beside him.

"You are horrible, Lord Carlisle!" And she swatted him lightly.

"Justin," he reminded her. She'd called him by his Christian name first in the chapel, when…

"Then you must call me Rhoda."

"Not Rhododendron?" he teased.

"Definitely not Rhododendron. Only my mother gets away with that." At the mention of her mother, her mood subdued. "Tell me about this estate of yours."

She was quite good at that. Changing the subject when things got uncomfortable.

Justin released the reins just long enough to adjust his hat. "It was built in the early 1500s. And I don't think it's had a lick of maintenance done on it since then. But it's beautiful in its own right."

"Your poor cousins!" But she was laughing.

"I wouldn't feel the weight of it so much if it weren't for the poor tenant conditions. I only stopped into a couple of them, but both needed new roofs."

"You poor dear." She patted his arm. "You've only been responsible for the spiritual health of others up until now. It must all seem rather daunting."

Her words comforted him. So simple and yet... such truth. "I imagine I left the bulk of my responsibilities up to God until now."

She laughed again. "Perhaps you ought to continue to do just that."

His heart warmed at her words. That a girl painted a tart by a few idiots of the *ton* could see such a simple truth.

"Where are you taking us... Justin?" She remembered to call him by name. This afternoon already was improving his mood.

He turned the vehicle onto a darker, narrower route. "Along with the debts I've inherited, I now own a townhouse in Mayfair."

She examined their surroundings, craning her neck to peer up at the flower boxes hanging over the cobbled street. "The outskirts of Mayfair, I take it?"

This time, it was he who chuckled. "Where else would it be?"

"Cheapside?" She slanted him a dancing smirk.

He couldn't help but lean closer to her. "Watch your

mouth, minx. This might very well be your future home."

RHODA'S HEART SKIPPED a beat. *My future home. My future husband.* She'd not ever enjoyed spending time with a gentleman so much as she was enjoying Justin's company. She'd never felt she could trust someone so much.

He spoke to her as though what she had to say was relevant.

The thought brought her up short.

She'd spent hours, hundreds of hours perhaps, in St. John's company. She'd flirted with him. He'd flirted back. They'd spoken of the dismal London weather, of whom was betrothed to whom, of the theatre, for heaven's sake. But they'd never spoken of personal matters.

Even when she'd lain with him.

He'd called her beautiful. He'd compared her hair to the mane of his favorite horse. She smirked at this memory. She'd thought it a compliment at the time.

He'd rambled on and on about the smooth quality of her skin and the depths of her eyes. He'd even complimented her bosom.

He'd never discussed his feelings, his thoughts about life. About the two of them or any future they might have had together.

She'd made some grand assumptions based on all that frivolity. Some grand mistakes.

Justin joked about himself. About his empty pockets, even. He allowed her words to bring him comfort. The tension had left his body when she'd offered her suggestions. She'd felt it. And then he'd leaned toward her and joked about their pending betrothal.

He maneuvered the high-perched phaeton into an even smaller driveway and drew to a halt behind a weathered but rather grand townhouse. The brick was covered with black grime, and the windows had been boarded up. Other than that, it appeared to not be tilting in any one direction, and the roof seemed intact.

A groom appeared from behind the mews and after a word with Justin, immediately went to securing the cattle. After tilting his head back to study the house for a moment, and looking a little uncertain, Justin climbed down and came around to assist her.

Her hands landed easily on his shoulders while he grasped her waist tightly and lifted her to the ground.

They hadn't been this close to one another since he'd left Eden's Court.

When he'd kissed her.

She enjoyed these brief moments, innocent though they might be. Allowing her body to slide along the length of his, the contact stirred up his spicy scent so that it tickled her nostrils.

She didn't step away when her feet hit the ground.

Instead, she enjoyed the feel of his breath on her forehead. If she placed her cheek against his chest, she would hear his heartbeat.

She was supposed to be breaking off their betrothal, and all she could think about was how to entice him into kissing her again.

"I missed you." His voice came out gravelly sounding and so he cleared his throat.

Rhoda tilted her head back and could not help but be caught. His blue gaze nearly took her breath away. How had she missed this when they'd first met? How had she not been affected by not only his looks but his goodness?

His character?

Her gaze shifted to his mouth as it seemed to be dipping toward hers.

"My lord, Should I take the horses off or—"

The groom stifled his question and quickly retreated when he realized he might be interrupting something.

At the same time, Lord Carlisle dropped his hands from her hips and took a long step backward.

Rhoda nearly toppled onto her backside without his support.

First her mother and now this!

"We won't be long. They should be fine." He'd stepped over to run his hands along the back of one of the horses.

Rhoda reached up and collected her reticule from the high seat. Was he relieved to not kiss her? Had she embarrassed him? She wouldn't stand around to wait and see. She removed her gloves and edged toward the stoop leading to the back of the house.

"I have the key here somewhere." He swept past her almost indifferently and began jiggling the lock. After considerable fussing, the door finally swung open. "I'd normally allow you to enter first, but I'm not certain it's safe," he explained over his shoulder and stepped inside.

Rhoda followed. "I'm not an invalid," she snapped but didn't think he heard her.

"What's that?" He peered around the door and flashed a smile, melting her insides again.

"I'm not afraid to go in." She climbed the steps and followed him inside.

Her eyes required nearly a full minute to adjust to the darkness. This room had obviously been utilized as a kitchen at one point. Gradually, she made out the shape of a large stove and two conveniently placed counters.

Justin took her hand and led her through the threshold

to the rest of the house.

He'd removed his gloves as well and their palms pressed into one another, flesh upon flesh.

He squeezed her hand, and, at that moment, she knew she'd not embarrassed him. He'd wanted to kiss her. Warmth spread from her chest to her limbs.

"There are two drawing rooms and a ballroom. It's in horrible condition but quite large."

Rhoda murmured something, she couldn't think what, and followed him from room to room.

She enjoyed the sound of his voice. His congregation must miss him something fierce. Especially those of the female persuasion.

"And the master chamber." A large bed sat in the middle of the room, draped in sheets. "It's rather substantial." He released her hand to begin opening some of the doors that lined the walls. "Ah, a dressing room." And then he returned. "And another bedchamber through here."

Rhoda wandered slowly toward the window. "You can see the park from here!" she exclaimed in surprise.

It was a beautiful house.

It *would* be a beautiful house.

After a few thousand pounds was dumped into it.

He'd returned to the room and was watching her, a grimace on his lips. "It is in horrible repair."

She couldn't pretend otherwise, and so she nodded. "But it could be a wonderful home." It was so much larger than her father's townhouse. "It seems solid enough."

He smiled at that.

"I cannot marry you," she blurted. "You need to marry money."

He went still at her words. "I need to marry you."

A sob nearly tore past her throat. "We would be broke. Worse than that, your cousins would be broke. And your tenants would remain in squalor."

He rubbed his chin thoughtfully. "I spoke with my solicitors, regarding some investments I might make." He shifted his gaze to the floor. "Let's not be hasty."

That's what he'd said before. She dared not to breathe while waiting for him to continue.

"Do you not wish to marry me?" His question took her by surprise.

"You are insane for wanting to marry me!" She closed her eyes. "I'm no prize, that's for certain."

And then she was in his arms. And his hands roved frantically over her back, down her sides.

A shudder ran through him as he buried his head into the crook of her neck. "But I do. I do wish to marry you." His voice came out in a harsh whisper. He was practically trembling.

Rhoda swallowed hard and slid her hands around his waist. She almost felt as though he cared about her.

He was not St. John.

He'd not brought her here in order to bed her.

"I—" His searching kiss cut her off. Almost violent at first, demanding, desperate. Rhoda tightened her arms around him as she tilted her head back.

Everything about this man felt real. His kiss wasn't choreographed; it was all emotion. Their teeth clashed a few times.

"I'm sorry," he gasped. "I'll stop." But his mouth tugged at her lips, and then his tongue delved inside again. One of his hands slid beneath her bonnet, and he threaded his fingers between the loose strands of her hair. His other hand splayed low on her back. A growl vibrated against her.

She'd never felt so beautiful, so absolutely necessary to a person in her life. A moan escaped her parted lips.

"Not be hasty," he mumbled into her neck. His lips trailed around her jaw, her throat. "I'm sorry."

"Not sorry," she whispered. He had nothing to apologize for. Her heart bled at the thought of losing this man.

He stilled after a moment, his lips no longer searching, but his breaths ragged. "I shouldn't have. I don't want you to believe—"

"Hush." She squeezed him tighter again, and in doing so, became acutely aware of his desire.

"I'll find a way." His promise. His faith. He was nothing like St. John had been. She'd been a fool to fall for the marquess's falsehoods. All last year, she'd experienced guilt over breaking the unpardonable sin. Guilt and fear. She'd berated herself for giving in to St. John's seduction. She'd worried that she'd murdered a man, although she hadn't felt tremendous remorse.

What kind of a person did that make her?

For the first time, she felt a genuine sense of regret. She regretted that she did not have her innocence to give to Justin. Remorse that she wasn't a better woman. He deserved somebody who would ease his troubles, not bring him more.

Breathing in the scent of him, of soap and spice and something uniquely him, tears stung behind her eyes.

She'd give everything that she could.

"Justin."

He stirred but didn't answer.

"You mustn't marry me. You are so honorable, so full of good will. You'd berate yourself in the years to come that you'd not provided properly for those who depended upon you."

He nodded but then shook his head.

"My mother has forbidden me to marry you." At these words, he pulled himself up, confusion in his eyes. "She says it would not be fair to you." Her mother's changed opinion had surprised her as well. Likely Mother considered her decision to be a practical one. "I imagine she knows the pain of a troubled marriage."

He searched her eyes. She hated the uncertainty behind his blue depths.

"You need protection." His statement sounded almost like a question. As though she'd implied that she didn't trust him. As though she doubted his ability to care for all that was his.

"I will be fine. I've weathered worse."

But he was shaking his head. "Nothing like this. Jackals will be after you from behind every corner. You are not safe."

Rhoda couldn't meet his eyes. Because she *was* afraid.

She *wanted* his protection. She *wanted* to marry him, and she didn't care how broke he was. "My mother says—"

"Rhododendron."

She bit her lip.

"We won't make any announcements. We won't have any banns read yet. You needn't tell anyone, even your mother." He swallowed hard. "But leave the betrothal in place."

He pinned her with his gaze, willing her to give in to his request.

How could she argue against something she wanted more than anything else? If a miracle happened, surely it would happen for Justin White!

She nodded slowly. "But I'll have to tell my mother we've broken the engagement."

"I understand." He took both her hands in his and raised them to his lips. "And you must know you'll have my protection, even if I'm obliged to provide it from afar. Promise me you'll not go out alone. Promise me you won't trust any man."

Was it possible such danger truly existed? And yet she knew. It did. It had already touched her.

"I promise." She nodded, feeling hopeless nonetheless.

CHAPTER TWENTY-ONE

In or Out

JUSTIN HATED THAT Rhoda was right. Partially right anyhow. He'd wallow in guilt if he couldn't find a way to improve the conditions for those who depended upon the Carlisle estate. He could find another lady to marry, one with a larger dowry. Logically, he knew many titled gentlemen did just this.

But he wasn't like other titled gentlemen. In fact, he still looked over his shoulder when anybody deigned to call him 'my lord.'

It was one matter to see other men undertake such a mercenary course, quite another to contemplate it oneself.

Besides that, he rather liked Rhododendron Mossant.

She brought him to life. He ought to feel guilty for practically mauling her. He'd attempted to halt his coarse desires, but she'd held him tight against her. She'd hushed his apologies.

Yes, he rather liked her. Rather a lot.

After extracting her promise to be careful, Justin found himself feeling even more protective than he had before. He'd guided her gingerly down the rickety stairs, assisted her to the vehicle, and then tucked her arm into his as he drove them through the streets of Mayfair.

In her bonnet, she was almost unrecognizable. Wearing his hat, he was indistinguishable as well. He wasn't exactly a known commodity in society.

And when he returned her to her mother's home, he'd bent low over her hand and held his lips against her glove only a moment. He'd do nothing to bring her further shame.

Driving away, his heart swelled, only to feel empty at the same time.

Her mother had instructed her to break off their betrothal. Mrs. Mossant must have hidden her misgivings earlier that morning. Perhaps she had hoped her daughter would give him the heave-ho on her own.

Justin had no doubt that Rhoda could find a gentleman who would provide well for her. How could she not, despite the scandal surrounding her? Such vibrancy and beauty would be snatched up in a moment.

Likely, her mother knew this.

Blast and damn but if he hadn't inherited, none of this would be an issue.

Steering the vehicle back toward Prescott House, Justin searched his brain for any answer other than the one involving gambling on a lady's—on his betrothed's—virtue.

Again, nothing came to mind. His choices, it seemed, were charity, gambling, or losing her forever. The last he refused to contemplate. Neither could he accept money from Dev.

He handed off the horses and, rather than meet with his cousin again, slipped out the back of the mews.

The thought of never holding her again, of giving her up to another, or her going away left him ice cold.

He strode along the sidewalk, not meeting anybody's stare. He couldn't make idle conversation feeling as he did now. Those fathomless warm eyes of hers, so serious and yet lost. She had an independent spirit about her, and yet she needed him desperately. He'd convinced himself of this on more than one occasion.

She needed someone steady and true. She needed someone who would value all of her, laugh at life's ironies with her.

She needed *him*.

Oh, hell, who was he kidding? *He* needed *her*.

Justin stopped and looked up at the plain façade of the building looming above him. But for the small sign by the door, no one would ever guess at what manner of transactions and meetings took place within.

With a deep breath, he entered the club.

It was their only chance.

"DID YOU TELL him?" Her mother peered up from her embroidery and awaited Rhoda's answer.

"I did."

Well, she had. She bit her lip and pretended to be interested in a book that lay on one of the end tables.

"How did he take it?"

Rhoda opened the book to a dog-eared page. "Oh, fine." Best to say as little as possible.

"And that is why you are suddenly interested in propagation techniques?"

Propa... what? "What are you talking about?"

"You are suddenly captivated by my book on grafting." Rhoda turned the book over. *Propagation Techniques: A Practical Guide for Grafting Nut, Fruit, and Ornamental Plants.*

Oh.

"You did break it off, didn't you?"

Rhoda wasn't handling this very well, and her mother

was far too clever to not catch on to her halfhearted efforts.

"I told him. He isn't happy. I am not happy. But I told him."

"So, it is broken off then?"

Blast her mother's uncanny abilities! "It is no longer officially on." Rhoda stared at her mother defiantly.

Her mother's steady gaze narrowed. "So, he was not eager to move on to other chits?"

The memory of his eager mouth on hers, of his trembling body pressed against hers, sent tingles of warmth swarming around her heart. "He was not eager to move on." The words came out almost a whisper.

She awaited her mother's recriminations, but none came.

"Well then." Her mother sounded surprisingly unperturbed. "So long as he knows where you stand. I'd tell those other girls as well, the duchess and Mrs. Nottingham, that the betrothal has been terminated."

Except it had not been. It might just as well have.

He expected her to wait. It had been her own suggestion that he simply put it all in God's hands.

Something Rhoda could never do.

"Speaking of which, Sophia and Prescott have returned." Rhoda closed the book with a decisive snap and placed it on the table. "I'm going to go 'round, find out what's happened with Emily."

"Take a maid. Better yet, ask Miles to tag along." This was most unusual.

That frisson of fear slid down Rhoda's spine again. If even her mother thought she needed protection…

"I will," she promised for the second time that day.

Damn St. John to hell.

"EMILY IS NOW a countess then?" Even though Rhoda had known their destination was Gretna Green, she hadn't quite believed Emily would return a married woman. This was Emily, for heaven's sake. How many times had she disdained the idea of marriage?

And now she had married Lord Blakely, of all people.

Sophia nodded emphatically. "She is!" She leaned forward. "And not in name only."

Rhoda raised her brows at this. Well, of course, when one married…

"She was positively glowing!"

Rhoda felt her brows rise even higher. Of all people, Emily was not one Rhoda would have ever imagined…

She would not imagine.

"But they have left for his father's house?" Emily's husband's future estate was near Southampton. Rhoda had hoped they'd return to London soon.

Sophia nodded again. "With Cecily and Mr. Nottingham."

Rhoda grimaced. "I suppose Emily fears meeting her in-laws." She tried to be charitable but couldn't hold back the sound of her disappointment.

"She wouldn't say." But Sophia seemed to be studying Rhoda intently. "You cannot go out alone. Are you afraid?"

"We haven't been here all that long." Rhoda hated admitting that she was fearful, but this was Sophia. "I am. A little. But do you want to know the worst part of it all?"

"Feeling as though it's all your fault?" Sophia surprisingly supplied exactly what Rhoda had been feeling.

Of course, Sophia would understand.

"So many things I would have done differently if I'd only known. I call myself stupid every day. I never used to do that before."

"You aren't stupid, Rhoda. And it most definitely isn't your fault." She pinched her lips together. "It's the men who are idiots. Not only idiots, but louts, villains, monsters. Greed tends to have such an effect."

Sophia and the duke must have discussed the status of the stupid wager.

"I know. I will be fine. I miss going to parties with you."

"You know I'd go with you, but I've already been far too active for a lady in mourning. It offends Harold's mother."

Of course, it would.

"I have Mother, of course."

Sophia wrinkled her nose. "Your mother is nearly as bad a chaperone as Mrs. Goodnight was. Dev says you and Lord Carlisle have yet to make any announcements. Surely, that will provide you with some protection."

Rhoda moaned and then explained their unfortunate predicament; the financial despair the Carlisle estate was in, how her father had withdrawn her dowry, her mother's insistence they not go ahead with it.

Sophia furrowed her brows. "You are still engaged, are you not?"

"Not officially, and not according to my mother, in case the subject arises."

"Dev could help him."

But Rhoda already knew this. She had suspected it anyhow. "I think this is one of those things, Sophia, you know. I think Carlisle believes he needs to solve this himself. He already believes Dev's family has given him too much."

Sophia tapped her chin. "He believes he must earn it himself, then?"

Rhoda recognized this devilish gleam from when they'd been planning the parlor games.

"The wager." Rhoda stated the obvious. "I've thought of it. Mother forbids me but—"

"Why ever would you seek your mother's permission?"

"Well, I would need assistance, and I didn't expect you to return so soon." Rhoda bit her lip. She'd just instructed Justin to trust in God, for heaven's sake. And here she was contemplating...

"Do you have a sample of his handwriting?" Of course, Sophia's mind had already caught up with her own.

Rhoda pulled out the copy of the contract Justin had handed over this morning. Had it just been this morning? "His is the second signature."

Justin White, Fifth Earl of Carlisle and Viscount of Dorwich.

"I didn't know he'd inherited more than one title." Sophia pondered this new information.

"I hadn't either."

Their gazes caught and held. Would Sophia truly be willing to assist her? "If we were to get caught, even you might suffer from the scandal of it," Rhoda warned her friend.

"Even more important, if we get caught, might you lose Carlisle's affections?"

That indeed, was a good question to ask. He'd already once told her he did not appreciate female manipulations. "I'd rather not find out."

They both fell silent, considering the ramifications of failure.

"We are speaking of the same thing, are we not?" Sophia's expressive blue eyes were rather serious.

Rhoda drew in a deep breath. "Sneaking into White's? Placing the wager on Lord Carlisle's behalf?" She nodded. "I've been unable to come up with anything else."

"Chancy," Sophia stated.

"I don't want you to take the risk. I'll do it on my own." Good Lord, what a scandal there would be if the Duchess of Prescott were caught sneaking into the exclusive gentlemen's club! This was most unethical, perhaps criminal.

"I wouldn't think of allowing you to have such fun without me." Sophia lifted her chin. "When do you want to do it?"

Rhoda opened the marriage contract once again. "I'll need to perfect his signature."

Could she really forge his name? "I'll take a few days. And we'll need disguises. We'll need to look like gentlemen if we're to stand a chance at gaining entry."

"Dev says Kensington usually enters with an entourage. I think perhaps we could attach ourselves to such a group."

"With Kensington? As in Flavion?" Rhoda raised her fist to her mouth. This might be trickier than she'd originally thought. Perhaps her mother was right…

Sophia shrugged. "We'll fit right in with that group of dandies. Half of them look like women as it is."

How could Sophia seem so undaunted by all of this? "Will you tell Prescott? Surely, he wouldn't support his wife undertaking such a dangerous prank?

"Of course! I tell him everything."

Rhoda groaned. "Let's wait a few days. Let me see if Carlisle stumbles on his miracle. If God fails to lend him a hand, well, then I suppose we'll have to do it ourselves."

CHAPTER TWENTY-TWO

Still Undecided

VISCOUNT OF DORWICH.

Too much flourish. Rhoda made another attempt and cursed beneath her breath when the ink bled from the r to the w. Two days had passed since she and Sophia had discussed sneaking into the exclusive male gentlemen's club to forge her fiancé's name in the betting book.

At least she believed he was still her fiancé. She'd done naught but slip out for a turn about the park early in the mornings since arriving in London. With her maid and one of her mother's manservants, of course.

The first *ton* affair they planned to attend was tonight. Perhaps she could feign a megrim—or female troubles. Her heart raced at the thought of entering the Primroses' ballroom.

Not that she'd never entered it before. She'd attended numerous balls at the elaborate mansion, ironically enough, set right next door to Lord Kensington's townhouse.

But she'd not attended even one since the Snodgrass' garden party.

Hearing a knock, Rhoda stuffed the contract and her abysmal attempts at forgery into her top drawer. "Enter."

"You aren't dressed yet?" Her mother's hair had already been styled high atop her head, and she wore a pearl taffeta evening gown embellished with silver ribbon. "I'll send Lucy down, so you can ready yourself. Important that you look your best. Not that you ever have anything to worry about."

Rhoda winced. "Must we? Can we not simply return to Pebble's Gate? Forget this Season ever happened?" She knew the question was a ridiculous one. Firstly, her mother would die rather than reside in the same home as her father, and second, Rhoda was not a coward.

Her mother strode across the room and tugged on the rarely used bell-pull. "Turn around. Let's get you out of this day dress."

Rhoda lifted the long strands of hair off her nape while her mother began unlacing the comfortable gown. "What should I wear?" She felt like a small child, her mama forcing her to go to her first party.

At that moment, Lucy appeared and strode toward the large wardrobe. "Oh, Miss Mossant, the artichoke taffeta. It brings out the little green flecks in your eyes and makes the copper in your hair stand out."

Rhoda peered over at the looking glass. She was completely unaware of any green flecks in her eyes. She did have red in her hair though. And red was the opposite of green.

And green was her favorite color.

With a deep breath, she nodded. "Very well. Green, it is."

TWO HOURS LATER, Rhoda *felt* green as she waited to climb out of the carriage behind her mother. Dozens of familiar faces mingled in the drive, milling about waiting to climb the wide staircase.

The men wore combinations of bright silks and woolen

blacks, separating the dandies from the soberer gentlemen. The ladies tittered behind fluttering fans, some with tall feathers in their hair, the younger ones dressed in pastels and whites.

Oh, how she wished Sophia had been able to attend with her! Or Emily or Cecily! She'd not realized how reliant she'd come to be upon her friends over the past two years. And tonight, of all nights, she needed them more than ever.

And then a gloved hand appeared in the doorway.

Masculine, at the end of an elegant black sleeve.

Not the hand of a footman.

"Lord Carlisle?" She couldn't prevent the sound of relief that escaped her exclamation.

She'd considered that he might be in attendance but hadn't expected to be able to speak with him.

And now he was here.

"Rhododendron." His face appeared, oh so dear, merriment in his eyes and a reassuring smile.

She covered her mouth to hide the answering smile that had burst from somewhere deep inside of her. Oh, but she'd been dreading tonight and now she somehow felt she had absolutely nothing to fear.

She allowed him to assist her to the pavement and then tuck her hand inside the crook of her arm.

Her mother had already located one of her friends and appeared to be in deep conversation. Her mother never had quite embraced the duties of a dedicated chaperone.

"I trust you have been well." His voice rumbled near her ear.

"I have been holed up in my bedchamber like a mouse," she admitted. So very unlike her. "It is high time I face the felines."

He laughed. "You're no mouse, Miss Mossant."

She couldn't stop herself from turning to meet his gaze.

Oh, how she'd missed his face.

She wanted to ask if he'd had any luck with his finances. He seemed quite jovial for a man in dun territory. "And you, my lord?" She tilted her head. "You appear ever so cheerful this evening. Have you met with any luck?"

He winced and shook his head. "It's just the sight of you, I'm afraid."

Oh, my. How could words set one's heart to flight and then send it plummeting to the ground in one fell swoop?

The news, however, made her stumble.

She and Sophia might have to sneak into White's after all.

At the same revelation, she wondered if a lady would be sent to Newgate for doing so. For a female to enter into such an iconic male domain might be right up there with breaking the Ten Commandments. Or even worse, the King's laws. Or the Regent's laws, be that as it may.

He steadied her and chuckled. "You've nothing to fear tonight." He must have mistaken her expression for trepidation of the evening ahead.

He must mean to watch over her, protect her.

Ah, yes, she'd have to break into White's with Sophia's assistance or without. For Rhoda was tired of keeping herself hidden away, and it was time this wager came to some sort of conclusion.

Rhoda would rather thrive than survive.

"At least I'm aware, tonight." She turned and smiled up at him. She'd ignore those who turned away from her.

Would they be willing to shun an earl as well?

"None will have even an inkling of opportunity. As for myself, however, I would ask for a few places on your dance card."

She'd not tied it to her wrist like she normally would

have. With her free hand, she dipped into her bodice and produced the pristine card for his perusal. He paused, plucked it from her fingers, and ordered her to turn around. When she did so, she felt the paper on her back, along with the pressure of his writing.

He was signing her card on her back.

"Lord Carlisle!" She twisted to look over her shoulder in mock disapproval.

How could he so handily put her at ease with all these people watching? Nothing had become known publicly regarding their aborted betrothal. Sophia had assured her of this.

Prescott could always sniff such information out, and he always shared it with Sophia.

When Justin handed back her card, she immediately recognized his careful handwriting. She ought to, she'd been attempting to replicate it for two days now.

He'd selected both waltzes and the supper dance.

Three dances! He might as well have had the banns read. Would her mother take exception to him?

Rhoda would deal with her later if that was the case. For now, she decided she'd bask in his company.

They entered the Primroses' large and elegant foyer together, her mother casting her a disapproving glance as she slipped past.

It didn't matter that many avoided meeting her gaze. The only eyes she cared about tonight were blue, and comforting, and right beside her. She didn't want to think about next week, or last year, or even tomorrow.

He led her through the receiving line, a few raised eyebrows met their greeting, but nothing she couldn't handle.

And then they drifted into the glowing ballroom, lit with hundreds, perhaps thousands of candles, and draped in so much greenery that it resembled the outdoors.

"It's as though the Primroses decorated tonight with your gown in mind."

Rhoda glanced down at her dress and like a silly debutante, felt herself blushing. "Thank you," she murmured, annoyed at this unfamiliar bout of shyness.

"How is it that every color seems to bring out your beauty more than the one before?"

At this comment, she laughed and turned to challenge him with her gaze. "Very good, my lord." Now she could flirt. She batted her eyelashes and simply enjoyed the attentions of so handsome a man.

Of *this* man.

They were in public and she felt the gazes of several eyes upon them both. Likely, they believed she was attempting to corrupt the poor vicar turned earl.

She refused to give their suspicions any credibility.

Although she wouldn't mind corrupting him just a little.

"What else have you done with yourself in the two days since we last met? In between searching for your fortune?"

He turned her to face him in a flourish. "Count the minutes until I would see you again."

His delicious compliments delighted her. As did his smile. She knew this game well and enjoyed playing it immensely.

She'd not enjoyed much lately.

"Ah, but Lord Carlisle. I counted the *seconds*."

"I refused to eat until I saw you again. Refused to drink."

Rhoda licked her lips. "I refused to *breathe*."

He stared at her as though mesmerized and then tilted his head back with a hearty laugh. Oh, but she *liked* this side of him.

"How is it that I can laugh with you without knowing

what the future holds?" she whispered without thinking.

He turned serious as well but did not completely relinquish the twinkle behind his gaze. "Perhaps that is why you feel joy. We must value what we feel in the moment. Your heart knows this."

The stringed quartet nearby chose that moment to begin playing. It was not a dance, not yet, of course, but the music seemed to enhance the emotion clouding the space around them.

"So, we must embrace the joy of today, and when the hopelessness comes, pin our sights on tomorrow."

"Well said. When did you put off your cynical ways?"

"When I met you." Was she flirting again or pouring out her soul? "I think I'd forgotten how to laugh."

"Nothing gives me more pleasure than hearing your laughter." He swallowed hard, as though he, too, were caught up in emotion.

"But what if...?"

At her question, he merely shook his head. He did not have the answers to everything. Likely another attribute that had endeared him to his congregation in addition to all of his others.

"I like that about you." Rhoda did not check her words. "That you do not know everything. That you admit to not having all of the answers."

He shrugged at her compliment. "No one does. Those who do are likely the most uninformed of us all."

"My father considers himself all-knowing." She hadn't meant to talk about her father. "He blamed my mother for not giving birth to any sons. Because, of course, he had nothing to do with it."

"Ah. Men. Horrid creatures." His ready agreement drew a surprising giggle from her. The two of them had somehow come to be standing by a brocaded wall, and he leaned casually against it as he teased her.

He teased her and yet showed understanding in his gaze.

"Not all of you." Her mouth had a mind of its own tonight. "Not all of you are horrid. And might I add that there are a fair number of unpleasant females as well."

"Ah, but they appear so much better."

She swatted at him with her fan. "We hide it well."

At which, he gazed at her steadily. "You have never been horrid, Rhododendron. Never."

His intensity sent a shiver through her. She wanted to lean into him, inhale his masculinity, and feel his hands on her skin. How had he become so very dangerous?

She needed to change the mood before she did something untoward. "I wish to know what you like to do when you aren't fretting over this new earldom of yours. Do you enjoy horses? Archery?" She determinedly clasped her hands behind her back and began strolling along the perimeter of the ballroom.

And he fell right in line with her. "Horses, yes, but I am no expert like Blakely. And archery? I'll admit I do rather well. My secret vice, and I swear you to secrecy?" He turned, and she nodded in all seriousness. "It's drawing. Not very manly, I'm quite aware. But not much brings me so much pleasure as capturing the images of my imagination."

"Watercolors? Painting?" Rhoda was horrible herself. In all honesty, she couldn't remember having much aptitude for anything other than socializing and fashion.

"Do you doubt me or are you merely expressing disappointment?"

"Neither, my lord." Instead, she asked about his favorite subjects and mediums. How long he'd painted and what he was painting now.

In return, he answered her questions and, in doing so, shared a little more of himself. Before she realized it, the dancing had begun.

"My dear Lord Carlisle!" Her mother's voice drew Rhoda's attention back to their surroundings. She approached most determinedly with a simpering blond debutante in tow. "Have you met Miss Dillingham? And wouldn't you know, no one has yet to claim this set with her."

Mother!

How could her mother *do* this to her?

Justin, being his most affable self, turned and greeted them both with all manner of politeness. "Miss Dillingham, ah, yes. Indeed, we have met." He admitted. "Will you do me the honor of partnering me for this set?" He'd dropped Rhoda's arm as though it suddenly burned and bowed to the lovely heiress.

Of course, the girl tittered and accepted with all false modesty. Rhoda could not keep herself from scowling and did not care much at all who witnessed it.

And then Prescott appeared at their side with Lieutenant Langdon. "Are you not supposed to remain at home with your wife, in mourning?" Rhoda asked the duke somewhat petulantly. It wasn't fair that he made appearances at social functions when Sophia could not.

He grinned, not at all put out by her veiled insult. "I only came to introduce my comrade about. You needn't worry. I shall be departing within the hour."

Of course. Prescott was kindness itself. "Duly noted." She made a halfhearted attempt at being pleasant but her awareness of Miss Dillingham flirting with Lord Carlisle perpetuated her displeasure.

Blast her mother and blast Prescott.

"If you'll pardon me." Lord Carlisle turned to make his

excuses to her. "I shall return later to find you for our waltz." He, too, seemed to have laughter lurking behind his gaze.

That was, until the gentleman beside her spoke up.

"Might I impose upon you for this set, Miss Mossant?" Lieutenant Langdon bowed with an eager smile.

Who was laughing now?

Rhoda curtseyed. "But of course, Lieutenant. I'm honored to dance with one so decorated as yourself."

Prescott burst out laughing, drawing a scowl from all of them, whereupon he held up one hand. "I'm leaving. I'm leaving." With a casual wave toward Rhoda's dance partner and a wink in Carlisle's direction, he pivoted on his heel and disappeared as quickly as he'd arrived.

Miss Dillingham tugged at Carlisle, drawing him onto the dance floor, and Rhoda turned to her own partner, hoping her smile didn't look as forced as it felt.

She did her best to give the lieutenant her attention but could hardly keep her gaze from straying to the other line. A golden-blond masculine head seemed to stand a few inches above all the rest.

Was it her imagination, or did that blue gaze of his drift in her direction more times than was appropriate?

The dance felt as though it went on for hours. And when it came to an end, she was quickly surrounded by eager suitors.

None of whom she trusted, of course.

Not Lord Moggersley, with his hands that seemed to have multiplied, nor Lord Odwick, who surely must have inhaled garlic before attending, and certainly not Sir Morris of Clopcott, with his exhortations of undying love. All of them did their utmost to lure her to some secluded place away from the dancing.

She'd never been so happy for her mother's company.

She imagined her mother would be exhausted before the night was over.

By the time the first waltz was announced, Rhoda hardly felt like dancing anymore. Strolling, on the terrace, however, was not an option.

In addition to being exasperated with nearly every male in the vicinity, she couldn't help but note that her vicar danced every set with some new simpering debutante. It seemed not one of them had not set their cap for the poverty-stricken earl.

The evening had lost the magic she'd felt earlier.

Until, that was, he took her in his arms for their waltz.

She felt as though she'd come home.

Sinewy muscles tensed beneath her hand when she placed it upon his shoulder. He gripped her hand tighter than was absolutely necessary, and a line furrowed his brow as his gaze scanned the room. "Damned blighters, every one of them."

He cared!

"They will give up eventually and nothing shall come of it." She'd reassure him as much as herself. They'd all seemed awfully determined.

And Lord Kensington, Flavion, had been watching her with eagle eyes. Would he never cease to cause trouble for them?

The thought sent a shiver through her.

Justin pulled her slightly closer than was appropriate as the music began. "They'd better. Still, I'm glad to see your mother has been vigilant this evening."

"She's concerned about the wager." The urge to bury her face against his chest nearly overwhelmed her. "You are exploring your other options this evening?" she stated baldly.

He chuckled. "There are no other options for me." But

did he mean it? Did he have a choice? They'd been over this.

And yet with his hand steering her, the warmth of it at her waist, and with his face only inches away from hers, she could not imagine ever wanting any other man.

She'd go to her grave a dried-up old prune rather than seek any other than her vicar.

She held his gaze and nodded.

And forgot everything else in the world but him as he steered her around the floor with long, elegant steps.

"How does a vicar learn to waltz so well?"

The thought struck her in the final dance of the set.

Oh, how she loved it when he grinned like that. "You think I'm a good dancer?" He winked. "You forget, I was raised at Eden's Court under the tutelage of the Duchess of Prescott." His humility attracted her more than a thousand boasts ever could, but when he allowed himself a moment to be brash, her heart sang.

The dance ended all too soon. She'd have to wait two more hours until the supper dance and then at least another two before she and her mother could leave for home.

CHAPTER TWENTY-THREE

Too Far This Time

BY THE TIME the supper dance was announced, Rhoda had had quite enough of the supposedly besotted gentlemen swarming about her. But that wasn't her greatest irritant. Bitterness filled her at the sight of so many empty-headed twits fluttering their eyelashes at Lord Carlisle.

And so, when he led her onto the dance floor, she determined to put an end to all of this.

They stood facing one another, lined up beside the other dancers, and the music commenced.

With her flattened palm pressed against his, moving around one another in a slow circle, she took a deep breath. "The wager has risen to over seventy thousand pounds."

His eyebrows rose, but they both were required to partner another for the next few beats. When they returned to one another, his blue eyes held more than an ounce of suspicion.

"There will be no winner," he asserted and then lifted their hands above her head and twirled her.

"But somebody must win," she insisted and then backed away from him to line up again.

They lost sight of one another for a few minutes, and Rhoda considered her next words as she followed the ladies around in a slow line. Ought she to simply come out with it? No one else seemed to be listening to them, each couple intent upon their own flirtations. Dancing had always been one of Rhoda's favorite things to do on earth. After that, she liked to flirt. Or perhaps it was the other way around.

"What if someone were to place a wager upon you?" she blurted out when he took her hand again. "After all, I—"

He scowled, and his face darkened. "Absolutely not. I forbid it."

Rhoda raised her brows at that word. *Forbid.*

She'd never taken well to such a notion.

"You *forbid* it, Lord Carlisle?" At his stern look, a surprising bolt of heat shot through her and then settled between her legs. It was as though her body approved of his high handedness, reveled in it, in fact, even though her brain took offense.

He touched her waist and twirled her again.

"The wager is an abomination." And yet when she glanced at him, she saw other emotions flicker across his features. Doubt. Disgust, Yearning. And when he met her gaze, she was certain she saw lust.

She clenched her inner muscles in response and then stepped back into the line. When she turned, she nearly barreled right into the lady beside her. Wrong way! Good heavens, he'd befuddled her mind.

And other parts of her.

When they came together again, she could think of hardly anything but how his scent tantalized her senses, the warmth of his hand as it skimmed her shoulder and arm.

Oh, but how she wished he could kiss her. Would they ever have that opportunity again?

"I ask you not to pursue this train of thought. Trust me." He leaned forward and whispered the words near her ear. So closely that his breath moved some wisps of her hair. "Please."

He stepped away from her and the music stopped.

She nodded.

Before he could take her arm and lead her into the large dining hall, cool fingers grasped her elbow from behind.

"I'm afraid Lord Carlisle will have to dine with somebody else." Her mother again! "I'm in need of your companionship myself." The strength with which her mother could drag her away from him was surprisingly forceful. "I asked you not to appear in public with him." This time, it was her mother's breath filling her ear. "Two dances! Two dances, Rhododendron? Does that sound to you like avoiding him?"

Rhoda cast one apologetic glance back toward Justin, who appeared rather as though he'd just lost his best friend.

His melancholy warmed her.

RHODA WASN'T NEARLY so bothered when ladies swarmed Lord Carlisle after that. He didn't look at them with any longing whatsoever.

As he did with her.

He must hold her in his affections!

And although she ought to have guessed this from all of their other encounters, she'd had a difficult time trusting it. She'd grossly misjudged St. John's regard; how could she trust her conclusion now?

But this was different. Ah, yes, Justin cared for her. She was not mistaken.

And so, she could enjoy the rest of the evening, pretend even, that the ridiculous compliments she received did not stem from the bilious wager someone had found necessary to initiate.

When the rather young Lord Turlington bowed his thanks for a particularly lively set, Rhoda decided to forgo searching out her mother in favor of a trip to the ladies' retiring room. She sashayed past a group of tittering girls, all of whom she'd once believed to be her friends, and slipped into the darkened corridor leading to her destination. Part of her hem was coming undone and her hair needed repairing as well.

She ought to have located her mother first but nothing untoward had happened all evening, and there were moments when a girl needed a moment to herself.

Just as the thought niggled at her, a hand covered her mouth and another arm wound around her waist, lifting and pulling her into a dark entrance she'd not been aware of.

She recognized that scent. It had nearly choked her once before.

Rhoda kicked out behind her and twisted and squirmed.

"Be still! I'm not going to hurt you, for God's sake, Miss Mossant!" Both hands tightened around her, the one about her mouth pinching her lips and cutting them against her teeth.

Blasted Lord Kensington! She ought to have known better. He would not play this game fairly. He would not care how he won the wager. All he'd ever cared for was himself.

His hand blocked her cries as the door closed her into an empty room alone with him. It wasn't a library or any room she remembered ever visiting before.

She raised her hands and tugged at his upper arm. Just enough.

Once she'd gotten a much-needed breath of air into her

lungs, she exhaled with the loudest scream she could manage.

His hand clamped over her mouth again, just as quickly.

She would not allow this to happen.

Anger. Frustration. Outrage. She shot her elbow backward and connected with what she hoped was his rib.

His hold loosened, and Rhoda grabbed his hair and tugged his head toward the ground.

Yelping sounds escaped his mouth now. "Odwick, I could use a little help here!"

Two of them!

Not now! Not tonight! This wasn't happening!

Rhoda broke free and dashed for the exit, her heart racing. It was a wonder it hadn't burst out of her chest. She managed to swing the heavy door inward just as another hand grasped at the back of her dress.

A tearing sound rent the air when she kicked a foot behind her, and then pushed herself into the foyer. She didn't wait around to see how far they'd follow her. Instead, she set her legs pumping until she burst into the light of the ballroom.

It felt rather like awakening from a horrible nightmare.

A lively set was playing, those around her laughed and smiled and continued to converse. No one noticed her appearance. If they did, would they realize what she'd nearly endured a mere dozen or so steps away? Would they be horrified to realize that some of their guests were such villains?

What would happen if she attempted to tell her hostess that the Earl of Kensington had just accosted her?

Dismay? Disbelief? Judgment? Likely, all three, but would they be directed at him or at her? At his accuser?

It wouldn't be worth it. She and her family would be

dragged even further through the mud and Flavion would continue to go unpunished.

She could tell Justin. He was a man of honor. But then he'd call Lord Kensington out, likely challenge him at dawn.

Icy cold fear gripped her at the thought of something happening to the man who had comforted her, protected her, trembled in her arms with wanting.

She'd give him up to another rather than have him meet with any harm.

No one else would believe her, if they even listened to her. Men of the *ton* lived lives of entitlement, and part of what they considered themselves entitled to included women. Another aspect of their privilege was an unpardonable lack of consequences for their crimes.

Some could even kill with impunity.

Her mother would believe her, but she would likely respond as others would. Flavion was a man. Not only a man, but an earl.

She swallowed hard and attempted to slow her breathing lest anyone approach her before she could decide what to do next.

She knew one thing for certain. This wager must come to a conclusion, and that conclusion would be decided by her and only her.

She pushed some stray hairs behind her ear and searched the room for her mother. It was time to leave.

And tomorrow, well, come tomorrow, she would take matters into her own hands, determine her own destiny, blast them all. She was tired of being subject to what others did, what others thought. She'd not only survive. By God, she'd thrive.

CHAPTER TWENTY-FOUR

Girls Can Be Boys, Too

FIRST THING THIS morning, she'd taken it upon herself to make a visit to Prescott House. Sophia had been up already, having fed Lady Harriette in the early dawn hours. Since the babe was down for a morning nap, the two of them sat in Sophia's favorite drawing room while Rhoda told her of the events from the night before.

Sophia quite agreed. The wager needed put to rest once and for all.

"Dev says the last time he looked, no one had placed any wagers upon Lord Carlisle. He isn't even listed."

"That's a good thing, though, right?" As Rhoda understood the nature of betting, it would mean anyone who placed their money on Lord Carlisle would take the entire pot.

After Lord Carlisle won, that was. And she'd make certain he did. But how? She hadn't worked that part out yet.

Sophia was nodding. "The minimum bet allowed is a thousand pounds."

Rhoda bit her lip. Technically, her mother had allotted her that very same amount. "Would I need to have the money present to place the bet?"

"Members are not required to make any such deposits. If you wager in Lord Carlisle's name, nothing shall be required. But his signature must be true. And there is a man who keeps watch over the book. That's the tricky part."

They sat in silence together, both attempting to contrive some plan for this additional obstacle.

"You might be able to create a diversion. Knock something over, pretend to faint: anything to divert attention. And while you do that, I'll write the bet in the book."

"Both of us dressed up as gentlemen, I take it."

"But of course." Rhoda was already racking her brain to think where she might come up with a waistcoat, jacket, breeches, and a hat that might work for her. And for Sophia.

"Dev forbade me to do this, you know."

Rhoda's head snapped up at this. "You mean you *told* him?"

Sophia shrugged her petite shoulders, a few blond curls dangling around her face. "I tell him everything. And he's always deigned to give me advice. But he's never *forbidden* me to do anything."

Rhoda recalled how she'd felt upon hearing that word from her mother. And then later from Carlisle.

"I'm going to do it, of course." Sophia tilted her chin up just a notch.

"Of course." Rhoda understood completely.

"We can watch from across the street for a group of dandies to enter together. I think we'll fit in best with that sort. It might be tricky, but it oughtn't be so very difficult."

"Dev told me that the wager has taken on of a life of its own. A separate ledger has been tucked into the betting book. The betting book sits on a pedestal near the front drawing room. You'll have to locate it. Once you've done so, I suppose I can create the diversion."

"What sort of diversion?"

Sophia wrinkled her nose in thought. "As we discussed already, I'll do something to draw attention. Run into a waiter…" And then with a twinkle in her eye, she said, "Initiate a fight."

"Good Lord, Sophia, that's the last thing we need… you being called out. Challenged to meet some blighter at dawn."

The laughter they shared wrapped around her like a warm blanket.

Sophia was going to do it with her. Rhoda gave into the overwhelming urge to embrace her friend.

"Rhoda, remember, please, I'm not using a wet nurse!" Sophia pushed her away and glanced down at her bosom. Sure enough, two spots of moisture had appeared on the front of her gown.

"Now that would be an interesting diversion." Sophia looked irate and then they both erupted into another fit of giggles.

When they finally brought themselves under control, they'd decided to set the plan into motion for tomorrow at eleven in the morning. Sophia would send over clothing for Rhoda to wear later today. She'd said so many wardrobes had been left at Prescott House by Dev's relatives that she'd have no troubles locating two sets of disguises. Rhoda's task was to perfect Lord Carlisle's signature. They would place the bet using his Viscount title so that others wouldn't question him about it. Best the bet remained anonymous for as long as possible.

Tomorrow morning it was to be then.

Rhoda left terrified, but also with a skip in her step. She wondered what Cecily and Emily would think when they discovered Sophia and she had broken into White's.

A gentleman gave her a curious glance when she giggled out loud as she passed him. Rhoda's maid likely was scowling as she followed behind her.

Tomorrow!

RHODA HADN'T SLEPT a wink, various scenarios playing out in her mind not allowing even a moments rest. She wondered if Sophia fared any better.

The night before, Rhoda had used up the remainder of her ink practicing the notation she was to make in the book. Hopefully, nobody knew Lord Carlisle's secondary title. If anyone caught her forging it, she'd be challenged upon the spot.

She spent the early hours of the morning working on her disguise. She'd first thought to pin her hair atop her head and keep it under the hat but if she were to lose her hat… She realized it could look more natural tied into a simple queue at the nape of her neck. She tucked it under once, hiding the length.

What with the cravat, waistcoat, and jacket, she even managed to hide her other feminine assets. After wrapping a long piece of muslin around her chest, that was.

She wondered how Sophia would manage to hide this sort of preparation from her husband.

When Lucy knocked on her door, Rhoda climbed beneath the covers and pulled it over her head. "I've a megrim this morning! I've no wish for breakfast or chocolate!" she murmured as though half asleep. She only hoped her mother wouldn't see fit to check on her.

In truth, she was starting to feel like she might vomit. This had nothing to do with her health, however, but everything to do with her nerves.

What if they were caught?

What if Dev discovered the plan and kept Sophia from assisting her? Would Rhoda have the nerve to undertake it on her own?

She had to!

The alternative was unthinkable! More days, possibly weeks, of fending off advances that had become violent in nature. And even worse, having to relinquish Justin to some other lady.

After Lucy had closed the door behind her, Rhoda wanted to cry. She needed to pull herself together.

And then another knock sounded at the door. "Rhoda?"

It couldn't be.

She sat up in her bed, momentarily forgetting to stay hidden and called out. "Cecily?"

The door cracked open and sure enough, Cecily peered in with a cheery grin. "Whatever are you doing dressed that way?" She opened the door farther and strode across the carpet, taking in Rhoda's strange costume with questioning eyes.

"Oh." Rhoda tugged at her cravat in an attempt at nonchalance. "Sophia and I are sneaking into White's today. I'm going to place a bet on Carlisle, so he can pay off the bills he's inherited along with his title." Might as well come right out with it. Cecily would get it all out of her anyhow. "I thought you were with Emily."

Cecily waved her hand in the air. "We left her with her husband. She and Lord Blakely had quite the adventure." She regaled Rhoda with an unbelievable turn of events and then absentmindedly began retying Rhoda's cravat. "You need a valet, Rhoda. Tell me all about what you have planned because I'm going with you! I can't allow the two of you to sneak into White's without me!"

"Hm..." Sophia *had* sent over a rather large assortment of clothing. Rhoda pointed toward the worn carpetbag sitting outside her dressing room door. Cecily's assistance certainly couldn't hurt. "Let's see what we can put together for you. But we have to hurry. I promised Sophia I'd meet her a block away at a quarter till eleven."

Cecily finished the cravat with a flourish and then examined the contents of the bag.

"Aren't you going to chastise me for manipulating too much?" Rhoda asked her somewhat skeptically, the disapproval Cecily had expressed at Eden's Court still stinging.

Cecily looked over her shoulder with an apologetic smile. "I was only worried for you both. Since then, I see that Emily has found herself in something of an unusual love match and Sophia wrote that you seem to be rather enamored with Lord Carlisle. I've realized neither of you would have trapped yourself in a marriage you didn't really want. I ought to have trusted you both." She stood up, holding a pair of black breeches.

"These ought to fit. Your hips are larger than mine since your confinement with Little Finn." Rhoda stepped forward and held them up to Cecily's waist but couldn't stop herself from grasping her in a tight hug. "I know you were just concerned. I've missed you, Cecily."

After holding tight to one another for a moment, they both awkwardly stepped back and became quite interested in the remainder of Cecily's costume. Rhoda and Cecily had always been the least demonstrative of their foursome. Sophia was always hugging everyone, and Emily was quite affectionate as well.

They caught one another's expressions and let out some nervous laughter.

"Oh, this one is perfect!" Cecily had pulled out a rather elaborate waistcoat. "The embroidery on this is magnificent."

Between the two of them, they pinned and tucked and scrutinized until both of them looked passably masculine.

Again, Rhoda wondered how Sophia was faring, on her own through all this.

"You aren't concerned that Mr. Nottingham might be angry if he discovers you committed such a crime?" More and more, Rhoda was beginning to consider the entire enterprise to be more than a little illegal. Trespassing, forgery, fraud.

Beads of perspiration broke out on her forehead at the thought of all they were undertaking today.

But Cecily only shrugged. "He'll find out, all right. And then he'll likely have a laugh over it." She gritted her teeth together in a wince. "As long as we don't get caught. Oh, but this is so exciting though! I absolutely adore Little Finn, you know, but it all can feel so tedious at times!"

"I'd imagine the theater would suffice." Rhoda would not be attempting to do this if it hadn't been absolutely necessary.

She took one last look in her glass and then stepped back. "Are you ready?"

"Ready as I'll ever be!" Cecily was far too cheerful for this. Rhoda's future, Justin's future, *lives* were at stake here, for heaven's sake.

Well, perhaps not lives. But reputations, and happiness, and whatnot.

Rhoda peeked out the door and the two women slipped down the back stairs to the servants' exit. The true test as to the effectiveness of their disguises was yet to come.

"Oh, no, Rhoda!" Cecily said in her regular high-pitched feminine voice and then again, "Oh, no, *Dorwich*." This time much deeper. "You mustn't sway your hips. Walk like a man, like this."

Rhoda burst out laughing as Cecily attempted to walk with her knees apart, as though she had to accommodate a masculine appendage between her legs. "Too much! And what shall I call you? Warwick? I rather like Warwick for you." And then she took several steps in a less exaggerated manner than Cecily had. By the time they reached the street, both of them had found their rhythm.

An elderly gentleman glanced at them twice, causing Rhoda to pull her hat lower. It felt odd walking down the street without taking Cecily's arm. She wished she'd thought of a walking stick for both of them. At least that way they'd have something to do with their hands.

White's wasn't far, and they both strode down the sidewalk with more haste than usual.

"A diversion," Cecily confirmed in a low voice that only Rhoda would hear. "Sophia and I will create the diversion and you get that wager down. We'll only have one opportunity."

Rhoda felt faint.

She never felt faint.

"Justin's going to kill me."

Cecily grasped her arm reassuringly. "It'll be fine. You are destined for happiness, just as I was, and Sophia, and even Emily."

Rhoda nodded.

"Aye, mates." A small man edged up behind them. "What's yer business?"

Cecily glared over her shoulder with narrowed eyes that quickly opened wide in astonishment. Behind the mustache, pipe, and lowered hat peered an all too familiar blue gaze.

"Oh, my heavens, Sophia! How simply marvelous!" She eyed the duchess from head to toe.

But for the rounder bottom than most men, Sophia perfectly resembled an elderly gentleman. Of course, Sophia *had* thought to bring a walking stick. And a pipe. And how on earth had she managed to locate such a perfectly crafted beard and mustache?

Sophia grunted, not budging out of her character. "You two lads ready?" She flicked her gaze toward the doorway to White's.

Rhoda's stomach about dropped to her toes. A group of gregarious young gentlemen approached the club. They had the air of young lords about them. They looked quite similar to Rhoda and Cecily, in fact. Sophia would stand out simply in that she had taken on the disguise of an elderly gentleman.

"This way." Cecily sidled along the walk with Sophia closely behind. Rhoda truly understood the meaning of the term cold feet at that moment, as hers seemed to have frozen to the ground.

"*Dorwich*!" Cecily's scowl jolted Rhoda into motion.

"I'm coming, Warwick," she responded in a deep voice. Oh, heavens, she sounded nothing at all like a gentleman. She hoped she wouldn't be required to speak once inside.

With heads down, they casually fell into step with the lively group of lordlings. One of them even dropped his arm around Cecily's shoulders. "Haven't seen you in a long while, Huntly."

It seemed Cecily would now be Huntly. Her new friend had obviously had a few too many drinks this morning. Perhaps he'd never quit the night before. Nonetheless, his manner and lack of ability to distinguish his old friend Huntly from Cecily worked rather well in their favor.

"It has indeed," Cecily answered in her man voice.

"I want to up my wager today. My understanding is that Kensington is coming close. I'd hazard that's what brings you around finally." He stumbled slightly and seemed to be leaning heavily on poor Cecily.

The stench of his breath was strong enough to inebriate everyone within five feet of him.

Nobody questioned them when they stepped through

the hallowed entrance.

The interior far surpassed the rather ordinary design of the outside of the building. Rhoda did her best not to gawk at the luxurious settees and grand tables. A gigantic fireplace took up one end of the room, and discreet waiters attended to the gentlemen guests. Rhoda wondered that nobody could hear her heart beating.

Even more so when a footman stepped forward to take their hats. She handed it over and quickly turned her back on the employee. If they were going to be caught, surely, now would be the time.

Being insignificant, in this situation, rather seemed to be something of a blessing. All attention was currently directed at Lord Kensington, who was drinking and boasting to another cluster of young gentlemen.

The one who'd latched onto Huntly, aka Cecily, wasn't all that interested in the joviality surrounding Flavion. Instead, he proved to be of further assistance by leading them straight to the betting book.

"Got to get this down before it's all over," he explained with a wink in Cecily's direction.

Fool.

Rhoda peered over his shoulder and watched the idiot add another thousand to his wager upon Lord Kensington. Sure enough, the wager on her was deserving of a leather-bound book all its own.

Another employee hovered nearby but recognized their newfound friend and didn't question him as he made his notation in the book.

Cecily and Sophia moved toward a billiard table and Rhoda took some tentative steps backward in hopes of disappearing into the wall tapestry.

The employee, the one watching over the betting books, moved away from the book, on alert as another gentleman had approached Flavion.

Justin!

This was her perfect opportunity.

No one was watching the book, and yet she couldn't bring herself to look away from her vicar-turned-earl. He appeared determined and solid as he faced the man who'd caused so much havoc for Cecily and now, her.

Whereas Lord Kensington's complexion was powdery and pale, Justin glowed healthily. His thick head of golden hair standing tall above the rest. His shoulders seemed broader and the energy of his character crackled in the air.

"Stand down, Kensington. You think it noble to besmirch the reputation of an innocent young woman, a genteel lady?" His voice broached no argument, but Lord Kensington had never recognized the wisdom of walking away from one so determined.

A movement behind Justin revealed Prescott standing at her fiancé's back.

"You've been cossetted in your little church for too long. If you hadn't, you'd know for certain that Miss Mossant is no innocent." A ripple of guffaws ran through Kensington's entourage of hangers-on.

Rhoda glanced to her left. The book sat unattended just a few feet away. Now was her chance. And yet she was frozen in place, unable to tear her gaze away from the spectacle across the room.

Please don't do this! Rhoda begged silently. She did not want bloodshed over her. She knew enough guilt to last a lifetime. She wanted to step between the two of them. No! No! If anything were to happen to Justin because of her stupid decision last year, it would kill her.

"You wouldn't know innocence if it jumped up and bit that arrogant ass of yours." Justin took a step closer. He now stood inches from Kensington.

"Or if I cut off half your bollocks." The third voice sounded terrifyingly familiar.

Oh, good God! Cecily! No!

A gentleman beside Prescott whipped his head around to see who'd dare to say anything so impudent, as did Kensington.

Justin was undeterred from his mission, however. "Hold your tongue, Kensington, or I'll meet you at dawn."

The gentleman who'd stared so hard at Cecily turned his attention back to Lord Kensington. "Flave. I've no control over your behavior, but I do hold the strings to the funds you've chosen to wager with." Mr. Nottingham! Cecily's husband! No wonder he'd stared at her so hard.

This was Rhoda's chance. The pen had grown damp against her palm. She need only turn and carefully scrawl the signature she'd been practicing for three days now.

"She's not worth it." Lord Kensington's voice raised an octave as he responded to Justin. Perhaps the earl's confidence was dissipating at the memory of the last duel he'd participated in. "I'll not speak of her again, but have my word, the winnings shall fall to me."

Not if I have any say in the matter.

His bragging prodded her into action. She would save herself. She would make Justin the winner so that he could pay off the debts of his estate.

What was the name? *Dorwich. Dorwich.*

She set the tip of the pen to parchment but couldn't make her fingers move.

The disappointment she'd seen on Justin's face, when he'd learned of her and Emily's machinations at Eden's Court, froze her hand.

She'd betrayed him.

Would he trust her again if she did this?

Trust me?

She shivered as she remembered how his breath had stirred the wisps of hair at the nape of her neck.

Please.

He'd corrected his demand and turned it into a request.

Blast.

Rhoda stared at her hand as it hovered over the book. It was shaking. Her heart pounded loudly in her ears and a bead of sweat trickled down the back of her neck.

Please, he'd said.

CHAPTER TWENTY-FIVE

What's It Gonna Be?

JUSTIN COULD NOT remember the last time he'd been so angry. He was a man who preferred to settle disputes with rational conversation, open-mindedness, and understanding.

He'd wanted to plow his fist through Kensington's face.

Even now, marching through a small path he'd found himself on in the park, his blood boiled. He'd like nothing better than to use his sword to cut off what remained of that bastard's manhood.

Damned if he even deserved to be called a man. Kensington possessed the mental capabilities of an adolescent but, due to his place in society, wielded power and influence. Both of which ought only ever be afforded to individuals who'd proven themselves deserving by exhibiting wisdom and character.

He swiped his walking stick at a branch that dared to dangle in his way. Each day that damn bet persisted dishonored her.

Endangered her.

He was not fool so much to believe men wouldn't resort to violence over such a large sum of money. It seemed nearly every gentleman in London now had a stake in the outcome.

None that mattered so much as his own.

His head knew what needed to be done, but it hadn't

lined up with his heart, and with his soul.

If he were to participate, it would mean he approved of such behavior. Even worse, if he were to take any winnings from the wager, she'd always doubt his affection. It would stand between the two of them throughout their lives.

God knew his desire had absolutely nothing to do with winnings and could only be attributed to her allure and his own weaknesses.

Which beckoned altogether differing bouts of guilt.

He'd wanted her for so long that he questioned his motives for wanting to marry her.

Was it only lust or did his feelings amount to something more? Protection, yes. Compassion, of course.

"Carlisle! Wait up!"

Justin turned in time to see his cousin practically running to catch up with him.

He'd not wanted to speak to anyone. He'd needed time to himself. But this was Prescott. This was Dev, who'd always been there for him.

He waited until Dev was even before turning to march along the dirt path once again. He'd not make conversation unless Dev insisted.

"Why don't you just marry her? Put an end to all of this?"

Ah, so Dev had something to say.

Justin swiped his stick at a perfectly innocent flower that dared to be blooming prettily this afternoon. "Damn them all to hell, you know why, Dev." The mountain of bills he'd met with at Carlisle House came to mind, along with the leaking roofs and leaning walls that plagued the tenant dwellings he'd come across.

He remembered what it had felt like to be hungry. He remembered once again what the desperation had driven his mother to do.

"And yet you won't allow me to assist you in any of this?"

Justin refused to acknowledge the question.

Dev persisted. "You have provided comfort and guidance for my family for as long as I've known you. You have always been a sort of spiritual touchstone. You've a strength we all lacked. And that has bolstered us. Nothing we've done for you has been charity."

Justin appreciated the sentiments of his cousin, but he could not continue to depend upon others to meet his responsibilities. It made him feel less of a man somehow.

At that moment, he stopped suddenly, nearly causing Dev to barrel into him. "Would you do it, Dev? Would you allow another man to pay for your family's needs?" Justin swiped his hat off his head and found himself wanting to pitch it into the trees and shrubs nearby. "Especially if there was something you, yourself could do to absorb the costs?"

Dev stared at him with narrowed eyes.

"I'd do whatever it took to take care of Sophia and our child. I'd lie. I'd steal. I'd kill."

"Fuck you!" Justin exploded, sending his hat flying.

He had spent the last decade studying the word of God, teaching others the difference between right and wrong. How could he now disregard everything he valued?

"I've refused to wager upon her honor, not because I care for her so little, but because I care for her so much."

Dev shifted his weight from one foot to the other. "Does no good to care for her if you cannot be with her every night. If you cannot hold her in your arms, protect her from harm, make her smile."

Justin had imagined all of those things and more. His eyes stung at the thought of giving her up. "I more than care for her. I love her."

Prescott's hand landed upon his shoulder. "Then do whatever it takes to keep her." And just like that, Dev turned around and headed back in the direction from where he'd come.

"I love her," Justin whispered in awe. Could the answer truly be so simple as that? He glanced down at his feet, at the flower he'd all but shattered with his temper.

Pink petals lay tender and exposed in the dirt. Without their stem, without their life source, they might just as well already be dead.

Until he'd obliterated it, the flower had been a rhododendron.

THE THREE GIRLS did not wait around after the altercation began to settle down. Rhoda had been the first to exit, forgetting to retrieve her hat or even give the signal to Sophia that they'd agreed upon earlier. The plan had been for them to leave separately and meet up later at Prescott House.

Rhoda broke into an unnatural sprint the moment White's door closed behind her. She couldn't face them yet. Her mind and heart forged an epic battle that she couldn't control.

And so, she ran toward the park and didn't stop until a stitch in her side prevented her from running any farther. Feeling faint, strangled almost, she tore at the cloth wound around her neck. Thank heavens no one else had chosen to walk along this section of the park this morning. If she were to be seen like this...

And then she let out a snort of hysterical laughter. Would it even matter? She was already fodder for all of society. Would she? Wouldn't she? Had she?

She'd long since passed the stage of mortification that came with knowing what others imagined about her.

At least she liked to believe she had.

A lady and her maid came into view. Despite the hopelessness of her scandal-ridden life, she truly did not wish to add to it.

She spied a dirt trail ahead and turned to enter the privacy it afforded.

She should not be in the park alone.

She should not be dressed as she was.

So many "should not's" that she'd ignored in the past, one would have thought she would have learned.

Glints of sunlight danced on the leaves and flowers that lined the dirt-trodden path. In the past, she would have been grateful for such a beautiful day. She would have made plans to go to Gunter's, or perhaps shopping on Bond Street. Life had once seemed so very simple.

Having loosened her cravat, she went one step further and unbuttoned the heavy coat she wore.

How did men outfit themselves thus in such warm weather? She'd always imagined that women had the worst of it.

"Rhoda?" An incredulous male voice had her jerking her gaze up from the ground.

"Justin." The first thing she noticed was the absence of his hat and how his hair nearly looked on fire where the shafts of sunlight struck it.

The second thing she noticed was the empty, bleak look in his eyes.

"Is it really you? I was just thinking..." And then he shook his head in confusion.

He appeared so very lost. And tormented.

Rhoda stepped across the weeds in her path and into

his arms.

It seemed the most natural thing in the world. His warmth, his scent, his very essence. She slid her hands up his chest and wound them around his neck.

He'd defended her to Flavion in front of all of White's. He'd been willing to call the man out for his casual insults.

And now his arms held her tightly against his solid length. She tilted her head back so that his lips could find hers.

She belonged here. She'd belonged here all along.

His tongue tasted, plundered, demanded. One of his hands grasped the back of her head and the other had found its way to her bound breast.

Rhoda arched into him. He'd brought her back to life this spring, reignited a hunger she never imagined she'd feel again.

No more waiting.

No more delaying.

No more doubt as to whether this was meant to be or not.

"Justin." Her voice rasped on his name. He moaned in response. He was walking her backward, off the path. She didn't stop until she felt herself pressed up against the trunk of a tree.

He'd released her head by now, both of his hands frantically caressing her body, searching for access she had no intention of denying.

He'd hitched one of her legs up. Rhoda opened for him; she wanted to feel his arousal. She wanted nothing between them.

"Why are you wearing breeches?"

The words fell like cold water on their passion. He also seemed to take notice of how she'd done her hair and examined her wardrobe in confusion. "Is this a joke?"

She did not want to lie to him. "I was there. Today." She hated that he'd dropped her leg and stepped back. Where she'd been hot a few seconds before, frigid air hit her now. "At White's," she added.

His brows lowered as she added to his confusion. "But, how? And why?"

"I saw you, heard what you said to Lord Kensington." She was afraid to answer his question. "Sophia, Cecily, and I—"

"You snuck into an all-gentlemen's club?" He didn't sound as though he thought it was very amusing.

"I needed to place the bet." Her heart plummeted. The shame she felt wasn't nearly as heartbreaking as the betrayal she saw in the depths of his eyes.

He lowered his brows. "I asked you not to. You gave me your word."

She hadn't spoken any such agreement, but to be fair, she'd nodded. She'd indicated that she would accede to his wishes.

"But it is the only way—"

He took another step away from her. "I see you have so little faith in me that you deemed it necessary." And then realization narrowed his eyes. "Whose name were you wagering in? Not your own. That would never be allowed."

"Viscount Dorwich," she stated baldly.

"Mine?"

She'd gone too far this time.

She'd ruined everything. He'd never trust her again. "I *do* have faith in you!" She could not fight the tears that had accumulated behind her eyes. "I do! More than you know! So much so that I had to! You would not do it for yourself! You would never do it for us."

He had turned his face away from her, and she could

see his jaw clench and then unclench again. When she thought he wasn't going to say anything, he surprised her. "I don't even know what honor is anymore," he said so softly the wind could have easily carried his words away. He swallowed hard and then a mask dropped over his features, hiding any emotions he'd shown moments ago.

"Justin." She wanted to beg him to understand, but... his very goodness, his purity was part of what drew her to him. She did not want for him to change. "I didn't do it. I didn't go through with it."

But she had doubted him, and, by his lack of reaction, he apparently didn't recognize any difference between the two.

She'd been willing to do whatever might be necessary. Because she'd wanted him. She'd wanted it all. Had she been so very wrong? She wished she felt more certain of her position. She wished such questions could be answered more easily. Perhaps then, she could defend herself.

"Best repair yourself and I'll escort you to your mother's house. I don't imagine she knows you went out in public like that."

He suddenly appeared very tired.

Rhoda buttoned the top of her shirt and her jacket, and then smoothed down the creased fronts of her breeches. She could not take his arm while they walked. People would think two men were...

Well, she would walk a little in front of him.

CHAPTER TWENTY-SIX

Time's Running Out

JUSTIN FELT SICK inside. A failure. She'd not believed in him. What sickened him further was that he'd not believed in himself either.

He'd disparaged her for her costume and yet with her walking just ahead of him, hips swaying, he wanted nothing more than to run his hands along the sweet, round curve of her bottom. He wanted to lay her on the grass and remove that ridiculous disguise inch by inch.

He wanted to bury himself inside of her, claim her for himself once and for all.

Dev had said he'd lie, steal, and kill for his duchess. Suddenly, Justin had similar urges.

But she didn't believe in me.

He swallowed hard. Why did honor even matter? Or character? He struggled with the terrifying notion that he could not live without her and yet, if he went against his own conscience, could he then live with himself?

He glanced from side to side as they emerged from the forested path. A few members of the *ton* had begun to assemble early. It would not do for Rhoda to be recognized by any of them, especially dressed as she was.

Good God, she and her friends had stolen their way into White's! He didn't know that any other woman had ever done so.

How had they gone unnoticed? He shook his head as

he watched the sway of her hips, not hidden nearly enough by the length of her masculine jacket. Did men only see what they wanted to see? Were they so arrogant as to not believe a woman could slip by their defenses so easily?

Damnable men and damnable women.

With a flick of his hand and a quick whistle, he summoned an approaching hackney. Already the two of them were attracting curious glances. Best to get her hidden away, if only in a vehicle.

He gave the driver her address, along with payment, and then resisted the urge to assist her up the steps. She was dressed as a gentleman, for God's sake.

When she realized he was not going to join her, she frowned. Her lashes fluttered, and she looked as though she wanted to cry.

She looked how he felt.

"Can you not forgive me, Justin?"

Her words nearly broke him. He wasn't as bothered by her deception as he was by the fact that she had so little confidence in him.

If she couldn't trust him... "There is nothing to forgive." He met her gaze, willing her to understand.

Oh, how he wished he could simply forget everything except this woman.

"Then I don't understand."

This was not the place to have such a discussion. He merely shook his head and smiled with regret heavy on his chest. "Try not to be seen when you get home."

She rolled her eyes.

Of course. She wasn't a fool. She didn't need to hear his words in order to know something so simple.

His heart sank as he watched the rundown carriage pull away, Perhaps, she didn't need him either.

RHODA HAD BEEN inconsolable after St. John's death. She'd been sad. She'd felt abandoned.

She'd not been heartbroken.

Justin White had been the man to introduce her to this particularly painful affliction.

She'd managed to slip back into her mother's house and into her chamber to change without being noticed. She'd wanted nothing more than to don her night rail, climb beneath the counterpane, and cry herself to sleep.

But she'd promised Sophia she'd visit Prescott House. They would want to know if the plan had worked.

She owed them that much. They'd risked their own reputations to help her.

So instead of feigning illness for the rest of the day, she wiped her eyes and, along with Lucy, made her way resolutely on foot to Prescott House.

Mr. Evans told her she was expected and led her to Sophia's favorite drawing room.

She had barely stepped inside when she was nearly knocked over by Cecily, who'd bounded across the rooms and grasped hold of Rhoda's shoulders. "You are safe! We were so very worried. One minute we're watching Flavion attempt to defend his actions to Lord Carlisle and the next you have disappeared. I had hoped you'd met with success, but I didn't know. And we certainly couldn't ask anyone." Cecily laughed.

Rhoda could not meet Sophia's eyes, choosing instead to stare at the elaborately designed rug covering the floor. "I could not do it."

Silence.

"You mean you could not *do it,* or you *could not* do

it?" Sophia, Rhoda believed, had an inkling as to what Rhoda meant.

"I simply couldn't do it." She lifted her chin and looked from one girl to the other. "I wanted to do it. And I had every opportunity to do it. I'm quite certain we could have gotten away with it. It was just... he'd asked me not to. And there he was, defending my honor amidst all of his peers."

She awaited the recriminations Cecily would surely heap upon her head. And the justified complaints Sophia would have.

Neither of which came.

"I am so very proud of you." Cecily's smile stretched from ear to ear.

"You love him! I knew it!" Sophia's eyes had gone all dreamy, much like they normally did when she spoke of her husband.

Rhoda glanced from one to the other. "You mean you are not angry with me?"

But they were shaking their heads, most adamantly. "We were most willing to assist you, as you well know. But you walked away from nearly one hundred thousand pounds, simply because you'd given him your word." Sophia sighed. "Isn't love the most wonderful thing in the world?"

But Rhoda didn't feel that way at all.

"There is more," she blurted out.

Cecily's eyebrows rose.

"I ran into him in Hyde Park, while taking an um... detour coming home."

"Oh, this gets more interesting by the moment." Sophia's enthusiasm was not to be dashed.

"In my gentleman's garb." Rhoda waited for this to sink in. "I was dressed as a gentleman when I came across my unofficial, formerly official, now former officially unofficial fiancé."

Must she spell it out for them?

"He knows I was going to place the bet. He knows that I didn't have enough faith in his abilities to resolve our difficulties on his own."

"But you didn't." Cecily stated the obvious. "Place the wager, that is. You walked away, incredible character on your part, might I add."

"I told him I didn't go through with it, but he was so very upset. It was as though by doubting him, I'd killed any feelings he ever had for me." And broken her heart at the same time.

"But what is a lady to do?" Sophia burst out of her chair, throwing her hands into the air.

"He was so… disappointed that I'd considered going against his wishes. It was as though he didn't even want to look at me after that. He put me in a hackney and sent me away."

"Well, that is easily remedied." Cecily spoke matter-of-factly. "Nothing a conversation cannot repair."

"I hesitate to agree that it will be that simple, Cece." Rhoda couldn't shake the look of defeat she'd seen on his face when he closed the hackney door. She honestly wasn't sure it would make any difference anyhow. He'd wanted her absolute faith, her wholehearted trust. Which, to be honest, needled her. Both their futures were at stake; why should they only do this his way? He ought to have heard her out at the ball. He ought to have been willing to consider her ideas. She wasn't a complete nincompoop, after all.

Men and their fragile egos!

In a matter of twenty seconds, she went from utter heartbreak to exasperated frustration. Why should she feel guilty?

She was happy she hadn't placed the bet. She wasn't going to let him win anyhow. Holy heck, but she wasn't going to let anybody win! They could wait until the end of time, blasted bastards, every one of them.

JUSTIN WASN'T ANGRY with Rhoda nearly so much as he was disgusted with his own failings.

The person he'd thought he was, no longer seemed to exist. He'd considered himself a man of God. Did men of God lust after young women, sinning with them over and over again in their thoughts? Did they hunger for money? Were they willing to walk in the world's ways at the first hint of trouble?

He'd had her in his arms, alone, in a secluded place in the park. He'd not even realized she was dressed in men's clothing until he'd gone to slide his hand beneath her nonexistent skirt.

Blood surged to his groin at the thought of what her smooth thighs would have felt like. She'd been willing, pressing herself against him.

He wanted Rhododendron Mossant. He wanted to marry her and bed her and not necessarily in that particular order.

Unfortunately, he needed a windfall of money in order to meet the needs of his new responsibilities.

He'd preached about love on more than one occasion. On marriage. How those who had experienced it must have been silently laughing at him. Love, he was coming to realize, consisted of so much more than steady consistency and commitment.

It was messy, turbulent. It muddled one's thoughts and, at the same time, made things crystal clear.

Crystal.

Clear.

But did he have the stomach to do it? Justin broke into a run, as though chased by the hounds of hell themselves. Which was exactly where he might end up when all this was done.

He pumped his arms and ran faster. Perhaps heaven was overrated anyhow.

RHODA HAD THOUGHT showing herself in society would be unbearable. She'd thought the cut directs would wear her down. But her worries had been all for naught. Members of the *ton* were as nosey and curious as they were likely to judge. And they were fickle.

Despite the wager that everyone in London surely knew of by now, invitations continued arriving at her mother's home daily. In fact, they poured in. Every lady, it seemed, was vying to be the hostess of the party where the outcome of the bet was announced, if not won outright.

Madam Chantal had even opened up her schedule so that Rhoda would be wearing one of her newest creations when the moment eventually came about.

Tonight, she wore an emerald green taffeta creation, enhanced with gold lace overlay. She'd given in to Madam Chantal, even, and showed more bosom than she had in the past. Not a lot more, but enough to feed the rebellion growing inside of her.

She would have laughed at it all if she wasn't so upset over Lord Carlisle's noticeable absence. He'd not called upon her. He'd not sent any flowers, and when she did manage to catch sight of him across a ballroom floor, he barely held her gaze, nodding grimly and then finding something else altogether more interesting.

Someone else.

He'd not danced with her once in the week since they'd had their… disagreement.

He'd danced numerous times with a handful of heiresses. Their mothers had fawned over him while the daughters clung to his arms.

The arms that had previously wound themselves around her.

Rhoda recognized her feelings. She could even give a name to them. In fact, the color of her dress was quite appropriate.

Jealousy so powerful, it was likely to turn her eyes green.

"Miss Mossant."

Rhoda turned. One of the footmen stood before her and bowed. "The Duchess of Prescott insists she speak with you now but cannot enter, she says, as she is in mourning."

"Sophia?" But what could possibly be so very important? Was baby Harriette ill? "Where is she?"

"She is outside, at the edge of the gardens, by the fountain. She asks that you meet her there immediately. Alone."

For a moment, Rhoda hesitated at his final word. *Alone?* Why ever would Sophia insist she go alone? Rhoda scrubbed at the back of her neck.

"She says it is urgent, Miss."

If Sophia needed her then she must go. "By the fountain?" She vaguely remembered seeing it earlier from the terrace. And she remembered it from before. From that first ball of the Season.

The Crabtrees liked to host the first and the last.

"Very well. If I don't return shortly, will you please tell Mrs. Mossant, my mother, where I have gone?"

A gleam sparkled in the man's eyes, but he nodded. Rhoda didn't have time to mull over this strange request. Sophia would not send for her if it was not truly important.

Oh, how she hoped nothing was wrong with the baby. She and Dev had already experienced enough tragedy to last a lifetime.

Rhoda stepped nonchalantly toward the French doors. When Cecily caught her gaze, she smiled wanly.

Sophia had asked her to come alone. Otherwise, she would have gladly snagged Cecily away from the older baron who seemed to be monopolizing her attention.

The air outside was warm. June was just a week away and soon most everybody would be retreating to the country.

What would happen to the wager when nobody won it? Surely, it would not persist into a second Season.

Oh, Lord, she hoped not.

The sounds of the fountain grew louder as Rhoda made her way along the cobblestone pathway. This really was a lovely garden. If she weren't so worried about Sophia, she might have taken a moment or two to enjoy it.

"Soph?" she called out. Water poured from the spout at the tips of Lucifer's wings. In the moonlight, the face danced beneath the water, making it appear almost lifelike.

Such a dramatic sculpture, really. She preferred this one to others she'd seen with nothing but cherubs. But where was Sophia?

"Soph?" she called out again, making her way around the concrete pool.

"Ah, Miss Mossant."

Not again!

Lord Kensington really needed to seek out some other

means to fill his coffers.

When he strode toward her menacingly, she realized the missive had been a ruse. "Stay away from me," she ordered him, but he continued approaching her, almost like a panther preparing to pounce.

He jerked his head toward the trees. "I have witnesses watching nearby. Tonight is the night. I can't risk the Season ending, you see. It has to be tonight."

Rhoda bit her lip, real fear slithering down her spine. At the same time, anger surged through her core and into her limbs.

She would not let him win.

She would not.

She turned her head frantically. "Sophia?" she called out once more, hoping against hope that her friend truly awaited her nearby.

Flavion laughed but then grew serious. He was but three feet away from her. She would have backed up farther, but the backs of her knees pressed against the stone wall that encompassed the pool.

"It's not just the money, you know. Because of you and your friends, people laugh at me everywhere. They may not do it to my face, but they all believe I am incapable."

"Surely, that doesn't matter!" But she ought to know better. Flavion's masculine pride would have been devastated by such rumors.

"You'll swear to all of them for me. You'll tell them I'm the best you ever had. You'll tell them what a wonderful lover I am." Had he gone mad? But no, his eyes appeared more hooded than usual. He did not appear completely steady on his feet.

How foxed had he become before coming to undertake this diabolical mission?

"Relax, Miss Mosssannt." Oh, yes, he'd had more than

just a few. "And enjoy."

"Never!" She could only imagine the harm it would do to her mother and her sisters.

And what Justin would think of her.

"I won't do it," she asserted.

And then he lunged toward her.

He'd not timed his attack well, however, and Rhoda managed to slip just out of his reach before he could latch onto her.

His momentum tumbled him into the pool. She would not wait around for him to have another opportunity. Nor for the others who were hiding to come forth.

The path she'd only just been admiring for its beauty now became her roadway to safety. Why did the manor suddenly seem so much farther away?

Heavy footsteps pounded the ground behind her, pushing her to lengthen her stride. Likely one of Flavion's witnesses. What would he do if he caught up with her? Take her back to Flavion? Take her for himself?

She hated this! She hated all of this so very much. She wanted to cry but knew that she needed the safety of others.

A stitch formed in her side. Such a man would not be stopped. She could go to her hosts, tell them of his actions, but she knew they would do nothing about it. They would blame her for walking alone in the garden.

Even if they believed her, even if they wanted to. Nobody would challenge an earl.

Likely, her own father would merely laugh at her plight. He'd probably placed bets of his own on her.

A sob tore from her at the thought. She'd never be safe. She'd never be afforded the protection of a respected lady.

She wanted to leave London tonight and never return.

She felt so alone. So very alone.

CHAPTER TWENTY-SEVEN

Not Again!

JUSTIN WOULD GO to her today, this afternoon. He'd make his proposal. He tipped his hat to an elderly lady as he sauntered along the pavement.

Again. He'd propose again, but this time refuse to accept no for an answer. Over the past eight days, he'd done his best to leave her alone. He'd had to for his plan to work. He'd pour out his heart to her and then they'd head north.

It all sounded so much easier when he put it that way.

Pour out his heart.

He'd decided he'd do whatever it took. This morning, he'd relay his plan to Dev and then abscond with one of Prescott's more well-sprung carriages. The journey to Gretna Green would require two long days of travel, after all.

This was what he ought to have done to begin with.

Mr. Evans opened the door and led him to Dev's study.

Dev was not alone.

Mr. Nottingham and, surprisingly enough, Lord Blakely sat on two of the high-backed chairs around Dev's desk.

A somber mood hung over the trio.

Mr. Nottingham, in particular, looked paler than normal with dark circles etched beneath his eyes.

"Come in, Justin." Dev beckoned him. "I don't suppose

you've heard the news."

As always, in circumstances such as these, Justin's insides froze. Had something happened to Mrs. Nottingham? The child?

"Kensington is dead," Blakely announced bluntly before Justin's imagination could conjure up more horrific tragedies.

"Kensington?" Relief swept through him at the same time he realized the man had been Nottingham's cousin. "My condolences," he managed. The blighter had been sick in the head. Selfish, dangerous. But he'd also been someone's kin.

Nottingham dipped his head.

Justin had spent hours upon hours praying with those who mourned. He hoped to God they didn't expect this of him today.

"What happened?" Probably another duel. The rogue hadn't much caution when it came to offending papas and brothers.

And likely, husbands.

"Drowned. In the Crabtrees' fountain. No one is certain whether or not it was foul play."

Justin had been there last night. Kensington had been deep in his cups. Justin's attention had been focused mostly upon Rhoda. He'd had to make it appear as though he had not been, however, what with her mother's disapproval and other… rather important matters.

Rhoda had left the ball early with Mrs. Mossant. He'd not seen them depart but Lady Crabtree had informed him when he'd become worried.

The last he'd seen her, she'd been heading for the terrace.

She'd been alone, and Justin had intended to follow her but been caught up by the mother of one of the heiresses.

By the time he'd rid himself of her fawning, he'd lost her.

Rhoda had not been on the terrace. He'd assumed she'd returned inside and was lost in the crush.

He suppressed a shiver at the thought that she'd been alone in the garden.

It would not be the first time she'd had to fend the desperate earl off.

"When was he discovered?" Justin intentionally made himself sound only mildly interested.

He dismissed any foreboding the news brought with it. Kensington had made more than his fair share of enemies.

"A gardener came across him just after dawn." Nottingham stared into the bottom of his glass. "Face down in the water."

"No bruises? Or injury?"

"A bump on the head," Dev answered this time. "And Justin..." Oh, hell. Dev's voice contained a warning of sorts. "The last person he was seen with was Miss Mossant."

It was as though all the air in his lungs was sucked out in the fraction of a second. Justin met Dev's gaze, both of them remembering the revelation she'd made at Eden's Court.

"Sophia is readying to leave, as is Lady Blakely and Mrs. Nottingham. She'll need her friends."

He could not wait. He had to go to her.

Now.

Even if she'd done nothing to merit suspicion, she would need his support.

And if the opposite were true, she'd need him even more. "If you'll pardon me." Justin dashed out the door without another word. He hardly even noticed the startled glance from Mr. Evans when he ran through the foyer to the entrance and flew out the door.

What happened? Had Kensington succeeded in harming her this time? It had been the last ball of the Season; he would have been desperate.

And Rhoda was not completely vulnerable. She would have fought.

It took a moment for him to orient himself as to her residence. He'd not have a mount readied. He could move much faster on foot.

The notion that another tragedy might be too much for her to cope with terrified him.

Why hadn't he moved more quickly?

He jumped across a pile of steaming manure. Even Mayfair couldn't avoid some aspects of daily living. Dodging women carrying parasols and gentlemen clipping along with their canes, all Justin could think about was getting to her.

She'd looked more beautiful than ever last night. He'd wanted to talk with her, dance with her, hold her in his arms… but he had been forced to console himself with the knowledge that he'd have her alone in a carriage the following afternoon. They'd elope and return just before the Season officially ended. Just before all of Mayfair exited the city in pursuit of the cleaner air they'd enjoy at their various country estates.

He brought himself up short at her doorstep, breathing heavily, and pounded on the door.

The butler took his card and asked him to wait.

What if she wouldn't see him? What if she sent him away?

"Right this way, my lord." The butler's announcement jolted him from his concerns.

At the mere thought of seeing her again, away from the prying eyes of the *ton*, his heart raced.

God help him, but his attraction to this woman knew

no bounds.

Sun drenched the drawing room, allowing him to drink her beauty in unimpeded.

"Justin?" She rose as he entered. "Lord Carlisle?"

She looked pale, tired even, but not overly distraught. At a sudden loss for words, he bowed low but refused to refer to her formally. "Rhododendron." His mouth twisted into a smile at her exasperated expression.

"I..." She trailed off. "Won't you sit down? You are out of breath. Did you *run* here?"

"I needed to make sure you were all right." Hopefully, her calm demeanor indicated her lack of involvement with whatever befell Lord Kensington and not something else.

"Why would I not be all right?" She seemed only a little confused. "What have you heard?"

Those eyes of hers. He wanted them to smile at him again. He wanted them to gaze at him with passion-filled longing. He swallowed hard.

"You have heard the news, have you not?" At her blank stare, he continued, "About Lord Kensington."

She narrowed her eyes. "Lord Kensington is a worthless toad. He's not worth the space he takes up on this earth."

This comment surprised him.

She hadn't heard, then.

"He'll not be taking space—above ground, anyhow—for much longer. He was found dead this morning."

All the blood seemed to drain from her lovely complexion. No pink, no hint of cream. "How? What happened? Was it another duel?"

He was impressed that she didn't show any sort of glee at his demise. The bastard had done his fair share to discredit both her and her friend, Mrs. Nottingham.

"Dead. Found in the Crabtrees' fountain early this morning."

He'd not thought it possible, but she appeared to go even whiter, her skin appearing translucent almost. "They believe he drowned last night. There is doubt as to whether it was an accident or foul play."

She raised one hand to cover her mouth and stared back at him with horrified eyes.

Her response gave him cause to believe he'd been right to suspect the blighter's death had something to do with her. "Did he attack you again last night?"

She was shaking her head but not in answer to his question. "I didn't mean to! Oh, dear God, I didn't mean to! Tell me this isn't happening again!"

Justin crossed the carpet and dropped down beside her on the loveseat. Nothing in the world would stop him from holding her right now.

She didn't need to tell him it had been an accident. He didn't need for her to tell him she had been defending herself.

"Hush, hush." He tucked her head into his chest and rubbed his hands up and down her back. "This isn't your fault. Even if he died at your hands. I know, by God, I know with everything inside of me that it isn't your fault."

"But I didn't believe in you!" she wailed into his shirtfront. "I broke into White's with every intention of forging your name. How can you believe in me now? And after everything I've told you about Dudley Scofield."

He hushed her again, his lips finding the gentle curve of her cheek. "I'll always believe in you. Always."

And then her arms wound around his neck. "You cannot!" she moaned but clutched at him even more tightly.

He'd waited a lifetime for her. For this woman.

He'd fought his attraction from the very beginning, attributed it to an ungodly lust.

He was a fool!

A God damned supercilious fool!

He'd listened to gossip. A part of him had even blamed her for his own traitorous physical response to her. She'd done nothing to deserve the treatment she'd received. At the hands of others, and, by God, by himself.

"Forgive me," he begged as his lips captured hers. Ah, sweet. Nectar of the gods.

She sobbed. "No. How can you forgive me?"

His fingers soothed hot tears away. This woman. She was everything. Without her, he was nothing.

His hands ached to touch every inch of her skin. He needed to worship her. He'd beg her forgiveness for the remainder of his days. His mouth left hers, searching, craving her feminine curves. He gently bit down on the lobe of her ear, lust jolting him when she arched herself closer.

"My sweet, sweet girl," he murmured against the pulse beating frantically beneath his lips.

How had he managed to wait for so long?

When a warm small hand began stroking the material covering his manhood, he thought he'd died and gone to heaven.

JUSTIN HAD COME to her. Finally. All the need, all the pent-up emotion she'd tried to ignore broke free. "Justin," she murmured back, vaguely aware of the endearments he whispered against her skin. She tugged at his cravat, as hungry to devour him as he seemed for her.

In his arms, she could ignore the horrifying thought that she'd killed another man. In his arms, she could pretend her future wasn't in such peril. She would take this moment. She would embrace it with all of her heart.

She lay back on the settee, exulting in the weight of him on top of her, between her thighs. Both their movements had become frantic, urgent. Her skirts had made their way around her waist, his pantaloons unbuttoned. "I need you," he gasped, his lips latching onto her breasts.

"Now." She clutched him against her. So much pleasure spiraling with just a hint of pain. Was this love?

It was.

It was one part of it. It was the earthly, necessary part of love that wasn't discussed in polite circles.

His hand touched her, fondled her, and slid partway inside. And she wanted more.

She struggled to lower his breeches and smalls, caught up as though starving for him. "Now," she commanded again and clasped her legs around him.

He removed his hands and settled between her thighs. "Sweet, sweet flower of mine."

She could barely talk, and he was reciting poetry.

And then even those thoughts evaporated as he lunged himself forward, filling places she never knew she had. Touching her deep within.

He withdrew and then drove forward again. She arched and met him with all her need. "Justin. Yes." Her voice left her in whimpers.

And then they were moving together, like a great orchestra, building, slowing, louder, softer, all the while knowing something wonderful awaited them both.

"Rhoda, are you in here? There is a magistrate here to ask a few quest—Oh, my heavens!" Her mother's discordant shriek effectively brought all thoughts of crescendo to a screeching halt.

CHAPTER TWENTY-EIGHT

Interrogation

"RHODA! LORD CARLISLE!"

The words sliced through Rhoda's passion-clouded mind and, at the same time, Justin was tugging at his pantaloons and pulling her dress down.

As quickly as they'd been interrupted, the door slammed closed.

"Tell me that did not just happen." Rhoda groaned into his shoulder. Mortification set in along with disappointment.

And frustration.

A tender kiss landed on her forehead.

He was inside of me!

And Mother saw us!

"Are you all right?" He'd kept his arms around her, but the door could open again any minute. And then one word her mother had uttered struck an even greater fear.

"Magistrate. The magistrate is here." Her voice raised an octave or two, and she burst off the settee. Why was this happening to her? Nervous energy surged through her as she paced across the room. Ought she to run? Could she escape? She'd been the last person on earth to see Flavion Nottingham—an earl, for God's sake—alive!

"The magistrate." She came to a halt and moaned the word this time as Justin sat watching her. "What should I do?"

Tucking his shirt back into his breeches, he stood and crossed to her side. He looked so handsome, all ruffled and serious. She wished she could take the time to appreciate the fact.

"Did you strike him? Tell me everything that happened, exactly as you remember it." He took her by the elbow and lowered them both back to the settee. Sitting this time. With their clothes on.

She glanced anxiously at the door. "But they are returning."

"Tell me quickly." He rested his elbows on his knees but regarded her closely.

As coherently as possible, she described the events of the night before. The more she said, the more she sensed him relaxing. And just as she finished her narrative, a tentative knock sounded at the door.

"Rhoda?" Sophia!

"Tell them exactly what you have told me," Justin whispered in her ear. "You have done nothing wrong."

She nodded at his words. "Come in," she croaked.

Her face burned. Who had seen them? Who all had witnessed their lovemaking?

She wanted to bury her hands in her face at the sympathetic look on Sophia's.

"Would you like to withdraw to your chamber for a moment?" Sophia crossed to her and cast an apologetic glance toward Justin.

Her lover.

What had Sophia asked? Her chamber? Oh, no. "I'd rather get this over with now, if it's all the same to… everyone else."

"If you are certain?" Sophia stepped forward and began fussing with Rhoda's hair, removing a few pins and then inserting them again.

It would be more seemly, Rhoda supposed, to change her gown. And perhaps remove some of the wetness that remained on her thighs.

But no. She did not want to delay her reckoning. "I'm certain."

Her mother entered, looking more flustered than Rhoda could ever remember, followed by Prescott and an unfamiliar, very official-looking gentleman.

Justin squeezed her hand in reassurance.

"Rhoda, this is Mr. Bradley." Her mother glanced around nervously as though making certain nothing in the room was out of place. And then she stilled and clutched her hands together in front of her. "He has a few questions for you, about last night. The most horrible tragedy has taken the life of the Earl of Kensington, and he believes you might have been a witness."

"I'll handle this. If you don't mind, Mrs. Mossant." Mr. Bradley interrupted her mother and turned to make a quick bow in her direction.

"May I present you to the Earl of Carlisle," Rhoda supplied, doubting anyone else was considering proper introductions.

"I am Miss Mossant's fiancé," Justin added.

Warmth spread through her, but also disappointment. This was never the way she'd intended to become engaged. Without her consent, before her mother and one of London's disapproving magistrates.

By the look on the official's face, he'd been witness to... Oh, dear God, she couldn't really even think the words in her own head.

"My lord." Mr. Bradley's gaze flicked toward Justin in irritation. "I've a few questions for Miss Mossant?" He looked as though he'd like to have interrogated her without an audience but did not have the temerity to ask a duke, a duchess, and an earl to leave.

And her mother. She could not forget her mother.

"Please, sit down." Rhoda gestured toward the sitting area. Heat rushed to her face when she glanced at the loveseat, where Justin had been lying atop her… inside of her.

She noticed that everybody avoided that particular piece of furniture, leaving it for her and Justin to take.

Her fiancé.

Mr. Bradley removed a small notepad from his coat and then stared at her with a frown. "You were a guest at the Crabtrees' ball last night?"

She glanced sideways at Justin, who nodded in encouragement.

Just tell them the truth, he'd told her.

"Yes." She licked her lips, which had suddenly gone dry. That wasn't so hard.

"Can you please tell me where you were at approximately half-past midnight? The set after the supper dance?"

Ah, not quite so simple. "I was sitting with the wallflowers."

"But not for long, isn't that right, Miss Mossant?"

"No, not for long," she agreed. In a fit of exasperation, she was tempted to blurt the story out. He seemed to want to do this his way, however, and she didn't wish to draw his ill will any more than she already had.

"You went outside, for a walk, alone? Is that not correct?"

"I received a missive," she explained, unwilling to allow that detail to pass. Of course, under normal circumstances she wouldn't have gone out walking alone in the dark at such a late hour. Especially in light of everything that had already happened this Season.

His eyebrows rose. Ah, so she was telling him something he didn't already know. "A footman, at least I believed him to be a footman, told me that Sophia, er, that Her Grace, the Duchess of Prescott," she flicked a look toward Sophia, "needed to meet with me immediately. That it was urgent."

"Oh, no!" Sophia seemed horrified that someone had used her in their ruse. Prescott reached over and covered his wife's hand.

"And did you send any such missive?" The magistrate turned on Sophia now.

"Of course not! I'm in mourning! I could not attend a ball. Even if I could, I'd never put Rhoda into a situation like that." She frowned at the magistrate's impertinent question.

"Please tell me what you did next, Miss Mossant." He turned his questioning back to Rhoda.

Next? "I walked toward the meeting place. The fountain. Where the servant told me the duchess would be waiting."

The studious man wrote something in his notebook. "Did you encounter anyone on your way there?"

What on earth would that have to do with it? "No." And then she reached into her memory. Had she? It was difficult to recall what she'd seen while rushing to meet Sophia. Mostly she'd just been concerned about getting to her friend.

"No," she repeated.

"Are you certain?"

"No. I mean, yes. I'm certain that I didn't encounter anyone... I think." Likely, she would have asked them to come along with her. She'd had a feeling something was off.

She should have listened to it.

Mr. Bradley lowered his gaze and glowered at her.

"And when you reached the fountain, was anyone there?"

Rhoda shook her head. "I called out for Sophia. Twice, I think. And then Flave—Lord Kensington appeared."

"So, you were on familiar terms with the late earl? You addressed him by his Christian name? Had the two of you been intimate before?"

"I was not on familiar terms with Flavion. I mean. Well. He married Cecily last year, Mrs. Nottingham, but not really. He'd only done it for her money and once she found out, she didn't want to be married to him. We all hated him, actually, so we talked about him as though... I have *never* been on intimate terms with Lord Kensington!" How dare he insinuate such a thing!

Prescott dropped his head into his hands while Sophia watched her earnestly. "Rhoda would *never*!" her loyal friend inserted quite emphatically.

"You hated him?" The magistrate held steady.

"We all did! Of course, I would never do... that... with Fl—Lord Kensington! I would never!"

At which, Mr. Bradley raised his brows. Oh, yes, he'd just witnessed... as had her mother... and Sophia, and oh, heaven's, likely the duke had as well.

"*Not with Flavion Nottingham*! Not willingly. Not ever." Of this, she was certain.

Mr. Bradley narrowed his gaze again, and she felt Justin stiffen beside her. "The Duchess of Prescott did not set a meeting with my fiancée last night." Surely, Justin would bring this impertinent gentleman back to the matter at hand.

"But Lord Kensington *had*," the magistrate continued.

Rhoda nodded. "Yes."

"Had you planned to meet him there?"

"Did I not just explain to you that I thought Her Grace wished to meet me there?" He was making her angry.

Justin squeezed her hand again.

"What did Lord Kensington say to you?"

What had he said?

A frown pinched her forehead as she pondered the question. She remembered being angry. She remembered feeling foolish for having gone out there alone.

What had Flave said? Something threatening? She'd known he was up to no good.

"He did speak to you, did he not?"

Rhoda rubbed her head. "I think he said something about running out of time to win the wager."

"You *think*? You do not remember exactly? Ah, yes, you are the young woman who inspired the infamous wager this spring. You really should not put yourself in such circumstances, Miss Mossant. A woman invites such attentions—"

"I beg your pardon." Her mother burst from her chair. Prescott rose as well. "My daughter had nothing to do with that wager. Despite what you might think you may have witnessed here today, Miss Mossant is a lady of quality, and I insist you treat her as such."

Rhoda swallowed hard. She could not remember ever seeing her mother so angry at anyone other than her father. Prescott took hold of her mother's arm and lowered her into her seat again.

"I rather suggest you keep such comments to yourself, Mr. Bradley." Justin looked ready to pounce on the beady little man if he uttered so much as one additional word of… advice.

After an uncomfortable pause, the magistrate persisted. "Had you been drinking spirits, Miss Mossant?"

His question confused her. What did her refreshments have to do with Flavion's death?

"I don't understand."

"Is it possible that you were inebriated? Had you perhaps consumed a few too many glasses of champagne? Your memory seems to be failing you."

"I drank lemonade." She glared at him. One did not always remember every single detail to every situation. People remembered the big things. And how it made them feel.

"Very well." The magistrate cleared his throat. "You did not think to return to the manor at that time?"

Of course, she had! Did he think she was an idiot? "He frightened me. This was not the first time he'd attempted to..." Suddenly, she felt like crying. "He wanted me to attest to his manhood. Not only so he could win the bet... And I refused. And then he made a move to grab me." She remembered how quickly he'd staggered forward. "He lunged at me."

"Did you hit him with anything? Did you shove him?"

She'd stepped to the side.

All she'd done was step to the side.

"He lurched. I moved, and his momentum carried him into the fountain." It was as though a ton of bricks lifted off of her.

"You did not fight him?"

She shook her head. "I moved. He fell into the water, and I ran."

"You didn't so much as touch him." More a statement than a question from Justin. Of course, he'd realized this when she had told him in a rush. He'd told her to just tell the truth.

She glanced at him with a wobbly smile. "I didn't so much as touch him."

"Did the earl say anything after he fell into the water? Did you ascertain that he was not injured?"

"Surely, you're joking?" She'd had quite enough.

"No, Miss Mossant. I am quite serious."

"When Lord Kensington moved to attack me, my only thoughts were on escape. He'd said he had a witness nearby, and I feared I wouldn't get away. I did not care that he had fallen into the water. I did not care if he'd hit his head or hurt himself in any way." She leveled him with an unwavering stare. "I did not care if he was dead or alive."

For all of thirty seconds, all that could be heard in the room was the ticking of the clock sitting on the mantel.

"But you never touched him," Prescott reiterated.

"All I could think was to escape his touch. No. I did not *touch* him."

"Did you see this witness Lord Kensington referred to? Do you know who it was?"

She'd thought whoever it was would take chase. She'd almost felt somebody behind her. But she'd never seen anyone else, in fact. She shook her head. "No."

"Do you have any further questions, Mr. Bradley?" Rhoda had never heard such an edge of steel in Justin's voice, even when she'd told him what she and Emily had done at Eden's Court.

When the other man didn't answer right away, Justin rose, as did Prescott.

Sophia remained seated but sent a conspiratorial glance in Rhoda's direction. Ah, yes, her mother would wish to have a… word. *Don't leave me, Sophia!*

"We'll see you to the door then." Justin had firmly taken matters in hand. "If you ladies will excuse us."

When Mr. Bradley didn't protest, Prescott and Justin led him out of the drawing room, firmly closing the door behind them.

When the room fell silent at their departure, Rhoda dared to glance toward her mother.

"Oh, Rhoda. Well done."

Not the words she'd expected. Sophia had withdrawn a parchment fan and was waving it in front of her face.

"Mother?"

"I'll admit to nearly suffering apoplexy when I opened the door. That Lord Carlisle must do an abundance of riding…"

Sophia's fan waved even faster.

"I thought you did not want for me to be betrothed." What was her mother up to?

"Well, if you were betrothed then every gentleman with half a brain would be betting on Carlisle. We wouldn't want that, now, would we?"

Had the world tipped upside down? What was her mother talking about? "Don't tell me, Mother…"

"Well, yes. I admit it was something of a risk."

"You? Wagered? On your own daughter's…?"

Her mother broke into a huge grin. "And there were witnesses, by God. Not only Prescott and Her Grace." She gestured toward Sophia. "But a magistrate! A man of the law!"

She could not believe her own mother…

Did that mean?

"But how? When?"

"I probably shouldn't tell you this, but Cecily's father, Mr. Findlay, posted the wager on my behalf. Trustworthy gentleman for certain. Had his man of business draw up a contract for me so that it was all duly documented. And as to when, why the very day you planted the idea in my brain."

Rhoda lifted both hands to clutch the sides of her head.

"I, too, have a confession." Sophia's meek statement could barely be heard.

Surely not.

"When you told us that you hadn't placed the bet, well, I asked Dev..."

She had! "You and Prescott wagered as well?"

At this information, her mother looked more than a little chagrinned.

"There was a trust set aside for Lord Carlisle, by Dev's father. Carlisle had refused to take possession of it numerous times so Dev, well... decided to put it to use." Sophia shrugged. "All of the winnings will go to you and Carlisle, of course."

Rhoda blinked. "Of course."

"And the money I put up was to have been your dowry," her mother said. "So, of course, those winnings are yours and Carlisle's as well."

They all turned when the door opened. Behind Prescott, Rhoda could hardly believe her eyes at the sight of Emily and Lord Blakely, as well as Cecily and Mr. Nottingham.

But no Justin.

"Rhoda!" Emily barreled into the room, dressed prettily in a periwinkle blue muslin day dress, with what looked to be a new pair of spectacles perched upon her upturned nose. "I am married! And I am so happy! Tell me you are just as happily engaged! Oh, and Cecily is going to be a countess after all! Did you realize that, what with Flavion spending the night in the Crabtrees' fountain? Probably over imbibed if I were to take a gander at it. Can you believe it? I'm happily married! As is Blakely, right, Marcus?" And then she giggled unapologetically.

Rhoda had forgotten what a whirlwind of chaos Emily could bring to any situation. First and foremost, she squeezed Emily with all the strength she could muster. "You are not angry with me? For not staying to your plan? For not marrying Lord Blakely?"

This drew even more laughter from her friend.

Of course, Emily was not angry with her for that. Rhoda's mind struggled to keep up with all that was happening.

"And you are happy? Oh, I am so happy that you are happy!"

"And Cecily is a countess!" At Emily's reminder, all eyes turned toward Cecily and her husband. Mr. Nottingham's lips were pinched around the mouth and Cecily was shaking her head.

"I don't want to be a countess again! Must I?" Oh, but she must. Rhoda shook her head. No doubt, this time around would be more satisfying than when she'd been Flavion's countess.

"And, Rhoda, you must accept Lord Carlisle's suit." This from Emily, who obviously hadn't yet heard news of her and Justin's *engagement.* "Marcus has placed a wager on him. Any winnings are to go toward the Carlisle estate. After all, if it wasn't for you jilting him, Marcus would never have...." She flushed and dropped her gaze to the carpet.

"Seemed a decent way to show my gratitude to the vicar for not marrying my wife." Blakely's gaze settled on Emily with more than a little tenderness.

Utter. Chaos.

Had everyone wagered on Lord Carlisle? "Where is he?" She could not contain her curiosity even one second longer. Indeed, he'd yet to have officially proposed.

"He said he had an errand," Prescott answered almost as though such information was an afterthought.

Rhoda's heart lurched into her throat. He'd left her?

Alone?

To face her mother's recriminations? Not that he'd known there were none to come.

"He asked if you'd receive him later this afternoon." A

twinkle sparkled in the duke's eyes.

She would receive him. Oh, yes, she would receive him! "Of course." She nodded with a glance at her mother. And then she looked around to see all of her friends so very happy. They all loved her, and she loved every one of them.

"Oh, Em and Cecily!" Sophia's face burst into pure merriment. "You'll never guess what has happened..."

Whereupon, the men cleared their throats and promptly excused themselves with a promise to return in a few hours' time to collect their wives.

The four women had a great deal to catch up on.

And then Rhoda, well, Rhoda had an earl to receive.

CHAPTER TWENTY-NINE

Earning It

RHODA HAD DONE nothing wrong. When she'd told Justin she'd stepped aside and Kensington had gone tumbling, Justin had felt tremendous relief.

He berated himself for not protecting her sooner. For not putting an end to all this nonsense when they first arrived in London. Hell, he ought to have offered for her before leaving for Eden's Court.

He'd not miss his chance again.

It was over today. All of it. In more ways than one.

He adjusted himself and increased the pace of his stride as he made his way purposefully along the street.

He'd been inside of her. He tried not to conjure the recent euphoric memory. He was already struggling to subdue his urges and didn't need the added encumbrance of having to hide the beast.

A chuckle escaped at the thought.

God, but she'd been more than he ever might have imagined. As though he'd found the missing part of himself.

All the months of longing, yearning, and lusting. The thought that she'd wanted him—Justin White, former vicar and pockets-to-let earl—brought a lump to his throat and a burning sensation to the backs of his eyes.

Rhoda. His Rhododendron.

She'd been through too much this past year. More than

any lady, more than any person, ought ever to have to endure.

Dev had admitted proudly that he'd lie, steal, or even kill for his duchess.

Justin intended to do even worse.

Taking a deep breath, he burst through the doors at White's and marched over to the betting book. The atmosphere was subdued this morning, and the gentlemen present appeared downtrodden. Likely mourning the death of Lord Kensington.

Which was no loss at all.

"The wager has been won!" he calmly informed the employee who kept watch, just loud enough so as to be easily overheard. "And proof can be met with testimony from a Mr. Bradley, the local magistrate."

"By whom?" One of the lords seated near the betting book swiveled his head around from his hand of cards to see who dared to make such a claim.

"By me."

Laughter met his statement. "Weren't you a vicar up until a few weeks ago?" A few of the gentlemen had risen from their seats, however, and approached him curiously.

"Indeed," Justin said proudly. "But now I am Carlisle. And I expect to collect in a timely manner."

"You've got to be jesting." Another familiar-looking gentleman began flipping through the pages of signatures and wagers in the smaller leather book.

"My wager is on the last page," Justin pointed out. "Likely the last one made."

"And mine a few pages before that." Justin had not seen his cousin enter. But of course. Justin nearly burst out laughing. His cousin knew him all too well.

"How do we know he isn't lying?" the card player

asked. "The debt requires proof."

"Witness testimony from a local magistrate ought to be sufficient. I myself would testify but as one who stands to benefit, humbly defer to Mr. Bradley's statements." This from Dev.

"Send for this Mr. Bradley!" someone yelled out and a few of the younger bucks donned hats and made for the door. "And someone pour Lord Carlisle a drink!"

Cheers and groans of disappointment rang through the large parlor as glasses clinked and toasts were made. Likely, they had all anticipated having to wait until the next Season for any outcome.

A few studious-looking gentlemen sat down with pencils and began tallying the totals. Soon enough, they'd discover the bet Justin had placed in the wee hours of the morning.

"To love." Dev lifted his glass. Laughter rang out, but Justin raised his own tumbler along with Mr. Nottingham, Lord Blakely, and a few others nearby. Before he could echo his cousin's toast, murmurs went up around him, and the clinking of glasses echoed off the walls.

"To love," Justin agreed before sending the spirits burning down his gullet.

Love.

His heart raced at the thought. From here, he would go to Prescott House, clean up, and then return to Mrs. Mossant's home to make his official offer.

He'd taken a risk. He'd exposed her to ridicule and dishonored her immeasurably.

He hoped that was enough.

"WHERE IS HE?" Rhoda peered out her window to the street below for the ten thousandth time that afternoon. She'd long since bathed, donned one of her favorite gowns, and had Lucy fix her hair into an attractive style.

Three times.

At first, it had seemed too austere, pulled tightly at her nape. The second time, Lucy had added too many curls. Rhoda had insisted she brush it out and now it was casually piled atop her head with a few loose curls falling to her shoulders.

Likely, the curls would straighten by the time he arrived.

Rhoda wrung her hands in front of her.

The sun was already setting. She wished Prescott was still here. Then she could inquire as to whether he was certain Justin had said he'd be, in fact, returning today and not some other day later this week.

Where was he?

She turned away from the window to stare at herself in the mirror again.

If he didn't come, she would be devastated. Her heart would be broken. Yes, all of that.

But she would go on living. She was no longer afraid of the woman that she was.

A smile crept across her lips as she stared at her own image. He would return though. They would marry.

She would thrive.

"Lord Carlisle is here to see you." Her mother had peered inside the door without knocking. "Do you wish to make him wait?"

Of course, her mother would ask her that.

"He's waited long enough, I think." She pinched her cheeks and then inspected her hair once again. "I shall be right down."

THE DOOR HAD been left open, allowing Rhoda to stare at him unobserved before entering.

He was pacing the floor, dressed differently than he had been earlier in the day. Occasionally, he ran a hand through his thick blond hair.

And he was fidgeting with something in his hands.

At the sight of his rugged profile, she licked her lips.

"Justin."

He didn't turn to look at her right away but tipped his head and stared down at his hands first.

When he did deign to look her way, his expression drew a smile from her. So intense, this man. So sincere and filled with character.

"I must warn you," he finally said. "If you refuse to marry me this time, your reputation will remain in tatters."

She ought to be concerned at such words, but her heart lifted instead.

"Tatters, you say? And why is that, my lord?" She took a few steps forward. The room glowed a golden hue as the sun breathed its last glow before dusk.

"I'm afraid you've been thoroughly compromised at last, and all of London is privy to such information. In fact, the magistrate's account is likely to appear in the *Gazette* tomorrow." He strode across the room and lifted both her hands to his lips. "Along with the announcement of our pending wedding. If you'll have me, that is."

And then he dropped to one knee.

Nothing in the world had prepared her for the feelings she would experience as she watched Justin White kneel before her, grasping her hands, head tilted back so that he might allow nothing but love to flow from that blue gaze of his. "Marry me, Rhoda. Put me out of my misery. Make me the happiest of men. I beg of you."

This was the proposal she'd dreamed of. But even more importantly, this was the man of her dreams.

A man filled with goodness, character, and honesty. A man she could trust her life with, their future children's security, health, and well-being.

A man she loved with all her heart.

"I won the bet." He grimaced. "It was the only thing I could think to do that would convince you of my worth."

She dropped down to the floor before him. "You sacrificed your honor for me." She'd suspected as much but to hear him declare it took her breath away. "For us."

He nodded. "I love you. Now, are you going to put me out of my misery with some sort of answer?"

"I love you, Justin. I would have married you regardless. You didn't need to, you know." But she'd hold onto the fact that he had until her dying day. For she knew what his honor meant to him.

And then she was in his arms, his mouth on hers. "You are such a gift. My prize. My love. I refuse to wait for banns to be read. I'll obtain a special license. I hear that's a benefit of holding a title." His hands were in her hair. They'd both been on their knees but in a matter of seconds lay on the rug together.

"Oh, Justin." She pressed her body against his. She wanted to cry. "I believe my mother is just outside the door."

He froze, and she felt him take in a deep breath. "Of

course."

And then she couldn't keep herself from laughing. "Oh, my love. Ah, my love." She buried her face in the crisp folds of his cravat. "This is killing me."

And then he was laughing, too.

"It is my penance." He kissed the top of her head. "She is in the foyer? You are certain?" One hand was inching the hem of her skirt higher. Rhoda shifted so he could slide his hand beneath it.

"She told me she would join us shortly."

Rhoda's hand drifted down the front of his shirt, and then lower, locating the bulge in his breeches. The very large bulge.

"How shortly?" His hand grazed the tops of her thighs, just above her garters. All the while, he trailed hot kisses across her shoulders, her throat.

Logical thought fled. His mouth igniting an inferno of need…

"Do we have some news in here?" Of course, her mother's voice.

Cold air hit her as Justin began crawling around on the floor. "Absolutely, but my fiancée has dropped the ring I presented to her. Oh, here it is."

And sitting on his heels, Justin was grinning like a fool, holding out the most gorgeous piece of jewelry she'd ever seen. Twisted white gold, dozens of tiny rubies encircling a dazzling diamond, much like a flower. He tilted his head and grimaced. "Closest thing I could find to a rhododendron."

She threw herself into his arms again. *Oh dear, God. Thank you for this man!*

"Looks as though you've located it." Her mother stood looking down at them both. "For a moment, I was concerned that you were attempting to win the wager again."

"Mother!" Rhoda stared at her mother in disapproval. Who was this woman and what had happened to the mother she'd grown up with?

"Ah, no." Justin pushed himself to his feet and then assisted her off the floor as well. "That business can well be considered settled and far behind us."

Her mother laughed. "I doubt the highest wager ever to be won in the history of White's will soon be forgotten. It's interesting, however. A small scandal will attach itself to a woman for life, ruining her. An extravagant, outrageous scandal, however, has lifted her to infamy. You'd be surprised at the pile of invitations we've received this afternoon."

"Really?" Rhoda did not relinquish Justin's hand now that she was standing. Surprisingly, she hadn't considered how all of this would affect her social standing. She ought to have, for Coleus and Holly's sake. All that had mattered was that she not swing from the gallows, and that once allowed to live, she be allowed to do so with the man beside her.

Justin turned and took both of her hands. "Will you come with me for a drive?"

He looked so earnest. She'd do anything he asked her at that moment. "Of course, let me fetch my bonnet." Even the thought of being without him for a few minutes squeezed her heart. "Mother will keep you company until I return."

And then she dashed upstairs, donned her prettiest hat, and descended the stairs again as quickly as possible. All the while, the weight of the ring on her finger assuring her she wasn't dreaming.

"I'm ready." She sounded slightly breathless when she reappeared at the door.

Her mother fussed with the ribbon on her bonnet, and then sent them out the door with a happy sigh.

"I cannot count how many times you and I have been interrupted." Justin assisted her into a carriage. She'd expected a curricle, or something open aired for the drive but appreciated the privacy afforded them in the coach.

She wondered if her mother knew.

Justin joined her on the front facing bench and dropped one arm behind her. "Now. I have another question for you."

He looked smug, much like a cat who'd gotten his canary. She rather liked this expression on his handsome face.

"And once you've asked it, I'll give you an answer." She wouldn't cease to be cheeky, simply because she was to marry.

They gazed into one another's eyes like lovesick fools for nearly a full minute.

Then he reached into his coat pocket. "I have a special license on my person. Are you inclined to a grand wedding, with all your relatives and friends? Or will you multiply my joy today? The driver is taking us to a small church not far from here right now. And at that church, a friend of mine, another vicar, is willing to perform the ceremony."

Was he asking?

"Oh, yes. Oh yes!" She was ready to begin their lives together now. "And where will we go after?" Surely not Prescott House, where she assumed he'd been staying.

"That's a surprise."

It didn't matter where they went together afterward. All that mattered was that they would go together. No shadows lingering over their heads. Just the anticipation of a long life together filled with joy and love. And perhaps a few children.

"I can't believe it." It all dawned on her. She'd hoped and not been disappointed. "Everything has worked out after all."

This man. This man she would spend the rest of her life loving leaned forward and pressed his forehead against hers. "You are no longer a cynic, then?"

This close, she could see tiny lines forming at the edges of his eyes. She also noticed silver flecks hidden in those glorious blue irises.

Was she? A cynic anymore? "I think that would be impossible now. I didn't believe dreams could come true but now…" She shook her head in disbelief. "I do."

"I'm glad." His voice came out gravelly sounding. He cared so much that she believed in dreams.

"Even more importantly. I believe in you."

Ah, he swallowed hard upon hearing those words.

"I love you, Rhododendron." She loved that he called her that. It felt symbolic somehow. As though he loved all of her. Even her ridiculous name.

"I love you, Justin."

"My Rhododendron." His lips found hers. "Finally, mine."

EPILOGUE

Wednesday Afternoon at the Park

THE DUCKS WOULD never forgive them.

Conventional wisdom would dictate one leave very youthful offspring and pets at home, but the four women, dubbed long ago by their husbands to be devilish debutantes, preferred to bring those they loved out into the world. Along with their nurses, of course.

The small dogs were managed by the older children—older meaning nearing the age of five.

Ah, because, yes, Peaches had procreated as well, having given birth to a litter of four miniature versions of herself, ranging from a solid red to the blackest of them all, who sported only a few red spots and who was also the runt.

The Countesses of Blakely, Carlisle, and Kensington had each taken one into their home, leaving the fourth one to go to the Duchess of Prescott. And of course, the Duchess allowed Peaches to visit with her other offspring as often as possible.

As the rather ungainly party descended on the calming shores of the Serpentine, they drew more than their fair share of attention.

Of course, none dared censure them for their behavior. That sort of business was reserved for the nobodies and the upstarts. This collection of titled ladies and gentlemen held some of the highest titles in London. They were not only tolerated but fawned over—children and dogs included.

In fact, a few daring members of the *ton* even deigned to bring their own children along.

The park's custodians no doubt didn't appreciate the additional traffic on Wednesdays, but upon receiving a rather large anonymous donation, no one could complain.

The tallest of the fashionably dressed ladies opened a bag of bread, luring the more alert ducks to waddle out of the water in their direction. A few of the web-footed creatures eyed the dogs warily. Other, more experienced birds had realized their quacks could be as fierce as the short four-legged creatures' barks.

And their bills, even more so.

"I absolutely love this design, Cecily." Rhoda ignored the ducks to more closely examine the embroidery on the avocado green muslin gown that contrasted so vividly with her friend's hair. Although a countess, Cecily hadn't given up designing her own gowns. And Madam Chantal had become even more popular by implementing many of the young Countess's ideas.

"It's one of Stephen's favorites." And then she blushed. How was it possible her friend might blush when referring to her husband of five years? And then Rhoda knew.

"You are increasing again?" After giving birth to their son Finn, Cecily and the earl had failed to produce any more little Nottinghams. Although more than content with her family, her home, and life in general, Cecily had been unable to hide the growing disappointment it had caused from her friends.

A joyful light glowed behind her gaze as she placed one hand over her abdomen.

"How did we miss it?" Emily lowered her spectacles and examined Cecily's midsection. "Good heavens! How have you hidden it from us?"

Cecily laughed. "I didn't want to say anything until I was very certain."

Sophia covered her mouth with her hand, as though keeping a secret at bay.

"Not you, too?" Rhoda felt like giggling.

Sophia nodded. "Dev says he truly doesn't mind having only daughters, but I'd be so happy to have a son. A little boy just like him."

"He'd be spoiled to high heavens by Harriette and Little Lorrie." Although the girls were only two and four, Rhoda had no doubt as to the accuracy of this prediction.

"I'll bring Alistair and Creighton over if you'd like. They could show him how to be a man." Emily's voice carried no small amount of exasperation.

Emily's twins were three, and already as incorrigible as their parents.

Rhoda turned her head toward the grass, where all of the children played together, and smiled. Three children stood out to her more than the others, with their golden-blond hair and exceptional good looks. They all resembled their father, of course. And thank goodness they'd inherited his kindly disposition. Eleanor, nearly four, proudly held tight to Bruno's leading string; Sebastian, two and a half, was studying something in the grass; and the baby, Daniel, waddled unsteadily beside one of the nursemaids who'd come along on this outing.

She never could have hoped to experience such joy.

And then, quite out of nowhere, her Sebastian lifted what appeared to be a long ground worm into the air and held it obnoxiously close to Eleanor's face.

She promptly dropped the leading string, sending Bruno into a desperate flight in the direction of the ducks.

But these ducks were no cowards, especially when an entire bag of bread still awaited them.

In a matter of mere seconds, the peaceful grassy area transformed into a circus of nurses, children, fowl, and small yapping dogs running in circles after one another.

Just as Rhoda moved to jump into the fray, a warm arm wrapped around her from behind. "I'll not have you running after them in your condition."

"But Eleanor's dress!" Rhoda gave a halfhearted tug, but in truth had no desire to escape.

Her husband's breath caressing the skin behind her ears never failed to send tingles down her spine. That and the discreet kiss he'd placed on the sensitive skin there. "Look, see, Dev and Marcus already have the dogs mostly contained. And Mrs. Bobbitt has the children well in hand."

"Cecily and Sophia are increasing as well." Rhoda glanced over her shoulder to stare into her husband's beautiful blue eyes. She never failed to be surprised that they could appear even brighter than the sky.

Justin laughed, causing tiny wrinkles to appear at the corners. "Our children shall never lack friends, that is for certain."

Just as she would not. How lucky they had all been, at that first ball, to have been ignored by most of the gentlemen present. To have been left alone so that they might forge their own very special bond.

"They are more than just friends, Justin." She wondered that her heart did not explode from so much joy. "They are family."

She felt him nod behind her and together they watched the flurry of activity taking place near the edge of the water.

Prescott bent over to swipe one of the puppies away from the mud, and at that moment, a duck took purposeful aim at his ducal backside. Exhibiting more strength than one would attribute to the feathered creature, the poking bill sent the unsuspecting Duke of Prescott flying head first into the pond. Surprisingly, his splash was not all that impressive.

"What on earth are you doing, Dev? People are going to think we're a group of uncivilized urchins." Sophia rushed to her husband and reached out with a gloved hand to assist him out of the water.

"Oh, no!" Rhoda gasped, knowing she could do nothing about what was about to occur.

For the same diabolical duck was now rushing toward Sophia from behind with a decidedly wicked look on his face.

Sophia's fall, accompanied by a high-pitched scream, caused a much greater splash then the duke's had.

"Never a dull moment with all this family." Justin took Rhoda by the arm to lead them toward their muddied cousins. "Not when four devilish debutantes get together."

– The End –

DEAR READERS,

Thank you so very much for experiencing this journey of happily-ever-afters for all of my Devilish Debutantes. But does it really have to end?

Of Course not!

Remember Miss Louella Rose?

Ah, yes. She had her very own reasons for being out of sorts at the Garden Party. Her story will kick off my new series which I've titled, The Not So Saintly Sisters.

On a sober note, I feel it my responsibility to issue a trigger warning for her story.

I never wanted to know so much about the very alarming practice known as cutting. When you discover somebody near and dear to you, however, suffering from an addiction, you absolutely must learn as much about it as possible.

It is often misunderstood, mimicked, and criticized, but I've learned that for those who are truly compelled into self-harm, they cannot control it any more than an alcoholic or overeater.

Even more alarming, the more a cutter dwells on it, the greater the compulsion.

For that reason, I find it necessary to recommend that anyone with cutting compulsions NOT read the following sample chapter of my next book, THE PERFECT DEBUTANTE. Or the book itself.

I've done my best to write an accurate depiction of a young woman who struggles with cutting and the most realistic means she has to overcome it. Although cutting has been referred to by different names throughout history, the compulsion is nothing new.

Know that cutters rarely are suicidal and most leave off the practice in their twenties.

I am not a psychologist, nor an expert in any way. THE PERFECT DEBUTANTE has been written based solely upon my own personally conducted interviews, research, and experience.

And so, I give you the first chapter of:

THE PERFECT DEBUTANTE

(The Not So Saintly Sisters, Book 1)

By Annabelle Anders

CHAPTER ONE

A Little Relief

MISS LOUELLA ROSE huddled on the floor behind the large canopied bed taking up most of her chamber. If her mother took it upon herself to peek inside, she would believe the room to be empty.

Which was exactly what Louella wanted—what she needed.

But Mama would not come now anyhow. She and Papa knew she was not at all pleased with them. Not after Papa had told her his decision, giving her no choice but to consent to the betrothal he'd arranged for her with their neighbor's son.

And they expected her to be grateful! Of all things!

Anger. Frustration. Disappointment. The hopelessness of her situation made her want to be invisible. Black crept into the edges of her vision.

How could they do this to Olivia?

Cowering behind the bed, Louella opened the bottom drawer of the nightstand and reverently withdrew the sewing basket.

The tattered straw and old cloth lining provided a modicum of comfort, in and of itself.

"You are the beauty of this family, Louella. A perfect English Rose. This is your duty. And your mother assures me the marquess is quite handsome. You'll be a duchess someday, gel. Now stop your blathering." Her father's

words had been meant to placate her. A beauty! Perfect?

Louella knew what they saw.

A young girl with an unblemished complexion, chestnut brown hair, and blue eyes with thick lashes.

But it was only her shell.

She was not perfect; she was not beautiful.

Dizziness gripped her.

Closing her eyes a few moments, Louella inhaled deeply before opening them again and unraveling the ribbon from around her wrist. She'd tied the silk loosely, but it managed to leave an imprint on the tender skin nonetheless.

She would use a needle this time. Hopefully, that would be sufficient.

She could not access her abdomen during the daytime. Her stays prevented that well enough.

Rolling her arm to expose the tender skin there, she located an unscarred section and compelled the needle downward. As the sharp point drew a short crimson line, she felt nothing. Was this even her?

She pressed harder the second time, and a thicker line of blood oozed onto her pale, almost translucent skin. A sting. And tingling. Ah, yes. *I'm real.*

And the berating voices swirling in her mind began to subside.

Blood is real.

The blood is mine.

I am real.

She drew another line, this one longer, and just the tiniest bit deeper than the first two. The needle stung. It hurt even.

Her racing heart slowed.

It would be okay. Olivia would understand.

She could now feel the floor beneath her and the frame of the bed digging into her back.

The last cut was shallow, barely a scratch, really.

Her vision cleared.

As she watched the blood flow and begin to congeal, her breathing slowed. Her muscles relaxed, and her bones nearly melted onto the floor. She could almost fall asleep right there. Still holding the needle between her fingers, she dropped her hand to the carpet and tilted her head back, resting it on the side of the bed.

She could do this. She didn't want to, but she could. Papa would insist.

After what might have been a few seconds or several moments, Louella roused herself from the blessed lethargy enough to clean the needle and replace it in the sewing basket.

She then washed her wrist in the wash basin, dried it, and rewrapped the silk ribbon to tie it snugly.

Using her teeth, she managed a fairly decent bow.

Louella had done this before.

The devil didn't dwell inside her.

It was just.

Her.

"YOU WISH ME to marry *Little Louella Rose*?"

Captain Cameron Samuel Benjamin Denning, Marquess of Stanton, barely remembered the girl.

She'd been a child when he left, gallivanting about her father's estate, and often his father's property as well.

He vaguely remembered the older sister… blonde, she'd been on the verge of womanhood, sweet and pretty. But he'd been a cocky bastard at the time. All he'd noticed was that the gel had been cockeyed.

And the younger girl? Louella Rose? She had been all skin and bones, eyes too large for her face, dirt on her dresses, and ah, yes, stringy brown hair. She would have been most unmemorable but for her temper. She'd lobbed an apple at his head on one occasion. He scratched his chin. If memory served him correctly, he'd done something to provoke the attack. He'd been an ass that summer. Hating his father. Hating his father's new family. Hating pretty much everybody, including himself.

"She's not a child anymore," his father said without glancing up from the papers on his desk.

What had the sister's name been? Olive? No, Olivia, Miss Olivia Redfield, oldest daughter of Viscount Hallewell. She'd been closer to him in age.

"Truth be told," his stepmother, the duchess, piped in. "Miss Louella Rose is likely one of the comeliest debutantes in all of England."

Cameron wasn't certain he could believe that. The hoyden had been something of a tomboy, trespassing with her sister almost daily. They'd met with better luck fishing on the ducal lands than their own.

And Cameron had not treated them kindly. Ah, yes, he'd teased the older girl mercilessly for her eye. He winced at the memory.

At the time, he'd barely reached his majority. He'd been an irresponsible youth, willing to do anything to escape his father and all of his ducal expectations.

"What of the older daughter?" Cameron stared out the window, contemplating his past wrongs.

Again, his stepmother supplied the answer. "Something of a spinster. Doesn't move in society, as I understand. Hallewell keeps her well under wraps. I doubt they've brought her with them to London for the Season. If I were to take a guess, I'd say she's probably simple."

His father grunted.

Cameron knew neither of the girls were what attracted his father to such an alliance.

The Hallewell estate sat just south of Ashton Acres. Nestled in the low lands, unkempt and overrun with brush, it was aptly named Geyser Gulch.

But just inside of its borders sat the true prize.

An abandoned mine.

Abandoned and branded as cursed by the current Viscount's father, following a tragic cave-in decades ago. But that wasn't the end of it. No, the damn thing was rumored to be loaded with gold. A few of the men who'd managed to survive the collapse, but not their injuries, had spoken of a thick vein of gold discovered just before the collapse. Ancient tales warned that the cave-in had occurred because the gold had been exposed.

Locals scoffed at the notion of gold in the mine. Never, in the history of the area, had any precious metals been mined profitably.

Viscount Hallewell, like his father before him, believed the mine to be cursed.

He'd adamantly refused to reopen it.

Until now, apparently.

With pockets to let, and a comely daughter at that... Cameron guessed that Crawford, his own father, had finally discovered the bargaining chip to change Hallewell's mind.

His son.

And damnit, upon departing a decade ago, Cameron had promised to marry upon his return. He'd not hated his birthright; he'd simply needed to sow his oats. Such a stupid promise to have made.

"Isn't there a son in the family as well?" Surely, the son would have something to say about all of this. It was his inheritance, after all.

"Not anymore. Died shortly after you left." Cameron's father had no sympathy when it came to others' misfortunes.

Raising his brows, Cam glanced toward the duchess. She would know more about the family.

"His mother, the viscountess, was inconsolable for months. But the boy was always sickly. Nearly drowned but then took sick. I imagine he'd have died of some other malady if not for the accident." She answered the unspoken question. "William, I believe they called him, was only five years old."

Cam rubbed his eyes with the heels of his hands.

All of this seemed rather sudden, and yet, he'd known, before returning, that his father would expect him to marry and set up a nursery. And Cam had promised he'd do just that.

He intended to keep his promise.

Because, as backward as it seemed, the one thing he'd carried with him all those years serving his country had been the burden of guilt.

He'd known his family worried endlessly about him.

Well, not him, per se. The male son. The heir.

For the Duke of Crawford had failed to produce a spare. After bringing five young daughters from her previous marriage, the new duchess had failed to conceive again. Cameron was an older brother to five silly stepsisters.

Yes, the family had spent a good deal of time worrying after his wellbeing.

Hell.

Why the Redfield daughter?

He could only hope she had little memory of him.

Upon reaching his majority, Cam had been filled with

angst. He'd returned from school to discover his father remarried and a house filled with annoying little girls who'd managed only to remind himself of his mother's absence, and the peace she'd always given him.

Cam had responded by drinking, carousing, swiving whatever he was offered, and then ultimately threatening to enlist himself into the British Army.

Which would have been unheard of.

An unmitigated embarrassment to his father.

His father had taken the threat literally, and although it would mean sending his heir off to war, he'd negotiated a bargain with him. With the understanding that when Cam reached the age of thirty he would return home and marry the bride of his choosing, the Duke of Crawford had purchased Cam an officer's commission in the British Navy.

Thirty had seemed a lifetime away.

Cam brushed a hand through his hair. What an ass he'd been.

Damn his younger self.

"I'm to visit the youngest daughter tomorrow?" he asked. "And she is agreeable? How old is she now?"

He certainly wouldn't force the poor girl to marry him if she was unwilling. He would make his offer, formally, dispassionately, but… pleasantly. He would not insist, however, and by God, he wouldn't beg.

"She's ten and nine. A most suitable age. We'll visit their townhouse together. For tea," his stepmother responded to his first question.

"Of course, she's agreeable. Damned fool girl she'd be if she wasn't," his father answered his second question.

A social climber, then.

Hell, maybe she'd forgotten him completely!

"Tomorrow, then? At tea," he asked as though announcing his own execution.

"She's a lovely girl." The duchess patted Cam's father on the shoulder. "We'll allow the two of you a few moments alone, so that you can be certain you'll get on well together."

Well then.

Damn.

"Better yet, you'll have a chance to renew your acquaintance this afternoon, at the Snodgrass Party. I wouldn't think the Redfields would miss it."

Perhaps that would make tomorrow easier. Perhaps he could charm her into forgetting his actions before he'd gone off to war. His stupid and churlish behavior.

Might make for a less awkward proposal, anyhow.

Preview End

Acknowledgements

Thank you to Rebecca, the voice inside my head who keeps me going every single day. To Tracy, Kay and Manny for all of your edits, helping me prepare this book for public consumption. To my Beta Readers, Mary, Debbie, and Cassandra, for pointing out that which needs to be pointed out.

And as always, to my husband, for his unfailing support and encouragement.

I love keeping in touch with readers and would be thrilled to hear from you! Join or follow me at any (or all!) of the social media links below!

Amazon: amazon.com/Annabelle-Anders/e/B073ZLRB3F

Bookbub: bookbub.com/profile/annabelle-anders

Website: annabelleanders.com

Facebook Author Page: facebook.com/HappyWritingGirl

Facebook Reader Group: A Regency House Party: facebook.com/groups/AnnabellesReaderGroup

Twitter: @AnnabellReadLuv

Read More by Annabelle Anders

Devilish Debutantes Series
Hell Hath No Fury
Hell in a Hand Basket
Hell Hath Frozen Over *(Novella)*
Hell's Belle
Hell of a Lady
Lord Love a Lady Series
Nobody's Lady
A Lady's Prerogative
Lady Saves the Duke

Devilish Debutantes Series

Hell Hath No Fury (*Devilish Debutante's, Book 1*)
To keep the money, he has to keep her as well…

Cecily Nottingham has made a huge mistake.

The marriage bed was still warm when the earl she thought she loved crawled out of it and announced that he loved someone else.

Loves. Someone else.

All he saw in Cecily was her dowry.

But he's in for the shock of his life, because in order to keep the money, he has to keep her.

With nothing to lose, Cecily sets out to seduce her husband's cousin, Stephen Nottingham, in an attempt to goad the earl into divorcing her. Little does she realize that Stephen would turn out to be everything her husband was not: Honorable, loyal, trustworthy…Handsome as sin.

Stephen only returned to England for one reason. Save his cousin's estate from financial ruin. Instead, he finds himself face to face with his cousins beautiful and scorned wife, he isn't sure what to do first, strangle his cousin, or kiss his wife. His honor is about to be questioned, right along with his self-control.

Amid snakes, duels and a good catfight, Cecily realizes the game she's playing has high stakes indeed. There are only a few ways for a marriage to end in Regency England and none of them come without a high price. Is she willing to pay it? Is Stephen? A 'Happily Ever After' hangs in the balance, because, yes, love can conquer all, but sometimes it needs a little bit of help.

Hell in a Hand Basket (*Devilish Debutante's, Book 2*)
Sophia Babineaux has landed a husband! And a good one at that!

Lord Harold, the second son of a duke, is kind, gentle, undemanding.

Perhaps a little too undemanding?

Because after one chance encounter with skilled rake, Captain Devlin Brooks, it is glaringly obvious that something is missing between Lord Harold and herself... pas-sion... sizzle... well... everything. And marriage is forever!

Will her parents allow her to reconsider? Absolutely not.

War hero, Devlin Brookes, is ready to marry and thinks Sophia Babineaux might be the one. One itsy bitsy problem: she's engaged to his cousin, Harold.

But Devlin knows his cousin! and damned if Harold hasn't been coerced into this betrothal by the Duke of Prescott, his father.

Prescott usually gets what he wants.

Devlin, Sophia and Harold conspire to thwart the duke's wishes but fail to consider a few vital, unintended consequences.

Once set in motion, matters quickly spiral out of control!

Caught up in tragedy, regret, and deceit Sophia and Devlin's love be-comes tainted. If they cannot cope with their choices they may never find their way back once embarking on their journey… To Hell in a Hand Basket…

Hell's Belle (*Devilish Debutante's, Book 3*)
There comes a time in a lady's life when she needs to take matters into her own hands…

A Scheming Minx
Emily Goodnight, a curiously smart bluestocking—who cannot see a thing without her blasted spectacles—is raising the art of meddling to new heights. Why leave her future in the hands of fate when she's perfectly capable of managing it herself?

An Apathetic Rake
The Earl of Blakely, London's most unattainable bachelor, finds Miss Goodnight's schemes nearly as intriguing as the curves hidden beneath her frumpy gowns. Secure in his independence, he's focussed on one thing only: evading this father's manipulating ways. In doing so, ironically, he fails to evade the mischief of Emily's managing ploys.

Hell's Bell Indeed
What with all the cheating at parlor games, trysts in dark closets, and nighttime flights to Gretna Green, complications arise. Because fate has limits. And when it comes to love and the secrets of the past, there's only so much twisting one English Miss can get away with…

Hell of a Lady (*Devilish Debutante's, Book 4*)
Regency Romance between an angelic vicar and a devilish debutante: A must read if you love sweet and sizzle with an abundance of heart.

The Last Devilish Debutante
Miss Rhododendron Mossant has given up on men, love, and worst of all, herself. Once a flirtatious beauty, the nightmares of her past have frozen her in fear. Ruined and ready to call it quits, all she can hope for is divine intervention.

The Angelic Vicar
Justin White, Vicar turned Earl, has the looks of an angel but the heart of a rake. He isn't prepared to marry and yet honor won't allow anything less. Which poses something of a problem… because, by God, when it comes to this vixen, a war is is waging between his body and his soul.

Scandal's Sweet Sizzle
She's hopeless and he's hopelessly devoted. Together they must conquer the ton, her disgrace, and his empty pockets. With a little deviousness, and a miracle or two, is it possible this devilish match was really made in heaven?

Hell Hath Frozen Over (Devilish Debutantes, Christmas Novella)
The Duchess of Prescott, now a widow, fears she's experienced all life has to offer. Thomas Findlay, a wealthy industrialist, knows she has not. Can he convince her she has love and passion in her future? And if he does, cans she convince herself to embrace it?

Nobody's Lady (*Lord Love a Lady Series, Book 1*)
Dukes don't need help, or do they?

Michael Redmond, the Duke of Cortland, needs to be in London—most expeditiously—but a band of highway robbers have thwarted his plans. Purse-pinched, coachless, and mired in mud, he stumbles on Lilly Beauchamp, the woman who betrayed him years ago.

Ladies can't be heroes, or can they?

Michael was her first love, her first lover, but he abandoned her when she needed him most. She'd trusted him, and then he failed to meet with her father as promised. A widowed stepmother now, Lilly loves her country and will do her part for the Good of England—even if that means aiding this hobbled and pathetic duke.

They lost their chance at love, or did they?

A betrothal, a scandal, and a kidnapping stand between them now. Can honor emerge from the ashes of their love?

A Lady's Prerogative (*Lord Love a Lady Series, Book 2*)
It's not fair.

Titled rakes can practically get away with murder, but one tiny little misstep and a debutante is sent away to the country. Which is where Lady Natalie Spencer is stuck after jilting her betrothed.

Frustrated with her banishment, she's finished being a good girl and ready to be a little naughty. Luckily she has brothers, one of whom has brought home his delightfully gorgeous friend.

After recently inheriting an earldom, Garrett Castleton is determined to turn over a new leaf and shed the roguish lifestyle he adopted years ago. His friend's sister, no matter how enticing, is out-of-bounds. He has a run-down estate to manage and tenants to save from destitution.

Can love find a compromise between the two, or will their stubbornness get them into even more trouble?

A betrothal, a scandal, and a kidnapping stand between them now. Can honor emerge from the ashes of their love?

Lady Saves the Duke (*Lord Love a Lady Series, Book 3*) – Coming Early 2019

He thinks he's saving her, but will this Lady Save the Duke, instead?

Miss Abigail Wright, disillusioned spinster, hides her secret pain behind encouraging smiles and optimistic laughter. Self-pity, she believes, is for the truly wretched. So when her mother insists she attend a house party—uninvited—she determines to simply make the best of it...until an unfortunate wardrobe malfunction.

Alex Cross, the "Duke of Ice," has more than earned the nickname given him by the ton. He's given up on happiness but will not reject sensual pleasure. After all, a man has needs. The week ought to have been pleasantly uneventful for both of them, with nature walks, parlor games, and afternoon teas on the terrace...but for some inferior stitchery on poor Abigail's bodice.

And now the duke is faced with a choice. Should he make this mouse a respectable offer and then abandon her to his country estate? She's rather pathetic and harmless, really. Oughtn't to upset his life whatsoever.

His heart, however, is another matter...

Lady at Last (*Lord Love a Lady Series, Book 4*) – Coming Spring 2019

Penelope's Story

Manufactured by
Amazon.ca
Bolton, ON